CLAIRE ANGE

a

novel

by

D1516473

M.A. Kirkwood

SPIRIT STAR PRESS
SAN FRANCISCO
SPIRITSPRESS@MAIL.COM

ISBN: 978-0-9852379-0-5
Spirit Star Press
San Francisco

Cover art: detail from the painting, *The Stuff Dreams Are Made Of* by John Anster Fitzgerald, 1858; Private Collection/Bridgeman Art Library, London.

Grateful acknowledgment is made for use of the following:

"The Man I Love" by George and Ira Gershwin, Harms Inc. 1924
"I Will Survive" by Freddie Perren, Dino Fekaris, Universal Music Publishing Group, Warner/Chappell Music, Inc. EMI Music Publishing
"Someday, We'll be Together," Johnny Bristol, Jackey Beavers, Harvey Fuqua, 1961, Jobete Music Co., Inc. EMI April Music Inc., and EMI Blackwood Music, Inc.
American Express-regional trademarks, service marks of American Express Company
"Have it Your Way," Burger King jingle, Richard Mercer, David Berger, BBDO Advertising, 1973

Also by M. A. Kirkwood
Simon Lazarus

"And what is spirit-wisdom? A knowledge of God which blossoms like a flower in the depths of the individual soul. God, apparently vanished from the world, is reborn in the depths of the human heart."

Rudolf Steiner

"When I die I will soar with angels-and when I die to the angels, what I shall become you cannot imagine."

Rumi

For Gary Aylesworth
Thanks, friend, for the merriment and joy.
Humor loves you.

Author's note

The spirit world lives among us. Its denizens eavesdrop on our conversations. Often they watch with amusement as we text message away, or reach for the remote when the latest CNN headline is no longer holding our interest. And yes, sometimes a wandering spirit will stumble upon a story's very pages.

In fact, the one you're holding right now.

CLAIRE ANGE

This time, it was non-negotiable. Where previously mere threats had been made, today it became official: Claire Molyneaux was kicked out of the house, as stark and plain as any eviction notice a sheriff might post on some poor wretch's door. Still, it was odd, as it was only hours earlier that everything seemed so normal—a typical winter morning, with Claire sauntering out of the front door soapy fresh and ready for the day that lay ahead. But by afternoon, at about the time Claire usually returns, she found herself barred from entry, her things amassed in huge piles, her key no longer fitting the front door lock.

Strange—as it all felt so cold and final. Even the dead leaves on the doorstep seemed worse off than they were earlier in the day when Claire had nary a worry in her mind. Understand, this wasn't some penurious, nit-picky landlord she was dealing with, nor a cruel warden of a domicile for young, wayward truants—the kind you read about in 19th Century English novels. Truth be told, it was her own mother giving her the boot making it especially harsh being that the girl is a mere seventeen and the charming, Antebellum, mini *Tara,* the only home she's ever known.

What got all this started is not so easy to determine, as the world Claire inhabited seemed as still and sanctimonious as the occasional statuette or cool running fountain gracing the private backyards of its stately and elegant domains. Undoubtedly, many would agree that a girl from this upscale a neighborhood—attending one of the better, finer schools, even being *brought out* only last year as a junior debutante—isn't usually kicked to the curb with such devil-may-care insouciance. For girls who are brought up with such fineries there's usually a protocol one follows before that day of independence arrives. One must at least finish college and perhaps then she is given a few dollars from the trust mill before such a brush with the cruel world is to take place. From the way it all seemed one would have never guessed anything unusual was in the making. It was only earlier this very morning that everything appeared to be so calm and ordinary to Claire, at least, on the emotional front. It had only been a few days since there was the slightest altercation between Claire and her mother, Rita, the primary culprit in this new arrangement. But there it was, in plain view. As Claire walked up the winding, tree-lined walkway she could see that there was an imbalance in the usual symmetry of things. As she came closer, she noticed the boxes and suitcases labeled with her name on them all stacked on the brick steps and landing of the great house. Claire cried out and rapped her delicate knuckles on the great door—double-checking the car-less driveway in between futile attempts at entry.

After fruitlessly searching for more possible clues, Claire sat on one of the steps and thought about what she could do. Gentle leaves rustled down the walkway while Claire took stock of her new situation. Sweat began to emit from her forehead. Her brow furrowed as her thoughts intertwined to meet up at intersections deep in her very soul. Claire slowly began to realize that this really wasn't all that strange. Rita had done crazy, even insane things before. There was the time two years ago when she did a rampage on Claire's room and tore down her vintage *Green Day* and *Primitive Radio Gods* posters, took her CDs, books, stereo equipment, memorabilia, sheet music, clothing, and other such belongings and brought them to the back of the house to burn.

Rita did this in a rather odd, bon-fire celebratory fashion, laughing and cackling as she skipped and danced around the leaping flames as Claire cried and looked on in helpless despair.

And now, two years later, with new personal effects acquired, Rita was throwing her daughter out of the house for good. Was this really so surprising? Not entirely, but the sudden dramatic switch seemed too much to bear. Now the challenge was to go forward with the meager three hundred bucks Claire had in savings from her last part-time job, a low-limit credit card her dad gave her for *basics* and no car—just her sturdy feet and a few bus tokens. That was it for Claire.

She also had four and a half months left of high school and college was still pending. Her father only recently left for a nine-month assignment in Dubai where he is overseeing a sizable construction project. Could she email him? Could she just try to reason with him that his wife, and her own mother, had gone off the deep end and without Rita getting to him first? Now understand this was the trick. Depending on the balance of energies between the respective influence of the two of them, there was always an egregious, slippery thread that left Hilaire Molyneaux in a waxy loop, caught in an *Othello*-like sense of being loyal to his wife, (a true *Iago*, more than a *Desdemona*) yet loving toward his daughter, a mere innocent (a *Cordelia* if there ever was one), but depicted otherwise by the shrewd and deceptive calculations of her mother.

Claire's young mind reeled: *What lies would Rita fabricate this time?* Oh, theirs was an odd threesome. Odd, firstly, because Claire is hardly an only-child. She has two younger brothers. Yet when it came to her relationship with Rita, she always felt there was a forged threesome-ness between Claire, her father and Rita. What was with this unhealthy triangle? Perhaps some all-knowing, prescient psychiatrist in her distant, adult future would

3

know, but for now, Claire clearly had to figure out what she could do—on her own.

As Claire pondered the boxes, plastic trash bags and luggage so neatly stacked and assembled, she noticed a message attached to one of the bags. Of course, it was her mother's scrawl. In big letters it read:

"Had enough of you, Rochelle Claire. Time to go your way. Do not call us. Do not email us. Do not text message us. Your tuition was fully paid by your good father. So you can finish at ' Immaculate Heart'. Now college (if you get into one), still needs to be determined and I will discuss that with Dad. Do not bother him! No emails because he will not be responding. He knows what you've done. Leave your cell-phone in the mailbox. Remember. You were on the Family Plan. Well, not anymore. Mom"

Cut and dried Rita. It was not entirely so surprising to read her terse, cold words. It was an exclusive, private torture Claire had endured with her mother for all of her short life. And the false accusations—the allusion about her dad knowing what *she* "*had done*", was one of Rita's signature stabs. Claire wondered to herself: *What? What? Mom? What did I do? Live? Breathe? Want to play the piano—which you stole from me?*

Of course, Claire forgot about the pierced nose incident where being obedient to her mother about doing the non-debutante thing—which was to pierce her earlobes—she decided to come home with a hoop in her left nostril instead.

But that was almost four months ago, ancient history in the life of a teenager. It sure was frustrating. And exhausting. What was presented to the rest of the world via Rita—be they remote members of the family or the myriad upscale social clubs of which Rita so shamelessly aspired—was a show, a fabrication, a fiction, a put-on. As long as there was the correct audience, Rita would always portray herself with the utmost sweetness and motherly affection towards her daughter—all for show, of course. Rita valued the society page and the social columns and lately, Genevieve Du Valle's society '*Blog* far too much to put the slightest doubt in anyone's mind as to her true nature. Behind the polite courtesies and afternoon teas with the old nuns who would show up at the Molyneaux home for quaint conversation and exchanges of gratitude for the generosity Rita would bestow in her yearly financial contributions to their ancient, crumbling convent school was a lie, a flat-out lie. And no one knew about this lie better than Claire, as she was simultaneously the exclusive participant and witness to the lie.

But the others knew—others being her brothers who are all of fifteen and thirteen respectively, and Dad—if he bothered to come out from the folds of his financial pages and formidable magazines to pay any attention. Surely Claire was too embarrassed to call any relatives. Besides, what exactly would she say?

They, too, would never believe her, as they would most likely fall for the front Rita would put on in their semi-annual visits. Childless Aunt Lena and Uncle Ray were not even on the radar. They wouldn't get themselves involved as they never seemed to want to bother with anyone younger than thirty-five. Claire's grandmother was not an option, either, as she lived nearly two hundred miles away and in the country. And as for Aunt Nanette and Uncle Claude, Claire couldn't bear the thought of her stuck–up cousin, Nadine, faux-frowning at her misfortune while harboring the deepest glee at her beautiful cousin's cruel misfortune, so that nixed a good bulk of the extended family right there.

Claire sighed, surrendering her phone by dropping it into the mailbox, but only after calling some of her school mates, leaving nervous, "Hey…you wanna do somethin?" voicemails. Realizing that this was probably not the best approach in this time of complete and total distress, she got on with it and SOS'd a text message to her best friend,

Darva, who knew the situation she was dealing with far better than most. *"HELP! I'VE BN '86'D. RITA ON RMPGE. NO PL 2 STY. WL CALL LTR."*

Claire wondered if she was reaching everyone she knew before giving up her trusty little connection to the world, figuring she would attempt contact with her friends sometime after her piano lesson. There she would use her teacher's phone. By then, the girl would have some clues. So far so good, but Claire panicked when she thought of where on earth she would put all of her stuff.

Winter leaves cracked under Claire's cheap and worn saddle-oxford soles as she paced. At times, she'd pause and look around her as she strutted down the smooth, leafy, walkway, slowly mulling her thoughts over the low flame of a crushed and humiliated spirit. Claire realized that most of the neighbors had to know there was commotion going on at her house on a fairly regular basis, she only hoped they didn't know anything too specific. Like this. And it was too embarrassing for her to ask any of them to give her a hand, now that she was no longer going to be living there. If she could only convince one of the neighbors to simply hold on to her mound of belongings for a few days. That maybe she could say she was going abroad to study and was in the process of separating things that were going to be put into storage and those items she would bring along. But then she tried another tactic: *Mother somehow came down with an obscure illness and must be quarantined*…or something of that order. *Could work*, Claire fancied.

The sun lay low in the horizon in that hazy way of winter, it being only four in the afternoon. Claire's brothers, Marcel and Phil were probably doing their after school activities, and Rita was probably off to one of her clubs. Claire surmised: *Who would really be around at this time anyway*?

The only person that came to mind was old Mrs. Gaynor, a few houses down. She was about eighty-five, maybe ninety years old. She doesn't hear very well. Maybe she would be a good bet.

♦   ♦   ♦

"I don't know if I understand what exactly yew might be sayin to me, darlin. Culd yew come on inside here?"

Mrs. Gaynor slowly opened the huge front door and let Claire into the grand and spacious atrium of her elegant home.

"How're things? I take it you are preparin' to leave *Immaculate Heart* this year, young lady?"

Claire politely answered her neighbor, Mrs. Gaynor, with lots of *yes*, *ma'ams*, *pardons*, and such as this was her genteel training. Mrs. Gaynor seemed to like what she was seeing. The old woman munched on something crunchy as she spoke to the girl. Claire watched as she chewed, wondering if the old woman's teeth were still intact or if she were testing her *Poligrip*.

"Such a lady you are, Rochelle Claire. Now. How can I be of help to yew today?"

Claire painted her plight in dramatic but careful strokes. It would only be for a very short while that she would need to have her things stored, as her mother was gravely ill. Mrs. Gaynor cocked her ear as she moved closer to the girl:

"My goodness, that is god-awful. So what illness is it that yawr mama has somehow acquired?"

The old lady knew of the girl's situation as she recalled spreading her golden silk taffeta curtains that flanked the great window in her living room one evening two years prior to witness the bonfire flames flailing from the Molyneaux backyard, accompanied by a shrill cackle that pierced the night air. *That's that bitch*, Mrs. Gaynor muttered as she knocked back her evening cocktail, slinking away from the parlor window, barley catching hold of her walker to assist her back to the dinner table to join Mr. Gaynor, who was still living then.

Claire continued her nervous chatter almost non-stop, explaining to the kind old lady that it appeared to be a complicated infection that's highly contagious and that her mom would need to be quarantined and that it would be best if she left the premises for a while.

"I see...Well...what about yawr brothers?" Mrs. Gaynor inquired.

"It only seems to affect females." Claire quipped.

Mrs. Gaynor continued to play along with the girl:

"I don't believe I have evvah heard of such a thing before. Yew sure about that?"

Claire assured the old woman that it was true and even pointed to the pile of boxes and bags still stacked on the landing and stairs as she walked Mrs. Gaynor to the French windows in the parlor that overlooked the street. Claire gestured toward the boxes and suitcases piled high on the stairs.

"See? It's very serious."

"Well. I suppose yew could bring them to my spare room, then, dear girl. Just give me a ring when yew want to come by and get 'em."

Claire was so relieved she squeezed old Mrs. Gaynor's hands in hers. They were cold, slightly damp, and soft in that way common to ladies her age. A faint crushing sound could be heard as she clasped. Mrs. Gaynor opened her hands.

"Oh, have some. They're from my tree."

Claire looked down at the woman's soft, spongy, old palm and took a few pecans newly crushed in their shells.

Claire munched.

"Oh, gosh. Mrs. Gaynor. I'll just bring everything over and I'll call you in a few days."

Claire hurriedly ran out of the house. The lacey hem of her half-slip peeked out from her plaid hunter green and gray uniform skirt as she charged over to her piled belongings. She madly sifted through them to gather some things she might need for the forthcoming days and nights. Claire lifted the boxes and bags to carry over to her neighbor's house, breathing a tremendous sigh of relief, her knee socks now droopy and gathering at her ankles. Mrs. Gaynor lingered at the parlor window, watching the girl as she carried her things up the graveled drive, mumbling to herself, *" Infection, my rear. What on earth has that crazy woman done' to that girl this time?"*

But old Mrs. Gaynor maintained her cool demeanor and greeted the girl as she carted a large, oversized plastic bag into the foyer.

"That everything, Rochelle Claire?"

Mrs. Gaynor announced as the exhausted child dragged and pushed the last of the boxes in after her, breathing a sigh of relief. Claire's mind spun in all directions as she packed the last of the boxes into the old woman's spare bedroom and after thanking her a few more times, Claire fled, remembering to scoop up a few of the remaining pecans from the decorative bowl in the lavish hallway as she headed out for her piano lesson.

Or, at least, she had every intention of making it to her piano lesson. But it proved too difficult for the traumatized girl to bear. How could she paste on a mask of composure and proceed with a lesson today? As if nothing in the world had happened?

As soon as Claire turned the next corner for the bountiful and luxuriant Evangeline Boulevard she threw her duffel bag and plain navy wool coat against a languid Spanish Oak tree and plopped herself down on the leafy ground. It just couldn't be done. Not today. Drained, Claire rested her head against the gnarly trunk of the great tree and re-assessed her situation. So life was a tad inconvenient without her little cell phone, but she could deal with it. Claire figured she would call Mr. Logan to cancel in due time, but the events of the past hour still raced through her mind. Everything seemed to have happened so quickly. Surely there was something all too final here, something that's just not like Rita even when she *is* on a rampage. Despite the fact that there was never much of a warm and fuzzy relationship with her mother, Claire felt that, certainly, her home was a given. That when all was said and done Claire would have her cozy bedroom with it's canopied bed to greet her by the end of the day. Undoubtedly, being that she was still a minor, Claire had the basic right to have food, clothing and adequate shelter, despite the fact that there were signs that those very assumptions may be in jeopardy. Like the recent change in what the Molyneaux family called *R & R time*, short for *Rest and Relaxation*.

For the past two weeks, Rita had begun to leave a tray of food in front of her daughter's bedroom door—meaning that Claire was no longer allowed downstairs to eat dinner with the rest of the family, part of the *"R & R "* schedule. Ostensibly, the reasoning was Rita's wish to put an end to the arguments the two would have about the treasured parlor grand piano Rita had placed into storage in December, right around Claire's seventeenth birthday. Claire adored the antique piano, a rare model designed and built in the former Czechoslovakia and brought down through the generations by her paternal grandmother and given to Claire when she turned 14. Rita claimed that it was Claire's constant playing that drove her to take the instrument out. But Claire loved to play and spent hours on it after school.

"I've had three years of this!" Rita screamed and told Claire that enough was enough, fiercely blowing out the candles in the ornate, silver–plated candelabra her daughter would light every evening when she sat down to play.

Rita bellowed:

"Yeah. Like you're some Liberace. Ha! Fat chance. You have years and years to go. And I'm not enduring one more minute of that repetitive scaling and tinkling and scaling and tinkling, either. They'd have to put me in a nuthouse."

It was at that precise moment when Rita made her final and deadly decision. And ever since that chilly December afternoon when the storage people hauled Claire's beloved instrument away, the two would invariably get into an argument about it. And, so far, Rita was winning. And that's just how it was going to be. Never mind that Claire's playing had tremendous promise. Never mind that Claire was intent on continuing her studies and considering an emphasis in music composition when that glorious first day of college would arrive. Of course, this was an interest she kept from Rita for fear of ridicule and incessant criticism, but each evening before bedtime Claire would lie back and contemplate what life as a composer might be like, and as if seeking a safe harbor for those sweet wishes she'd imagine her desires kept and protected by some all-seeing, cosmic *Tooth Fairy*. She simply had no other name for this. This routine of sweeping away her cherished wishes to the lofty bosom of some imagined kind force at bedtime. Some might find this to be atavistic of the girl, as most assuredly, almost anyone over the age of twelve would give an eye-roll at such a prospect, but Claire never underestimated the power of wishes. Perhaps, a childhood of richly fecund imagination offsetting the blunt indifference of an emotionally distant mother is to blame, for Claire fancied the loftiest of spirited creatures: benevolent, gossamer-winged, creative helpers from a celestial realm gathering above her canopied bed to listen as she cried out in a soft whisper: "*Please, take these wishes with you and bring them to safety where that god-awful mother of mine can't touch them*". Claire patted her soft hand under her pillow, her glossy and languid black locks fanning the plump, lavender bedding as she gently drifted into her nightly slumber.

◆ ◆ ◆

The first night Rita left the tray Claire almost stepped onto a plate of meatloaf, a green salad, an apple, two baguettes, a slice of chocolate cake and a glass of grape juice as she was on her way to wash up for dinner. A note stared up at her as it lay between the glass of juice and cake. It read:

"*Bring the tray downstairs to the kitchen when you're done. And only after we've retired to the living room. Mom*"

At first, Claire laughed at this, but soon grew a bit dreary, as this ritual became an everyday routine.

"It's like you're Cinderella, girl. Only you have your nerdy, do-no-wrong bruthas, instead of the loser, barf-faced, bow-wow stepsisters our fairy-tale Cindy had to deal with. And your mutha? Well, *Attitude* wouldn't be sayin' it right. Nah-uh. Yo Momma? She's lookin' more like she's your typical, *thorn-in-the-side-troglodyte-medieval-as-an-iron-maiden-Bertha-butt-and-the-butt-sisters*-bitch!"

Her friend, Darva Jean, managed to say this in her usual rhythmic style into her phone while Claire held hers, picking at her plate as she listened. Darva was notorious for her often vivid and quite verbal descriptions, and, as usual, in a fit of mirth, Claire dropped her fork, gasping for air between hyena guffaws.

"Haaaaagh.Heeee.heeeeeya! Looks like you nailed that right on the head and here I am, helpless as they come, girlfriend. Well…at least we can chat while I chew."

After they got off their phones, Claire struggled to retain her friend's welcomed sense of humor as the regularity of this draconian routine was becoming all too dark and gloomy. Claire felt as if she were locked in a *Rapunzel*-like tower, removed from an exciting and thriving world below. All she needed was a gargoyle statuette or two to phalanx the over-sized window that looked out from her third story bedroom. Claire's only respite seemed to be her few friends. And during the many nights of Claire's dinner-time phone-chats, Darva, in particular, would invariably ask, "What's with Rita's game, girl?"

And on the evening of their most recent dinner time chat, Darva's words rolled out in rapid staccato succession like gumballs spilling from a broken gum machine.

"Ya gotta admit, the don't-mess-with-mother-nature-queen-bee is medieval on your hiney for some unknowable, unobtainable, unflinchingly and unobtrusively yet ultimately unfreakin'ly unfathomable reason that just no calculator in any Einstein-*Googlin*', 'round-the-clock-cyber-slide-rule-measurin-Quality Inn, Reno-Nevada-nerd-convention could ever compute."

The fork slipped through Claire's fingers before she could catch herself from breaking into a mini-earthquake right there at her dainty, lace-covered table. But now, things weren't so humorous. As she recalled that very conversation, it looked like Rita's *game* had taken a major shift and, of course, not in her daughter's favor.

But to…*this*? Whatever in the world motivated her mother, Claire could not say, but it certainly looked like she despised her very own daughter so completely that the girl found it mystifying that she wasn't left in a basket on a dirt road leading to some miserable, densely-wooded leper-colony as a gurgling infant, or perhaps, deliberately led astray at a shopping mall when a toddler, similar to the lurid tabloid stories Claire would read at the supermarket check-out stands when she'd accompany Rita on their weekly run to the *Piggly Wiggly*.

I mean, why the hell did she not simply ditch me: rattles, stroller, Huggies and all? Claire wondered, as she sat under a great Spanish oak, its gray, mossy entrails slightly dangling over her pretty face. Rita's controlling manner was one thing, her extreme unpredictability another. Claire pondered these sad facts a while, turning the recent scenes of the past week over in her mind. And there she dwelled until the late afternoon sun splayed itself into purple and magenta hues across the winter sky, reminding her that she had better get a move on and cancel her lesson. Claire rose to gather her things and headed to the corner store, amazed that she spotted a payphone so soon in her search, being that such things seem to have become recent relics from a not so distant, low-tech past. As soon as the voicemail picked up, Claire heard herself say,

"Mr. Logan. I'm so sorry. I've run into a situation here. I can't make it this evening."

Now Claire caught herself getting choked-up when she got off the phone. This was becoming the only time of the week when she could focus on improving her piano playing, an activity she always looked forward to. Sometimes Mr. Logan would let her practice for an hour or so after her lesson while he went about attending to other matters.

I will not have to cancel next week, Claire thought. *I will have settled this mess by then. Surely, I will be somewhere good. But... where? Where, exactly, is this good situation?* And how, pray tell, could she pull this off? Claire furrowed her fine, black brows, and took out her brush to stroke her long glossy black hair, fixing her gaze on a quaint café across the boulevard.

The problem, Claire pondered, as she settled into a small table with her mocha de-caf, *is working my way around the hideous truth.* Claire knew with no uncertainty that none of her friends' parents would believe her if she attempted to explain her new, locked-out situation. Not for a flat, *nano*-second. If she attempted to describe what had happened, things would be written off as a mere mother-daughter spat and such. More than likely, Claire would be invited to one of her friends' homes for dinner, light conversation, maybe a possible stay-over for one, possibly two evenings, then what? Claire squirmed in her seat imagining the possible scenarios that would most likely culminate in:

"Well. It's getting late, girls. School night. So...Mr. or Ms .Whoever parent—will take you home now, Claire".

◆　◆　◆

As our girl here ruminates on these things, I'm going to take the opportunity to introduce myself to you. Firstly, let me just say that I've been keeping watch of her. Usually on occasions when I sense there might be trouble. Odd, how it all started, though. If I could put it to you this way, in all the days I have roamed the various roads of existence, I don't believe I've ever answered to the call of 'Tooth Fairy' before. Imperceptible to her, of course, but I've been with her since that first wintry night of her current sorrows. When she made her wish that solemn frigid evening,

15

somehow I moved my way in, floating under heavy damask drapes that adorn her lovely bedroom window. I listened intently to her breathing until I finally had to whisk myself away, even if it were to simply catch a mere glimmer of her fair beauty.

At first, I lost myself in an intricate weave in an unnerving silk cord, but soon I broke free and my, what joy pulsated within me. And here I am, beside her once again as she blows her café au lait with her pout, cooing, rose bud lips. My. Truly, my fortune has run aplenty since I met up with her, I will be the first to say. Otherwise, it's been very lonely for me here.

Now I realize you may be wondering who I am. And I will get to that and tell you more—what little I truly know, but all in due time, of course—which I have a lot of, mind you. When you perceive life as you know it from my perspective, you realize it's the one thing you have in abundance. By the way, it's all true about time being a measure, a dimension relative to the physical world and its unique set of laws.

And now that I am here among you earth dwellers, I will speak in your terms. But I must caution that you may be a bit dismayed.

Now, how is it that I am here?

Was your ontological question answered in a day, a decade, a century? Is it resolved to this day? Well, then. In all honestly, I'm not so sure why I am here among you. As to who I am, the puzzle remains. As to my origins, let me just say that my most recent dwelling place has been in the silence of the world's dreams: a netherworld that serves as a sort of mezzanine between existences. I assume, that, perhaps, a sort of dissatisfaction has brought me back to life's starting point below. Understand—I am hardly in the hammock of a blissfully supine, existential retirement.

Vigilance seems to be in order. I wonder. I wait and wish. No longer can I affect anything. But there is the hope that I could, at least, follow along the lives of these curious individuals as a way back, perhaps, to unraveling my own mystery. Does this make any sense to you? Not to appear clever, but do you read me?

While you're deciding, an interesting scenario has just presented itself. Our famished waif has dropped her snack to the floor. If only I could scoop it up, brush it off and place it back on her plate. But this would not be possible. Besides, a floating baked treat suddenly lifting itself from the floor in an attempt to land back in her little plate would frighten the child. And I am not about to do that.

At this moment, I'm positioned exactly at her gaze. I appear as a pulsating, yet imperceptible, slither of light, but as our girl bends down, a teardrop falling from her eye, she remains oblivious to my concern and my very presence, of course.

"Damn!"

Claire slides the pastry back onto her plate anyway, looking around to see if anyone catches her brushing it off. She knows her money is meager, as she can't afford to toss her snack.

I can somehow empathize with this predicament. And I'm wistfully wishing: if only I could take a seat and initiate a conversation with our dear Claire. Perhaps, grasp her delicate hand and console her. Admittedly, my attention is transfixed by her soft as satin beauty—skin so supple, so porcelain flawless. Even the crumbs slightly brushing the side of her sweet mouth adds a certain sloppy attractiveness.

Of course, she cannot see me. She, along with all these other individuals, does not know I am here. If the girl could confide in me, I certainly would have no difficulty believing her. If I were that mistreated waif,

I would expose that wily woman. But to what just and all-seeing authority I would not know. Well, maybe I would know—but I don't believe it would be all that easy to request an immediate and just solution and right on the spot, being that I would direct things to a heavenly, all-seeing source. Divine hearings from the celestial realms don't happen so easily here. Not that I'm a complete stranger to the situation, mind you. I've observed all this—albeit from afar. And in my own quiet way—a most profoundly quiet way, I should add.

As I mentioned, I have been keeping watch of this lovely young damsel for what must be several weeks now. Sometimes I can't always tell how time moves. But in those early days when I felt called to the girl's home, I had a favorite place near the fence and weeds where I would survey the goings on in that grand house. The unpredictable, moistened air of this strange climate would hover about me, as the seasons seemed to alternate in a day's passing. Wild grass and weeds would penetrate what appeared to be a return of my senses. Sometimes distracting me so. Occasionally, I would twitch, scratching at phantom shins and ankles as I fixed my gaze on the goings-on inside.

My curiosity in this intriguing girl was complete and total once I noticed that exquisitely beautiful and rare mahogany parlor-grand piano being carried out of the front door and onto a moving truck parked in front of the former home of the young creature many weeks ago. You could say I just happened to be sauntering by—if my movements could be described as such. The young beauty was in tears as she buckled to her knees right there on the walkway in front of the house. It's still difficult for me to quell the memory of her nefarious mother staring down at the girl, relishing in the dominion she apparently had over her. I tell you, the child's cries were heart breaking. Somewhere inside myself I knew that place of anguish and I found it hard not to move closer in an attempt to rescue—but how? It was all too strange. With my new life being what it is, it's not so easy for me to interfere in these things.

And here I wait and helplessly observe this sweet ingénue, yet again, as she sips her café au lait or whatever, drumming her lovely sinewy fingers on the table as she attempts to figure out her own rescue. If I could, I would swoop down and snatch her up and bring the girl to a safe haven, but I am powerless to attempt such a feat. I was once heroic. I'm not quite sure how I know this, but I have a vague sense that there was a time when I could resolve conflict and the like in a matter of seconds, so many looked up to me. But not anymore. Not now. At least, not in the way I could before. Before I died, that is.

♦ ♦ ♦

Claire finished her pastry without leaving a crumb, picking at every flakey morsel on her plate. She stared down at the brown bag that held a sandwich for later. She wondered if it would be enough. *Well, it'll have to be*, Claire decided, figuring that she had to be on a strict budget now that she was homeless. But this didn't exactly freak her out. Claire busied herself with her notes and after putting her book away Claire sat very calmly for what seemed like an hour. She couldn't exactly tell which was more still: her body sitting upright in the stiff, wooden chair, or the potted fern on the plant-stand in the corner by the window. Occasionally, she took small sips of her de-caf mocha and observed the customers coming and going in the bustling coffee shop. One thing for sure, there was no way she was going to attempt a stay-over at the home of one of her school chums. She simply could not afford to waste energy on explaining the matter. Especially to somebody's parents. Claire felt that what she needed was a place where she could quietly make nervous, last minute plans. And it was at this very moment that Claire got a flash of inspiration to go into the café's ladies' room, change out of her school uniform and pull on some chic tights and a sweater from her tote. She would also re-apply her make up and head for the nearest youth hostel for the night.

After examining herself in the bathroom mirror—checking her countenance in an attempt to appear more sophisticated and after brushing her jet black mop of hair and flopping it back and forth in huge waves to make it appear more fresh and fashionable, Claire drew deeper lines around her obsidian eyes to give her that added depth of college-coed maturity and perhaps, a bit of a worldly touch. Claire strutted out of the bathroom and checked an old *Yellow Pages* directly in the back of the coffee shop. She called two numbers under the *hostels* category. Did they have reasonable rates for a small private room for a night or two? Did they also have weekly rates? Not that Claire could afford more than twenty or so dollars a night. It would at least give her time to figure out what to do, or where to run to next. The nearest hostel was only a streetcar ride away. Claire packed her notebooks into her bag, grabbed her coat and ran out of the café.

◆　◆　◆

And I am following our capricious one out into the chilled night air, double-checking through the café window to see if she collected her things, wool navy pea coat and notebook notwithstanding. Silly, though, isn't it? As if I could run after her to let her know of any item she might have forgotten.

So you won't be left aloft and forever curious, please come along with me and I will tell you more. Certainly, it's strange being who I am. And it took a while for me to understand it myself. In case you haven't guessed, I was once human and now exist as a complex thought and emotion form that can move.

I will give you a moment or two to digest what I've just said.

All right, then, if you prefer, I am now a spirit. And I am invisible as I move about your world. But you should know that I am keen on being as accurate as I can with you, and what I am is mental-feeling energy when I am closest to the earth plane as I am at present. If I were to go farther from this plane I may be a bit different. Not so much a thought formation that once had a human personality and a life, a history, a biography, and all of the things that concern humans when they are in human form. When one is post-human you'd be surprised at how things are. But I will get to these things as time allows.

Our girl just stepped onto a streetcar and is now sitting next to a woman of African descent who is now American. She has tiny white stoppers in her ears with wires attached to a small square that sits on her chest.

She is moving her head around and closing her eyes as if in prayer. Our brave girl—the one we are specifically following—is digging through her great canvas bag for coins and bills. She just pulled out a lunch ticket and threw it back into the bag. Now she is counting paper money and is folding it into her fist.

I realize you may be thinking: "Well, what are you doing hanging around here and being curious and even concerned about this Claire Molyneaux?" And I'd say, "Well, your guess is about as accurate as mine. And realizing that I can't exactly do anything to actually help the child, being that I cannot influence physical reality the way I could when I was last human, then why don't I move onward and upward?"

I wish I could tell you the answer to this. But I cannot. I am just as puzzled to be here as you are, perhaps, startled to see me here taking up space in thought formation in the way of words that are making up the reality of this very paragraph on this very page right at this very moment.

Rochelle Claire, our young musical aspirant, is now arriving at this homey domicile for traveling youth, and she is being told the expense for the night and her beautiful dark eyes are tearing up. Her newly applied eye makeup is forming black pools around her eyes, making her look like a baby panda. The young man at the counter is scratching the stubble on his chin as he listens to the girl stating her plea. He's handing her a wad of soft paper so she can wipe the mess around her eyes.

♦ ♦ ♦

And luckily for Claire, she was able to convince the handsome hunk at the front desk that when she called earlier, she was quoted a flat rate of twenty-five dollars a night for one of the single rooms and was told she could apply that to a weekly rate if she were to continue her stay for that length of time.

The attendant nodded his head and lifted the counter top partition so he could assist the girl to her room. Claire blew her nose into the wad of *Kleenex* he had given her.

" Where are you from?"

Claire sniffled, trying to re-capture her stride.

"Oh, not far. Around. I go to Erasmus U. in St. Peregrine."

"Oh, yeah? That's a good ways, isn't it?" The boy cocked his head, admiring Claire's long glossy tresses, fastidiously unlocking the door while ushering her things into the small, but cozy, wood-paneled room.

"All right, then, it's all yours!"

Claire hesitated for a moment, wondering if one should tip in a place like this. The young man stared down at the pensive girl as if reading her mind, announcing, "This is our prime suite," the young man looked at the receipt he was about to hand to her, "Miss Molyneaux!"

Claire beamed and blushed at the young man, but decided to hang on to her dough. After a slight pause, the attendant nodded his head "All yours." and politely handed Claire the key and left the room, gently closing the door behind him.

A rosy flush was still quite visible on Claire's cheek as she listened for the young man's footsteps to vanish in the hallway. A spontaneous rush of excitement now fluttered through her young veins.

Wow. Maybe this won't be so bad. Chortling now at the prospect of what could very well come her way. *Maybe we'll get involved*, Claire shrieked and got up to check herself in the mirror. Of course, her eyes were bereft of their paint, but she still liked the cool way she stood in her sleek, suede boots and the way her leggings made her look so svelte and chic. *I could go out and order a cocktail somewhere and hang out and play pool and no one would ever know.* Claire thought, but soon tempered such fancies for more practical matters. After all, it was a school night.

Claire took out the ham sandwich she bought at the café earlier, and leaping onto the little bed, she flipped open her notebooks. Claire actually looked forward to the task of completing some homework. She would call her friends in an hour or so from the pay phone in the hallway and she will tell them all is fine and well. And tonight, Claire liked the idea that she would forget her troubles and maybe even dream about the cutie at the desk. Maybe they'll get to know each other and he'll invite her out for beers at the nearby college bars. This time, Claire couldn't shake such a delicious notion and tossing her books aside, she gathered some coins for the payphone and darted out of the door. She just had to tell Darva Jean about her new situation.

♦ ♦ ♦

Since I have been allowed to take up such residency in these very pages, and to express myself as freely as I have been allowed thus far, it only seems that the honor should be yours as well. Now, would you, dear readers, care to share your thoughts on the prospects of this? Certainly, it's understandable that in times of turbulence, given what our dear Claire has just gone through, she would want escape in simple pleasures. And it's fine and well that our damsel wishes to spend some time catching up with her friends on the old horn in the hall.

But the idea of this fellow at the desk—that would clearly be out of the question, now, wouldn't you agree? Young innocent like that swilling sloppy ales and sudsy intoxicants with that lascivious young counter-top cowboy. Certainly, this should come as no surprise. Our Claire's life hangs by a mere thread. Her wicked mother locking the girl out to be left helpless in the streets all the while her sturdy white knee-sox and saddle oxfords are packed so neatly in her duffel bag so she will be ready for the nuns' instruction at her school come morning. Brave girl she is. While she frets with her coins at the payphone, her charming travel tooth brush and the silvery metal bar that she places in her mouth when she sleeps awaits her fastidious school-girl attention as they lay on the plain, but honest little dresser by the sad twin sized bed. It actually breaks my heart's memory, this. The girl is barely out of her pigtails, as they say. Such notions are mere passing flights of fancy to ingénues such as she is. And our stud muffin (I picked that one up recently) at the desk probably has a dozen or so little sirens already at his beck and his call, so why would he dare be interested? The wolf would be far too wild for her. Though young, surely he is older and more experienced than she. I must somehow protect her where and when and however I can. But I often forget what I am now: a light and slippery wisp of formless thought-emotion-impulses. Foolishly, I find myself attempting to intercept on her behalf so I can be of assistance when all I do is slip through materials—be they persons,

25

walls, moving automobiles, and yes, even a payphone hanging on a wall in some dark and dismal corridor, a single, bald, light bulb hanging from the equally glum ceiling. And as soon as I realize what has occurred, I am then ricocheted back to the previous scene as if nothing had happened. Just as helpless as before.

Perhaps, then, I should be comforted by the fact that I'm able to take sentinel of her. I will be in this room, up near the ceiling, floating lightly above her as her lithe young body rests under the scratchy and plain, coarse blankets tonight.

Surely, it may bring a tear to her eye to recall her former princess bedroom with its lofty canopied bed, and silken adornments. But I will be here, for it is she I am guarding. Maybe I'll watch and wait with even more fastidiousness than before, because somehow our darling Rochelle Claire holds a clue to something from my own most recent life, strange as that may sound. Yes, kind readers, in some inexplicable way, I feel this to be true.

♦ ♦ ♦

Rita Molyneaux , (nee Silvestri), sat patiently, aiming not to scratch her hands as she sat at the table near the window in the bar of the exclusive and for the most part, pedigreed, Bienville Club. Her doctor told her the hand scratching would subside if she simply tried the deep breathing exercises he showed her.

Rita was trying this out as she waited. After a few stabs, Rita took a long swill of her drink. Forget these silly things, she mused, as she emptied her glass. After all, she was due. Due a little pleasure after all she had been through. It was only a little after seven o'clock in the evening—not too soon for a second vodka. Rita nodded to the waiter, figuring it may be a while before her bridge partners showed up. It's not that Rita was ever considered all that popular or a person one would pointedly seek out, but she does play a mean card game, especially bridge. And there aren't many who actually play that old parlor game favorite anymore. Not these days, anyway. Yet the club was quiet this evening. For a Thursday night, that is. A few people lingered at the handsome mahogany bar. Ruenelle de la Houssaye and Mini O'Brien huddled together at a corner table, chatting away, Ruenelle, glancing over at Rita, waving a crisp hello her way as she flicked her Gitane cigarette—so elegantly poised in its elongated black holder—in the smoldering crystal ashtray near the center of the table. *Phony bitch*, Rita thought, as she sent the women a frozen lipstick smile their way. Finally, Anne Leblanc appeared, her stylish raincoat draped over her shoulders, laughing at Ronnie, the Maitre d' as she made her entrance.

"Well, I had no idea I'd run into that mess on Versaille Avenue comin over here, Rita. See you are situated with a…what's that you're drinkin', girl?"

Rita gave a slight wink.

"Oh, it's just a splash of vodka and a couple of olives in case I git hungry. Wanna order one?"

Anne settled in and pulled up her chair.

"Hang on there, Rita…let me git myself settled in here." Anne looked over at the empty table placements on either side of her.

" Well, I see we are up for a serious game tonight. Know when the others are comin' by?"

Anne was referring to Bob and Louise Knowlton, their bridge partners for a few weeks now.

"Well, then, maybe it's the traffic so…what's goin on with you, Rita? Am I sensing that things are a bit askew?"

"Oh, Anne. I don't know where to begin."

Anne piped:

"It's Hilaire's goin away, isn't it?"

Rita replied:

"Well, yes. That's never a joy. The boys always miss him. And they're at that age when they just need their dad more than they need me. It's just my daughter."

Anne pulled herself slightly away from the table, leaning back in the plush velvet chair.

" Oh, dear."

Rita continued,

"Well. It's a sad fact. And I suppose she's almost at that age when she can do this. But technically, Claire is still a minor. All of seventeen goin' on twenty-five, mind you! I've got to wash my hands of it. But, it's hard. Claire left, Anne. She moved out ".

Now Anne Leblanc sat there and took in Rita Molyneaux's chatter for going on a half-hour and slowly, as Rita talked on and on, Anne realized that she really didn't know the woman who was sitting across from her. Not really. Yes, she lived about mid-way on the block from her, and their children were roughly the same ages, and their boys had gone to the same schools. And yes, they had attended the same social venues. Warren, Anne's husband, would occasionally chat with Hilaire, Anne's devoted husband, as Warren thought well of him. But there was always something a bit vague about Rita, the clawing social climber, as she's been called, particularly by the rich bitch, Ruenelle de la Houssaye, still puffing away in the corner of the room.

Anne briefly looked up as she noticed the always-elegant Ruenelle rising from her table to greet her husband who had just entered the club moments before.

Anne turned her attention back to a chattering Rita, noticing slight beads of sweat formulating on her upper lip. Maybe the girl had good reason to leave, Anne thought, taking a quick swallow of her white wine. But what girl can manage to do such an impractical thing? She has no money.

"You sure she isn't plannin on elopin' or somethin' like that, Rita?" Anne intercepted.

Rita took a swill of her drink.

"Oh, I don't think so. She's not all that interested in boyfriends, cute as some of them are. She wants to be a musician—actually, a composer. Says she's going to be a working musician, playing wherever the work takes her. That might include some questionable places, mind you. We had fights over this. So she left."

Somehow, Anne couldn't imagine the scene. She thought her daughter was more on the classical music track. Anne had heard that Rochelle Claire was quite a capable musician, but such an ambition to play in such venues? Wasn't Claire *a Daughter of the Pre 1803 Society*?

Rita continued to explain her differences with her daughter. But Anne's concentration seemed to split. Suddenly, an image popped into Anne's mind. As she was walking the upstairs hallway in her home a few nights ago, she caught a glimpse of a movie her 20-year old son, Andre, was watching in his room. Anne paused at the door and looked in for a few moments. It was a David Lynch movie. And in this particular scene, Diane Ladd and Harry Dean Stanton are talking to each other on the phone. The Diane Ladd character looked like she was losing her mind, having completely covered her face in red lipstick, and while she sits on the floor of her bathroom, the Diane Ladd character nervously insists that she must confess something dreadful to her boyfriend, the Harry Dean Stanton character.

"I've done something awful, just awful." She blares into the phone. Her horrifying, clownish image reflecting in the bathroom mirror as she shrieks.

Anne lingered on that image a while before being called back to the table.

"Hello?" Rita asked, "Don, our waiter here, wants to know if you want another glass a wine, Anne?"

♦ ♦ ♦

Perhaps you should know that as I pulsated near the ceiling in the sad little room that now houses our Claire, my thoughts drifted to the girl's mother. I wondered if she were having a fine time of it while her daughter sniffled herself to sleep. But as it usually turns out, as soon as I think something, there I am.

I drifted into the elegant room of her social club and soon situated myself near the vaulted oak beams of the ceiling, high above the goings-on below. I looked down on Claire's mother as she actually attempted to cheat at cards with her fellow players. The crown of her head had dark roots sprouting. I saw no money spread out on the table, however, so I was a bit baffled, but remained intrigued. At one point, I shouted down at her. And do you know, dear readers, for a moment she lifted her head somewhat and looked upward? I spun myself, orb-like, in a rotating motion and said: "I see you! And you are not going to a very welcomed place when you become like me!"

And you know what else, dear readers? Rita emitted a tinny little laugh. Then she snorted. Of course, she was looking at her card-mates when she did this. As she left the premises of the club a couple of hours later, I followed her to her vehicle.

It's a big machine that looks like a small military vehicle, but has a smooth, brightly colored body. She started up the motor device. When she arrived at her home she stumbled up the stairs even though the front porch lights were on. As she was unlocking the front door, she noticed something shiny in the mailbox. She lifted the lid and retrieved our girl's metal device. The one she talks into and types little words on.

◆   ◆   ◆

It's been a very rough academic year for Sister Mary Boniface, principal of the *Convent of the Immaculate Heart School* and former Mother Superior of The Sisters of the Holy Sepulchre, the order that maintains the school. Originally settled in what was a rugged outpost back in 1712 when the state of Louisiana was formerly a territory owned by France, the Convent is a little under a decade shy of its 300th year anniversary.

One could surmise that such a notion would fill the good sister with teary pride, but these days such a sentiment seems rather trivial now that keeping one's head above water has become the order of the day. Yet, anyone would agree, the convent has had an extraordinary history. What originally started out as an orphanage later became a domicile for disobedient girls of unfortunate circumstances, the majority dealing with unwanted pregnancies.

It was later in that century, in 1760, that the school was founded by wealthy French settlers, most of them indigo and later, cotton plantation owners. Always a woman of the times, Sister Mary Boniface would often wince at the drawings that adorned the old hallways—most of them sketches of the plantations themselves.

Some of the older, historic depictions include representations of a slave or two holding baskets of material as they stand behind the school's wealthy white benefactors, heads inclined, smiles sheepishly plastered on their faces, lending an air of gratitude as the plantation-owner-benefactor stands in the foreground, arms held akimbo.

"We should take this stuff down. It's just not appropriate. Besides, we've had wealthy donors who are "pillars of the black community. It's just not the thing to have displayed, especially during a fundraiser, wouldn't you say, Conchetta?" Sister Mary Boniface was over heard saying this one afternoon while talking to the cleaning staff who are, nowadays, mostly from south of the Border.

But today, the usually sunny and optimistic principal had too many pressing matters on her mind than to worry herself over issues of political correctness. The school was falling apart. Literally. There were buckets placed in different sections of the old grand room that houses her office. Placed there in case of a sudden and brisk downpour. The good sister knew how well storms could blow in unexpectedly, so the buckets were often kept on hand.

Now where has all that good money gone? Boniface thought to herself, adjusting her tiny headpiece on the crown of her head as she pulled up her chair. Her brittle fingernail traced the columns in the opened ledger atop her great desk. They had just paid for the new air conditioning, heating and boiler equipment. The gymnasium had finally been renovated two years prior. Computers in the library and lab were now up to par and many of their long-standing teachers had received generous increases in pay and benefits. Let's not forget those dear benefits, the conscientious sister noted as she ran through the spreadsheets for a third time this morning. And then the dreaded thought: *Oh, dear…it's merge with St. Jerome's or bust*, crossed her weary mind.

The old nun pushed herself away from the screen, her chair rolling toward the window that overlooked the lovely courtyard. The very idea of an enforced merger seemed like a death sentence. For decades she has striven to keep *The Convent of the Immaculate Heart* a girls' school. She was so proud that hers was one of the last all girls' academy that has withstood the vicissitudes of the day: stay in business and merge with a boys' school. She also took pride in having the girls receive rigorous instruction that would empower them. And them alone. No co-ed environment could ever offer such a gift to the growing minds of young girls. Oh yes, the buzz word is and always will be: empower!

Odd as that may sound when one is referring to a Catholic nun. Actually, Sister Mary Boniface is the only feminist nun she's ever known. And long before the term comfortably nestled itself into the vernacular, thank you. Many an alumna would tell you that after they obtained their Juris Doctorates, or allowed to the bench, or serving as freshman state representatives (and one now a U.S. Senator, another, a candidate for Governor, and many others who are doctors, PhD's in various fields, judges of note, important scientists, journalists) they would invariably drop by their beloved alma mater to have a gee-thanks-for-your-inspiration chat with the beneficent and forward-thinking Sister. The problem now was most of those illustrious graduates didn't care for Mass anymore. In fact, many of them grew away from the Mother Church, spending their time meditating or reading books by Buddhists, Christian mystics, Sufi Masters, modern-day, self-styled gurus and this Indian physician turned spiritual/lifestyle advisor who's often seen on Larry King or the various PBS channels whenever there's a fund drive.

Sister murmured to herself: *They're giving their money to all of these save- the -globe, stop disaster in the Congo causes. Which isn't so bad. No, not at all.* Sister knew all too well as the good, apostolic church has taught her and her former students it was only right to care about the less fortunate in the world.

But the lofty alumna didn't seem to care anymore about the very institution that gave them their first flames of enlightenment. Yes. The life of the mind!

Sister thought back on the first class lecture she gave on the illustrious and illuminating philosopher/theologian, Blaise Pascal. Her competitor, *St. Jerome School for Boys*, had prided itself in churning out supreme intellectuals, so Sister sent a spy over to their school one day to eavesdrop on their classes and of course, to obtain some of their class schedules. That's when she had Sister Innocent III dress down in overalls, an old hunting cap and sunglasses pretending she was a mere custodian on the St. Jerome campus back in 1965.

Oh, those were the days! Sister Mary Boniface gained a reputation for being bold and innovative with her girls. She had many master the art of debate and turned the most whimsical and taciturn into young lionesses, roaring their points and fecklessly retorting with the best of them, including, of course, the boys from St. Jerome's, in the city and often state-wide debates. No. I will not have it! No merger! Especially with the arch rival, St. Jerome's, which was also floundering, though not as badly as the Convent, as her school was often referred to.

Nonetheless, Sister would not even give it a moment's consideration. Just then, a slight, almost velvety knock could barley be heard on the imposing door to her office. Boniface knew that knock. She emitted a slight sigh.

"Come in, Sister Constantine".

An old, creaking nun, smelling vaguely of cooked onions, crept into the vaulted-ceiling chamber. She was carrying a flat white box.

Sister Mary Boniface, now ensconced behind her great desk, looked up:

"What do we have here on this fine mornin?"

Sister Constantine grinned and announced:

"It's your favorite."

"Naw. That isn't what I think it is, is it? You little devil, you!"

Sister Constantine lifted the lid.

"Goodness. It's Krispie Kreme."

They both dug in.

"I figured you could use some cheerin' up around here."

Constantine smacked her old lips as she sat back in the luxuriant, silk upholstered chair. It was a relic from the old days. In fact, all of the furnishings in Sister Mary Boniface's office were antiques, indications from a wealthy past, when the Church was still so highly regarded.

When former graduates would bequeath their fortunes to the school. But now that the news was out about questionable sordid practices on the part of many a parish priest, it really shouldn't be any mystery as to why former Catholics were migrating to Buddhism or some other such practice and leaving their money elsewhere. Boniface found herself lost in thought again. Asking her associate, as she reached for another glazed donut,

"We were good. Good to the girls. Taught them to be assertive and strong. And to take up for themselves. Didn't we?"

Sister Constantine nodded her old head.

"Yes. Yes we did. And still do. Your point?"

Mary Boniface leaned back in her swivel chair.

"Oh, I would just appreciate knowing why we are so alone on the receiving end. Let's just put it that way. I thought we did brilliantly for our girls. Now I feel abandoned."

The older nun sighed and put down her half-eaten donut.

"Now. Stop all this. We'll be okay. You know that."

◆ ◆ ◆

I've been meaning to tell you that I watched our ingénue leave the premises just a while ago this frosty, late winter morning. Our lovely Claire discreetly strode out of the youth hostel in her street clothes, sashaying her duffel bag with its uniform skirt and blouse and saddle oxfords still neatly folded inside. She crossed the busy boulevard and strutted into the coffee shop and bee-lined for the ladies' room. There she transformed herself from gal about town to apt and proper pupil, affixing her grosgrain black ribbon at her crisp, white collar as she strode right back out of the busy café, duffel bag now flung over her shoulder. She looked so confident stepping onto the streetcar, as if she had nothing better in the world to do than to go to her convent school and act as if nothing had happened. Displaced? Kicked out of her home? "Why, me?" She seemed to be thinking: "Oh, you must be wondering about someone else".

And off she went, straight into the old courtyard that leads to the school building, and just in time for the first bell. Now perhaps, our girl here needs to keep up a mighty appearance of composure and calm, but I know better.

I believe it's best that I inform you that while our girl is making the best of things, courageously showing her more frolicsome side to her companion, school chum, the charming and witty American of African descent, Darva Jean Mobray, who is now greeting her with jumping-up-and-down-as-if-on-a-pogo-stick- school-girl excitement, our Claire, though laughing and giggling away with her, is completely hiding her truest anguish and sorrow deep inside of her lovely being. It sits inside her like a small, cold stone nestled in her belly. Believe me, readers. I know.

Last night, after using the hall phone, as Claire sauntered back to her humble domicile in the residency for whimsical, if not intrepid, youth, she fastidiously completed her lessons, and as she was placing her stack of books and notebooks on the dresser she suddenly broke down in a cascade of tears. It was difficult for me to bear witness to such weepy sorrow. The girl used up all of the soft white papers right there in its little box. Such was her desultoriness and sorrow that the child simply had to drown out any further tears by standing under a steamy hot shower. She didn't want anyone to hear her wails, for pity. I want to tell you that part of me boohooed with her. And a part of me didn't mind following her to her little shower stall, and watching her undress, but I left the premises. I truly did. She needed her privacy.

And I spun myself, (a miniscule orb of light the size of a child's marble, but at times, larger) in circles as I blushed, knowing that she had no idea of my presence, but I felt embarrassed for her nonetheless. I knew well of my potential transgression.

After she finally pulled herself away from the shower stall and quietly dressed, sniffling slowly ceasing, I stayed with her and bore witness that she would sleep soundly and peacefully which she seemed to be doing once she shimmied herself between the coarse and scratchy sheets of her simple bed. As she slept, I whisked myself about, spinning and circling above her as I sprinkled portions of hope all about her sweet, resting head. Now I have no proof of what effect I might have had. It was probably nothing. But I desire this anyway, for I was the one who first heard her cries. I was the one answering to her deepest wish that bleak frigid evening. Whether I can grant anything, I do not know. And so I remain.

♦ ♦ ♦

The two elderly nuns finished their donuts and set the box aside on one of the corners of Sister Mary Boniface's ancient desk. There were piles of papers underneath, but Boniface waved her hands in the air, dismissing the mess.

"I'm so overwhelmed, it doesn't matter much where I stack things anymore." Boniface shuffled some of the papers and slid them into file folders. Looking up from the messy heap, she lifted the receiver of her ringing telephone.

"Mary Boniface speaking."

The gentle nun nervously picked at the single, wiry, white hair jutting from her chin.

"… Yes, Mrs. Molyneaux. I'm sure your girl is here today, as she almost always is—may I ask why you are calling? No, nothing has changed. As I told you the last time you inquired, we don't take boarders anymore. The last year we did that was in 1952. I was just a young novitiate back then. People don't send their girls to live at Immaculate Heart anymore. Times have changed. Did you ever call Our Lady of Prompt Succor…out in La Fontaine Parish?"

Sensing that the call might be a delicate one, Sister Constantine removed herself from her chair, waving a goodbye as she made her exit. Boniface nodded her head at her fellow sister and listened intently, the receiver cradled in the crux of her ancient neck. There was an even longer pause before Boniface barked:

"…Yes there is a federal penitentiary near there, but the girls are protected, Mrs. Molyneaux, if I must tell you: there is no way any institution will take in a boarder at this late stage in the school year. Especially if the child is leaving us in a mere four months or so for the better pastures that university life offers. Isn't that right?"

Sister Boniface detected a slight blip on the line.

"…Hello? Mrs. Molyneaux?"

Sister Mary Boniface gently hung up the phone and shook her lightly covered head. It was a little circle of lace that now crowned her graying pageboy. Long gone are the days of the starchy collars and white, cardboard frames inside voluminous veils of black fabric. There have been times when Boniface actually pined for the old habits. Somehow, those floor-length gowns with the accompanying heavy wooden rosaries with their equally cumbersome crosses swinging away at the shins gave her an authoritative heft that was missing with the post Vatican II smocks and smart plain suits she and her fellow sisters have been reluctantly wearing for the past forty years.

Boniface swiveled her chair toward the great window that overlooks the courtyard and leaned back, gently tapping her pen on her lower lip. She did not know this Mrs. Molyneaux very well, except that she had given the school some fiduciary support over the years, of which Boniface was most grateful, even if she had to look away as she slid the check into her skirt pocket.

There were a couple of occasions where she and Mr. Donaldson, the school's comptroller, were invited to Mrs. Molyneaux's home for an afternoon of tea, sherry, assorted pastries and a check or two from the general neighborhood till of the school's attendees. But the good sister asked herself: Now why on earth would this woman want to send her daughter to a boarding school? Who, in this day and age, thinks of such things? Boniface pondered this a bit more, but wondered about something she had recently overheard one of the other girls talking about as she was walking the school halls one afternoon. It was something about a piano being removed. This girl's piano. And it was her mother who ordered the deed. Now why would a mother do that?

There was another knock at the door. Unlike Constantine's light, barely audible thump, this was a brisk, all-business rap a tap. Boniface knew this knock as well.

She swiveled her great chair back around to face one of the very few non-secular members of the faculty who still teaches at the academy. About ninety-five percent of the faculty were regular, civilian folk since there doesn't seem to be many who wish for a life devoted to our most Holy Mother, the Virgin, and her Son anymore, as Boniface has been known to announce on many an occasion.

"Antoinetta! How are ya? "

Boniface reached over and lifted the white box of donuts, presenting them to her guest.

"Look-y here. We have your favorite."

The nun shook her head and flapped her hands.

"No..no…Sister. New diet, remember?"

"Just testin' ya. So ..."

Srister Mary Antoinetta pulled up the antique parlor chair and got right down to the matters at hand, announcing:

"Well. I think we need to lock our heads, Sister. I have here a list of things that I've written out—things that may resolve some of our questions."

Sr. Antoinetta handed a notepad to Boniface. The elder principal smiled and placed the pad in front of her.

"I will certainly look this over. And I thank you so very much for caring, Antoinetta. But let me ask you something—that girl…the senior with the long, black hair. The pretty one who's always in some kind of mischief, the one who nearly gave us a heart attack when she was found with the little scholarship girl jumping on the bed of Saint Veronique of Arles a few weeks ago, the Molyneaux girl. She's in your Applied Arts and Arts History class. How's she doing?"

The pert, middle-aged sister wriggled in her chair.

"Well…I can't really tell that. You know how it is with these girls. Most of them are so worked up about the boys they're chasing. But we don't worry about that so much anymore, being that we constantly have to watch this business they do on their cell phones. This text messaging! I had to practically wrestle two girls to the floor yesterday before they finally gave them up. Cheating, you know. It's come a long way from the old crib sheet days."

Boniface raised her brows.

"They cheat in art class, Antoinetta?"

The usually jocular nun corrected her superior:

"It's *Art History and Applied Arts*. I do give them tests in the History section of the course and yes, unfortunately, they cheat. Even in my class. And passing notes just isn't what it used to be, either. This electronic stuff goes on and on all day long. And I'm exhausted trying to keep track of it all. But, let's see…Rochelle Claire. Is that who you're talking about? Yeah. She seems to enjoy the class. But I sense a melancholia with her, in spite of all the clowning she and that Darva Jean do all day long. But these days, I'm not so sure about her. Take a week or so ago. There was one morning where the girls were in their pastels just going to town. Very quiet in there when they get to work. I looked over at Claire and while it appeared as though she was gingerly streaking the pastels on the paper and such, she wasn't really doing such a thing at all. Actually, I noticed she was doing something else. Sort of on the sly. Underneath that massive sheet of sketch paper, and the drawing on there was quite nice, but, I got a bit curious and casually walked over to the window to adjust the shades some, and I looked down and saw that she was writing music like a little…well…composer. Scribbling all kinds of complex bars and notes with scrawls in the margins. She had pages and pages of it in her lap, too.

41

"And I stood there behind her with my eye glued there a minute or so. I wanted to make sure that what I saw with my own eyes was true—the girl was writing music, and without an instrument. Now how do you figure that?"

Boniface perused the good sister's notes as she spoke, and looked up.

" Thank you. Thank you for informing me of this, Antoinetta."

"Is there something wrong?"

The old nun smiled:

"No. Just looks like someone's missing her piano, that's all."

◆ ◆ ◆

And I have managed to creep in here as well. Actually, I'm going to interrupt here and...just call me the invisible eavesdropper of human souls, nuns notwithstanding. In this strange tenancy in this very world where I truly don't belong, humans appear so fascinating to me—quixotic, actually. In the way things look from my standpoint, there's a glowing ray of light that emits from the top of human heads.

You, dear readers, are apparently not aware of this. But it's something to see. Sometimes the colors are grayish and murky and have a humming kind of glow, like a low flame in an old furnace. Need I say, those are usually the questionable characters: petty thieves, cat burglars, politicians: high and low.

At other times, I've noted a plum-like hue emitting from some individuals in jet-like streams not unlike a miniature fountainhead of sorts. But these cloistered ones have an interesting assortment of soft light shows going on. It might be useful to imagine that spirits like myself have special goggles—as we see the unseen and perhaps, hear with an uncanny precision. If I must, I couldn't help tuning in on what that crisp little cloistered woman just said. And I will be so bold to say that I believe our Claire does, indeed, long for the mahogany grand.

And curiously, I, too, am drawn to what she is scribbling when the mood catches her. For some reason, I rather enjoy a cozy feel to what the girl is doing—but it all escapes me. And it's been a while since I last witnessed her musical scribbles. Seems our Claire is much too worried about how she will persevere through cap and gown day. And she has that little front she must bravely put up for all to see. Survival shunts such whimsy aside, for now, the girl must go forward. And miss her fine piano, she does. I have also seen her take out these sheets of paper and attempt composition without an accompanying instrument.

◆　◆　◆

But Claire was not in a frame of mind to take out any blank pages this morning and attempt a score. In fact, all inspiration seems to have left her as her focus has turned to the task of simply squeaking by. Questions like where Claire is to scrounge her next meal or how's her budget going to stretch into a few weeks' stay at the hostel and more simply, could she afford a latte or will it just be a house blend most mornings? These were the concerns that vexed her now. Claire also wondered if, somehow, this new set of worries would show. Would one of those nosy old nuns stop her in the halls today and ask questions, say, about Rita?

And being that she is frail and old, how long should she wait before checking in on Mrs. Gaynor? And better yet: Is there a quick job she could take during after-school hours, or weekends so she doesn't end up on the streets?

Yes, these were the grown up worries that pestered Claire now. Frightening images of racing through nocturnal streets with her things in tow roamed the dark corridors of her soul. The thought—"What did I do to deserve this?" looped through her mind repeatedly, not unlike a doomed caged gerbil as it fruitlessly charges its little body forward in it's toy, miniature, runner-wheel with no hope of ever making a final destination.

But Claire also searched for clues as to the origins of this new locked-out situation. Was it the nose-ring ordeal, or maybe the evening last month when Claire lighted one of her father's expensive Cuban cigars as she skipped down the driveway in the midst of another argument with Rita? And Rita, then, lifting her skirts and high- tailing it after the girl, resulting in a chase down Beaumont Drive? Was that the incident that tipped the proverbial scales? But, of course, any neighbor who might have bore witness gave the scene a shrug of the shoulders for it was business as usual at chez Molyneaux.

Claire scratched her pretty head as she attempted to cull that foggy episode from her memory bank. "Oh, that! Did that set Rita off in finally shutting me out?"

Claire honestly wondered: Aren't there other gals out there who light up a cigar once in a while? In her case, it was one of Hilaire's Romeo y Juliettas. Yes, those. The elegant and prized cigars he keeps in a miniature humidor by the bar in the living room. The ones he takes out only on very special occasions. But Hilaire grinned when Rita stomped back into the house, her nylons looking like a stray cat had caught hold of them, relieving its clawing instincts on her bystander legs.

"Where is she?" Rita bellowed, slipping out of her fashionable flats, now a mess with tufts and lumps of mud and grass.

Rita glared at her husband.

"This is not funny, ya know. Your daughter is bad. A bad girl. And she fights me tooth and nail when all I want is the very best for that brat!"

Hilaire briefly looked up from reading his magazine.

"Rita, give the kid a break. Besides, she's a teenager. Why don't you unwind and take it easy?"

Good, old, mellow Hilaire. As diametrically opposite of his rigid and status conscious wife as one could get. Some would say he appeared that way because a brandy snifter of Benedictine & Benedictine or Hennessey cognac would usually be at his side when these scenes would explode between his lovely wife and daughter. As these ordeals became more frequent, though, Hilaire began to call them his after-dinner theater hour. And his was always a front-row seat. Truth be told, the only seat as Claire's brothers were usually upstairs on their computers, playing violent video games or sending fresh, if not pugnacious, emails to strangers in cyber-space.

On that particular evening, when Claire finally reappeared looking like a Bosnian refugee, her hair a sweaty and matted mess, her school uniform shirt-tail hanging out, knee socks now wet and gathered at her ankles, legs cut from racing through weeds and dead, thorny rose bushes, she looked straight at Rita and casually announced:

"Dad, when are you divorcing Mom?"

Claire devilishly kicked off her muddy oxfords in the hallway aiming them at her mother with her soaking sock feet.

Hilaire watched the two of them hissing at each other from his favorite easy chair. For a moment, Rita paused and looked directly at her husband as if to say: How dare you let her get by with this?

Hilaire then bellowed, gesturing to his daughter:

"Hey. Fork over any extra cigars right here, girlie. You know you ain't supposed to take those. Come in here, Rochelle Claire. Come tell your Papa you won't be takin' my cigars anymore, ya bad assed kid."

Claire would often catch that barely perceptible wink in her father's gaze in those awkward moments when Rita would demand a fatherly scold from him. Such moments made Claire smile. And right now, she sure missed her Pops. True, Dad was sort of on the brash side, but he brought balance into the household with his down-to-earth style. He didn't worry whether his daughter bothered with frivolous things like selecting the correct suit for tea at Miss Duval's, the old social club of the debutante elite. The sort of venue Rita pressured her daughter in partaking. Dad was basically kind, so much so that he seemed to be impervious when it came to his wife's often under-handed malicious ways. Poor, nice-guy, Hilaire. How like Oedipus he seemed to be: blind to the truest of truths, good soul that he is.

Unlike Rita, though, he wasn't the type to kick his kid to the curb, no matter how many altercations there were between his wife and daughter. Claire could only surmise: Was it any wonder he took off for that assignment in the Middle East? Maybe he has a double life. Maybe he even has a mistress. Oh, how she would love to have a puff of one of those cigars right now. That and maybe a swill of beer, one of those expensive, foreign ones. But Claire was at school and this was an impossibility. Better wait 'til later, when I'm back in my street gear and in the hostel, my new home, and life, the life of an adult. She rather liked that idea, though. Sliding onto a bar-stool like a college gal and ordering a beer after finishing her homework. She could sort of understand why grown ups did that kind of thing. Living on your own didn't seem to be all that easy. Forking out that money for a roof over your head. Watching the bank account and credit card so you don't max out. Gads.

After managing to get through her first class, Claire strutted down the main stairway and headed for the cafeteria. The break bell had just sounded off and she had to meet Darva Jean for a private conversation in their favorite meeting place: the shrine-room of St. Veronique of Arles in the old part of the school, adjacent to the convent, the area where they have their art class with Sister Antoinetta. Claire had about eleven minutes.

A group of girls were standing near the register at the end of the cafeteria line. They all looked at Claire as she approached the counter. One of them, Andrea Paternostro, walked up to Claire and fingered her black locks.

" Hey, Girlfriend. What's up? How's your bag?"

Claire grinned, slightly backing away.

"The bag is over and done with. I'm not in love with you, Andrea. Move over, I need to get an orange juice."

Bag was a term the girls used for mother. Or really, any parent, be it mom or dad. Another gal also moved toward Claire:

" What? No more drawing her ass in art class?"

Claire grinned.

"Naw. No need."

A chorus of giggles emitted down the length of the break queue. Claire was referring to an incident last month when, in frustration, during a demonstration Antoinetta was attempting to give in charcoal line drawing in her

Applied Arts/Art History class, Claire leaned over, took a sheet of paper and announced she was drawing Rita's sagging ass. The way it looked in her sloppy gray running sweats.

It was the hoot of the day. Claire tucked her carton of juice in her coat pocket and briskly walked out into the courtyard area.

"Gotta go, you brats."

An anxious Darva Jean Mobray leaned on the little prayer table of Saint Veronique of Arles, in the room where the nun dwelled when she came to visit the Immaculate Heart convent in the late 1780's. Down through the ages, the nuns kept the saint's room as it was when she lived there. It was not unlike similar models one sees at wax museums where historical figures are displayed in their homey settings. When St. Veronique arrived at the port of New Orleans, she was only to stay at the Convent for six months, but this turned into years as the French Revolution broke out in her home country practically right after her arrival. This fact was one of the major selling points Boniface used in getting wealthy donors to the school to continue their contributions. Often Boniface would say, during these elaborate luncheon affairs after a silvery ring of the crystal goblets, "Imagine. We are the only convent in this fair United States that has ever housed a genuine, canonized saint. Now that should mean something to all of you. Yes, indeed-y."

But Darva Jean Mobray was thinking none of that as she leaned against the old saint's holy prayer mount, leafing through her mother's *Essence* magazine as she waited for her friend. As soon as Claire appeared, Darva Jean tossed the magazine on the little bed, got up and walked toward her friend waving her hands in the air.

"I know this has been a drag, girlfriend, but ya gotta hang tough. What you need to do is look at the new possibilities, hear me? It's good you got yourself away from the bitch. I say it's a blessin. Gimme a hug."

The two locked in a warm embrace for they were the best of buds. A slight tear emitted from Claire's right eye.

Darva widened her eyes and slightly backed away:

"You still got that allergy thing goin on? Must be. Cuz they sure ain't no reason any body should cry when she gits herself away from the bitch of rottin' witches in the most medievalist of hells."

Claire emitted a weak laugh, turning toward the window to check the premises of any penguin-wobbling nun in the courtyard below. She looked back at her friend who was now eating a chocolate croissant and lounging on the saint's little bed. Darva remembered to set aside the little wooden crucifix that lay on the nun's pillow.

Claire paced the room in little circles. "I'm worried about money. I have about two, maybe three weeks' worth for a stay at the hostel."

Darva Jean crinkled her brows:

"Nah. We'll take care a that. Even if you have to stay with us. I mean it."

Claire leaned over the little bed, lifting the cross and waving it over her friend: "Bless you, child. Saint Darva-girl!"

◆　◆　◆

It has not been the absolute worst of times, to paraphrase that famous English scribe, but it certainly hasn't been anything near the best, either. Freedom, as dear Claire has learned, comes most decidedly at a price and she surely seems to have paid up for hers. In the three weeks that have passed since Claire and Darva had that bonding conversation that first frigid morning of Claire's newly founded independence, it has been a rather rough ordeal to say the least. On a brighter note, somehow and quite amazingly so, Claire has managed to hang on and pay for the room at the hostel. The piano lessons, however, ended. This embarrassed and distressed Claire a great deal. Rita simply stopped her payments and after several unanswered phone calls to Claire's mother, Mr. Logan didn't have much of a choice but to let her go. But that was not easy for him. Mitch Logan liked Claire and thought well of her playing.

He even offered a payment plan, but Claire was too stretched financially as she also had a similar arrangement at the hostel. Her living quarters, of course, being a priority, but even that is soon to come to an end. The management only recently told Claire that she could stay six more days—max because of their by-laws.

"This ain't a long term residence, ya know. We'd get into trouble if we kept you longer".

The owner, J.J., looking like an aged Stanley Kowalski of Tennessee Williams fame, remarked as he caught up with Claire just as she was leaving the premises one unusually warm, late winter evening. He rubbed his enormous chest with his knuckles, his hairy arms bare as he had on a T-shirt—not unlike the depressing, thin-threaded, low-life kind that Marlon Brando wore practically during the entire movie of that popular 1950's play. Claire tried not to show her distaste for the man, who was old by Claire's standards. (Maybe he was about 55?) But the owner flatly told her, as he blew cigarette smoke into the night air,

"Yeah, we can't do no long-term stays heeeah. Besides, we got Mardi Gras in two weeks an' we need deeze rums."

Needless to say, Claire was trying her best not to panic. She felt that, somehow, she would find a new place, and lately, she was wondering about her friend, Darva, and her own home life. Now understand, this was not easy for Claire. She felt that living on her own was the best thing to do. Besides, she rather liked it. Yes, there have been occasions where college guys asked her out on dates, and Claire enjoyed some of those outings. And yes, there was even one brazen coed who offered a live-in, share-situation if she joined him in moving to St. Louis. It's right up the river (meaning, the Mississippi). Just look at it as an adventure, he kept saying over *Dos XX* beers one night.

But Claire wanted to finish school and get started with the pursuit of college. She had already begun the process of researching and making inquiries into various schools of music around the country. Claire felt that now that she was on her own, she might have to join the ROTC or something of the sort to pay for college. She didn't believe a scholarship could be possible. But these were the far-off plans. They had nothing to do with the gritty reality of paying the bills for life in the scary present. As things stood, Claire was amazed that she hadn't gone through all of her meager savings. And, true, there have been spells of employment for dauntless Claire these past few weeks, but the jobs began and ended rather abruptly.

It seems both managers told her, respectively, that she wasn't a "fit". Aiming to not take these things all too seriously and, at times, fighting back incipient tears, Claire has persevered. Actually, only a day or two after her latest firing, Claire nervously picked up where she left off and got right back to the task of landing a better job.

As they were both gleaning local employment web sites on a school library computer one afternoon, Darva Jean rolled her eyes and sighed:

"Girlfriend, I don't understand how your servin' soft ice cream cones to some after school brats would be such a problem for those butt heads. I mean, you just some ice cream dispensin' bitch just trying to git the job done. So what's this bs about fittin in? Fittin "into what? That dumb ass outfit you had to wear? What exactly do the bitches mean when they say that stuff? Did you ask them that?"

Claire shrugged her shoulders as she jotted down some of the postings on a notepad that lay next to the computer mouse. Ah, Darva Jean! Claire was grateful that she was around to give her advice and comfort, and she had everything to do with Claire keeping her sanity at school. Thanks to her, everything was kept under wraps at *Immaculate Heart*. Somehow, Claire felt it was all going to come together. Claire paused at one posting, figuring a hostess job at 'Round a Burger might be a good choice. It was only a few blocks from school, and midway to the hostel.

Darva quipped,

"You crazy? I mean, you already have a lousy- assed track record with those places. Try somethin else. How's about retail? I can see you sellin' perfume or CDs or somethin' besides havin' to wear some cowgirl outfit and seatin' some old men after they pinch yo' ass. Girl, you don't even git a tip for that stuff. You can ax my cousin, Rolanda, about that one."

Darva informed her friend that her cousin finally took her employer to court for encouraging such uncouth behavior to go on in his establishment.

"Those outfits were god-awful. I mean, not appropriate, thank ya, girl. Especially, for the Ronald MacDonald crowd. I'm talkin' like—"do you want some pole-dance action with that dessert" or what ? And them old men? Puuuuuleeeze! I mean a purty puhleeze."

Darva further explained that, eventually, her cousin won the lawsuit but it took her two years and after she got her money, her attorney helped herself to well over half of it. But, of course, Darva had to admit that the pay out really worked to her cousin's advantage as she used that money to become an X-ray technician and now she's in a nursing degree program to become an RN.

Darva reconsidered:

" Well…maybe it wasn't all that bad in the long run, okay? Let's see what they're sayin'".

♦ ♦ ♦

It certainly appears that she and Darva Jean, the girl of African descent who is now American, are having a time finding a way for Claire to subsist. I admit, I am also concerned about her bumbling attempts at procuring income. Alas, the ways of the young! It is certain that, in time, our girl will find her way. Maybe it is only because I am spared the realities of physical upkeep—one of the advantages of non-material existence, true, but in these past few weeks, I have made some remarkable discoveries. Foremost is the recent revelation that I am in the new century that marks a new millennium. Now, I realize you may be unimpressed by this. You may even find this to be amusing. Maybe you're even laughing at me, wondering to yourselves:

"Where did he think he was? Ancient Greece?"

Well, I must tell you, this is not so easy to tell from my perspective. If you point out that I must have been able to detect the time period and what modern country I am inhabiting by the way things look, or the language, the way it is spoken, or the way language sounds, I must tell you that spirits see the impulses in the mental plane before they formulate into words. So it doesn't matter the language. You see? I understand the information as content, before the utterance of any vowel or consonant.

As far as the way the environment appears, it's human life, all right, but objects and things that are different or unfamiliar do not register right away. Yes, moving vehicles sport all of these unusual colors and varying shapes and sizes and there are so many of them. Food is packaged in a strange way.

Small machines that cook without fire or electric coils. Large metal boxes made of materials that keep things frozen and cold. And, of course, there are things I find a bit baffling and peculiar. Like these little screens. And big screens. And middle-sized screens that have the moving pictures inside of them. They seem to be attached to a device that's sitting on a flat surface. Then people gather together to sit and pass around these silvery elongated rectangular devices and when they pick them up, they punch buttons and new pictures and sounds appear on the screen.

I notice the people in the room watching the screens often get into arguments and disagreements about what they want to watch, but much of the time, what they end up viewing are more people on the screen disagreeing while one person, usually an attractive woman or man, is trying to keep control of all the chatter by asking testy questions or pausing to face the viewers, informing them that he or she must break away for these little skits where the idea is to sell a product in a very short amount of time. A depiction of a talking reptile convincing a silver haired entrepreneur to buy a certain insurance; a cartoonish mop and broom making wise cracks to a befuddled patron scrubbing floors; an impossibly attractive young woman, painted and powdered , pouting shellacked red lips into the screen as she announces how long they can stay this way if you would only buy the product now flashing atop her bare shoulder. This would not be so bad, actually, if there weren't so many of them. Eventually, the program returns with the same people arguing and disagreeing.

I tell you, I don't see why humans would want to do this with their time. (I'd rather be cuddled up in a wooly throw on a comfy sofa and reading a good, old- fashioned book like you are right now, sensible sober-minded, readers, yet that, too, is morphing into tablet-sized, hand held screens).

So I have learned that this is one type of screen: the usually large ones in sitting rooms or parlors in people's homes. Then there is the smaller screen that sits on a desk and is attached to a typing board. I find these things to be practically everywhere, but when no one is sitting in front of these desk screens, I notice these odd little objects that show up and sail around the screens when there's just a black background. It's as if they are there to take advantage of free time and are out to express themselves when the words and moving pictures have vanished. I love those things. The ones that show up and flutter around when no one is there. In fact, I'm in a relationship with one of them. I believe they are called, "screensavers".

I will tell you all about it. Just give me a moment while I attempt to describe it to you. It's a little multi-hued box that moves and then turns into a ball and then blooms into flowers and eventually splits and reproduces itself into more blooming bursts of colorful flowers and then it becomes a moving box all over again to start the process once more. The first time I noticed it, I thought it was trying to tell me something. Being that I appear in a similar shape—an orb of light that can shrink and enlarge at will, as I once told you—I thought something was malfunctioning on my end. So I attempted to mimic its movements. But to no avail. In frustration, I somersaulted my way forward and slipped onto the surface of this screen and then found myself rolling about with this object and somehow became enchanted. In fact, I stayed there for quite a bit and ever since, I figured out a way to intercept some of its movements. It's quite fun.

Actually, it helps me to forget what I am doing here for a while. I rather enjoy it, as these objects don't seem to have the complications that come with human beings. Not to insult you, but since I am sort of midway between that cool world of detached and colorful objects and the cumbersome world of humans, I rather enjoy having a choice.

Sometimes I wander around certain environments looking for clues to just what sort of human I could have been. Now what do I mean by this? Things that may help me understand who I was, what I might be doing by being among your world, in the first place. Well, yes. I am on a quest and romping around and looking at things and reading people's thoughts can trigger certain memory impulses.

Or so it seems. But no pictures really come to me. I still seem to be baffled as to why I am here. Oftentimes, these little adventures turn out to be educational processes of discovery. And that is not such a bad thing.

Take the other day, for instance. I was roaming about the old neighborhood where Claire formerly dwelled. I became curious and wanted to investigate as to the goings on in her old home. So I entered through her upstairs bedroom window. Similar to the way I had when I first heard her cries. Swiftly, I floated among the familiar effects of our dear Claire. Porcelain dolls and fluffy toy animals from her childhood sadly remained on her little shelf. Her posters, the stacks of mirrored, musical discs, her books and picture albums, her sloppy piles of sheet music (both her own compositions and others) were no longer there, of course, being that they are now stored away in those strange, oily, slippery black sacks at the old woman's house, I forget her name.

The one who drinks spirits in tall cold glasses and walks with an assisted device. Anyway, those things are no longer about, and neither are our girl's clothing and such. It was sad.

But I managed to roam the hallways and slipped through the locked door of her mother's boudoir. I saw a figure lying face down on the fluffy, buttery-hued satin bedding. She seemed to be sobbing. So I paused and wondered what the matter could be. There were a number of photographs spread out on the bed where the woman lay.

I attempted to get a closer look at the pictures, but soon found myself inside one of them, which was of a girl in gym shorts tossing a ball to another and laughing. It seemed to have been taken a while ago. I wasn't sure how I was going to slip back into three-dimensionality, so I paused and looked over at the puffy-eyed mother of my little friend. She looked like she had fallen asleep. Now, understand, sometimes I can enter that domain of a human sleeping. It's strange. But something told me not to attempt this. So I left.

And I drifted back down the hallway and into the room where Claire's brothers dwelled. Much to my chagrin, the screens were completely off. I was already missing my orb and flower-box companion who sometimes shows up on one of them. I then wandered into a closet and fell into the boys' laundry hamper. I was stuck in there for what seemed to be hours, but I am sure it was only a few minutes. The smelly socks and undergarments made it seem interminable. But then I thought of the elderly neighbor and immediately found myself right at her dining table between two glowing brass candlesticks. The old woman was cooling her soup, a chowder of some kind. I swiftly investigated the little bedroom that held our girl's belongings. They were all still there. On my way out, I noticed a scrawl on a paper near the telephone. It said: "Claire to call in morning".

◆ ◆ ◆

It was about half past six in the evening on a school night. Darva Jean was still clad in her *Convent of the Immaculate Heart* school uniform, much of it a wrinkled mess as she slumped herself in the recliner in the living room as she watched television. Her mother was tired and not in the best of moods. She was changing out of her work clothes in the next room as she attempted to get supper going for Darva and her twin brother, Dan. Darva could hear her mom fussing away. Finally, she stuck her head in the living room doorway and blurted:

"Ain't no white girl comin' over here, Darva Jean. Especially, with that upscale 'hood she's coming from. No way. I don't want any trouble with some society white woman, either. It's enough I got you and your brotha on my hands. Besides, where in the hell would we put her? Now no more about that stuff, hear me, girl?"

Darva Jean rolled her eyes and slid down the cool leather recliner, her crumpled plaid skirt now practically gathered at her hips, the tip of her lacey yellow mini-slip slightly brushing the floor.

Darva bellowed:

"Ma. You don't understand. This is an emergency situation. That ogress of a mother kicked her out in the cold!"

Lucinda Mobray stepped back into the living room holding a spatula at her hip.

" Why should you care 'bout that girl? She'll live. She has relatives, Darva Jean. What on earth are you doin to that skirt? Hey—go get your brother. He's over at Rodney Jeffers' again. Tell him to get his butt over here or he's the new appointed household chef. Go on, now."

Darva Jean slid a bit further down to the floor, waving her arms in the air.

"Mom. He knows when to come in. He has no money. What do you think he's goin' to do? Not come home to eat? You know…we could put my friend in the back cottage. Dad's old office. You were supposed to get a tenant in there, remember? Well it's just sittin' there. And Dan has his friends over. So why can't I?"

Her mother shouted from the kitchen:

"She's white, for one thing. And you and Danny are scholarship kids. You can't afford someone else's dramatics. 'Specially some white girl's. Your butt's goin' to a private university. A good, reputable, school where they will pay your way. Cuz, honey, I am tired of being a part time bus driver with no benefits. And your father being back in Michigan…up to I don't know what."

Darva's mom reappeared in the living room, salad tongs in tow.

" Stop slumpin' around. Go change. And get this place cleaned up. Tonight's my women's group."

Lucinda Darlene Mobray wanted so badly to forget that she gave birth to four children, even though two of them are now on their own and living away, experiencing relatively successful lives. She only had the twins left and was anxious to begin an exciting life of retirement and freedom as soon as they are off to college. Although, she admitted, she did not know where her income would come from if she were ever to leave her part time job as a bus driver, good, though the wages were, even without the benefits package she would have if she went on full time. Lucinda or Lucy as she was known, liked the flexibility of being able to go to museums and attend a sculpture or design class at the junior college and only complained about her "meager" wages to keep the twins focused on their A-B-plus schoolwork.

Lucy basically blew it when she was young back in the early '70's by running off with a good looking brother from

Kalamazoo, Michigan who was a leader on his college campus (University of Michigan at Ann Arbor) and later, an involved member of the radical, *Ebony Underground*, a matter he would later have to face and reckon with. (And of course, that is, indeed, another story).

But back in the hip '70's, when anyone who was a Black intellectual and supported the likes of Connie Chambers, the outspoken, feminist, protesting, and later incarcerated, Black chick with the wild Afro and fringe politics, Lucy was an open book. And Lucy Darlene had never experienced such a confident, smart, swash-buckling-ly handsome black man like her wayward husband before, so she was game. And, actually, ready for the Harlem Renaissance writers, the James Baldwin essays, the myriad Eldridge Cleaver and Malcolm X diatribes. College-educated, multi-talented, gifted in the gab department, and *a few others as well*, David Sterling Mobray was a catch, pure and simple. And Lucy had never encountered such a kind as he, quite frankly. Dave Mobray was exciting and a little dangerous.

They met near the center stage at the annual New Orleans Jazz and Heritage Festival in the spring of 1973. Lucy was in her second year of college, and all of nineteen. She, herself, was an excellent student. She wanted very badly to be a designer, a stylist, or a *professional* interior decorator. Her mother and grandmother and even her favorite *auntie* laughed at her. Made light of her ambitions. This hurt Lucy's feelings terribly.

"There aren't any jobs for a black woman doing such a thing, Lucy, child." Her grandmother joked. "Get yourself a practical degree. Be a medical transcriber. Be a corporate or legal secretary. Forget that stuff."

To this day, Lucy felt this was why she ended up dropping out of college. No one believed in her. No wonder she ran off with the good-looking dude from Kalamazoo.

And, of course, Lucy did not want to reminisce too much on all that that brought to her life: four children, a cheating, good-looking nearly ex-husband, dull jobs, hopes for a life as an artist dashed.

Well, looking over at her daughter gathering herself from the floor, dusting her green and gray plaid uniform skirt from a school that's considered the very top–drawer of the *top drawers*, with a feminist old nun at its helm, (it was why she wanted her daughter to attend—that and the generous merit scholarship that was awarded to her) Lucy could only hope the most excellent of lives for her baby girl. Baby genius. Smart and good looking like her dad, but maybe a tad impractical as well. (*Wonder where she gets that from?* Lucy mused) Darva liked language and turning it into this rapping and rhyming stuff.

What is all that? Lucy often wondered. What ever happened to *music*? *Like Stevie Wonder, and the Stylistics? Love songs. The kind we listened to?*

" You know what's the matter with you kids? With your downloadable, MP3 playin culture? You kids don't know what love is. Now isn't that something?"

Lucy made this remark to Darva as she and her brother came into the kitchen to wash up at the sink.

"Oh, and good to see you, Danny darlin." Lucy added.

The twins looked at each other and laughed.

Lucy threw a stern glance their way.

"I don't see what's so funny. At least, we *loved* when we were young. Yes we did. But maybe we messed it all up for you. We thought we *loved* and we married for *love* and practically every one I know is now divorced and that's not good. Maybe we ruined love for you kids and all you do is gripe and moan and rap about how much you—I dunno, hate. Hate the man. Hate the…I dunno…the "bleepin' chick that's two-time-in' away, the dude that stole your car. Your pimp buddy that's now servin time."

Darva and her twin gave out an even heartier laugh. Danny could only laugh so freely at home as he hated the shiny metal braces that fenced his teeth. His friends constantly gibed him about it.

Lucy wanted to get him the invisible kind, but they were almost fifteen hundred dollars more than the old standard ones.

She gently grabbed her son's chin.

"Those are comin off soon. Three more months and we are done with those. So keep smilin, Good Lookin."

Lucy glanced over at the wall clock. She couldn't wait for the girls to come over. Tonight's discussion was going to be on the wonders of Malta, the ancient civilization of the *Wise Woman*. Oh, Lucy would often daydream about getting away and traveling to all these exotic places. Although most of this was a fantasy, true, but Lucy so enjoyed imagining getaways to the Spice Islands, the ruins of Mexico, or, of course, an adventurous cruise to Malta. The gals in her women's group often chat away about the once powerful domain of women, of their lost power and rule. This seems to help Lucy come to terms with her life, being that she was pretty much decidedly single. "Not after *that* husband" she would often joke. But deep inside, she felt that men were too heartbreaking, too painful. Friendships with chicks were all right to Lucy. She looked over at Darva Jean and wondered. Actually, she realized she wasn't really listening to her daughter's chatter. What in the hell was she talking about? Darva's incantations seemed incessant.

"...well, her momma put her out in the streets. White people are bitchin, that's all you gotta know."

Dan rhythmically slapped his palms on the kitchen table as his sister rapped. Darva slowly blinked her eyes as she continued:

" ….yea, an I'm tellin' ya, bro. White people? Heck, yes. They torture and torment each other more than we could ever imagine. Take that movie star, Joan Crawford? She was one bitchin bitch with them caterpillar eyebrows. Those white bitches busta boom–a-rang, wid their bitchin, trippin, boastin and bamboozalin with a busta movin, and bodaciously bull-doazin', bum rappin, but with a boisterously bumblin, bale a' bull-dunk'n at 'em. Forcin' her baby girl to get on her knees and scrub the tile bathroom floors, but no buck's a stoppin' there. Nada—as in a negative notation. We got us here a most egregious situation. Justa wrappin her baby's head in a rope soap —then beatin her child with the bare, icy cold, coat-hangin' bobbed-wire. Just enough to give her a poke and that's no joke. Na, ah. That's a warm up, bro. I mean, we're talkin' disparagin', draconian dragons of despicable dribbles of drool dragging disproportionate distillations of duplicitous and deranged derelicts to the damnable, detestable, denizens of…"

Lucy set the salad bowl aside and walked over to her daughter, waving her arms in a referee fashion, wishing she had a coach's whistle around her neck, blurting:

"…Darva and Danny—dishin in the kitchen…Honey…. Stop! Breathe!"

Brother and sister now cackled even louder.

Lucy shook her head and chortled to herself as she sprinkled dried dill into a salad bowl.

"Okay you two…"

Lucy ordered, as she walked over to the stove to stir the spicy pasta primavera in the wok her kids gave her for Christmas. Lucy gave her daughter a stern look:

"Could you just peddle the metal on that stuff and come set the table?"

Darva smirked.

"You're a bus driver, Ma. It's cool. Stop and go lights all day long, with those customers rude and crude, slammin' brakes; always cuttin' to the chase, that's your metaphor and rhyme. But you gotta understand, mine is some serious sublime."

♦   ♦   ♦

Claire was hoping she'd be getting the signal from Darva Jean tonight. She had only two more days left at the hostel, and she had spent most of the evening organizing her things for the big move. Not quite certain where she would land, Claire was optimistic that Darva's mom would come through. But she had heard nothing so far. Claire went over the details of Plan B, which was to call old lady Gaynor. But the idea of having to sneak in and stay at the elder's with her mom and brothers just being a few doors away frightened Claire.

She also didn't want her mother to know that the old woman gave her a helping hand. Claire suspected that if Rita were to ever get wind of it, she might resort to some menacing and deceitful tactic that would inevitably mess things up for her even more down the line. She knew her calculating mother, all right, and she had reason to be wary. Claire wanted to get out and walk the neighborhood, maybe step into one of the college hang-outs, but hesitated. In fact, she took pause just as she was about to turn the knob on her cozy suite door. She so very badly did not want to run into Kevin, her companion who's become a little too interested in her over the past couple of weeks. Although he was a tremendous help in motivating Claire to fill in her applications and write essays and prepare her music to send to the colleges of which she applied, she was beginning to feel an annoying pressure from him; a pressure to make a certain decision, which Claire could hardly find favorable to herself and her overall life-goal.

Firstly, there was no way she was going to move away with him. Especially to St. Louis. What would she do there? Kevin would tell her that all she had to do is take the GED test and with her natural abilities, she could easily get into a college there. But what Kevin didn't seem to understand was that Claire was not at all interested in getting to know him any better, although she appreciated his musical knowledge and smarts, in general, he himself not yet graduating from college and taking a semester off by traveling to Mexico and the Yucatan and then stopping off in New Orleans to work odd jobs before heading back upriver, as they say. *Good riddance*, Claire thought to herself when he would talk about going back home right after Mardi Gras. In fact, Claire took out a calendar the other day and literally counted the days when he would be gone. Not that it so much mattered. Claire had to leave the hostel anyway, but he was still living nearby. And she didn't want to run into him.

Claire stepped away from the door and sat back down on the little bed. She picked up the phone she bought at the drug store. One of those disposable, pay as you go phones. She was waiting for a text message. But it had already been two hours since she last messaged Darva Jean and Claire could only assume the worse and started to re-think a possible situation with old Mrs. Gaynor. Maybe it would be okay. She could use her back door to come and go. And after all, the old lady is there by herself. Maybe she could use some company. But the more Claire thought about the prospects of this, she became depressed, figuring Mrs. Gaynor would retire about eight in the evening and Claire would be very restricted in her freedoms. Actually, Claire loved her new life in that it has afforded her flexibility and choice she had never experienced. How could she return to a life of rules and restrictions? Well, it would get her away from Kevin. That could be a plus, Claire figured. Claire glanced down at her little phone. A text message came through.

"Ansr is- No. Tom. wl xpln."

Claire tried to keep her cool. And she did for the most part, but inside, she felt that downward shaft opening. The inner maelstrom of emotions whirring uncontrollably while her mind was attempting to maintain a level of cool. Clear thoughts and calm perceptions—all will be well, she assured herself. But as Claire was attempting to settle her mind, her bony fingers nervously scrambled under the little bed like a wild crab escaping its captive fishing net. Surely, there should be a pack of cigs lying around under there, or maybe an old butt of a joint, Claire thought. But her delicate hand froze as it landed on the cool metal of a pillbox our girl had somehow forgotten she had placed there. *Oh, gosh, Mom's painkillers.* Claire wanted escape badly, so she snapped the lid open, took out two pills and popped them in her mouth.

Then she got a warm beer out of her closet and drank that, too. It was supposed to be a souvenir from her first date at the hostel A Canadian. A guy named Rolf. Now she liked this one. But he left after only two days. And, well, life certainly seemed to be more exciting in Montreal than in St. Louis. Claire swilled the warm beer and tried not to think of her meager prospects. *What's next? Life in a dumpster?* If Claire could not come up with another job and a new place to crash, life was going to get a tad messy, that's for certain.

◆ ◆ ◆

I believe we should take pause here and consider our dear Claire. She has been a paragon of bravery through and through. She has shown up, suited up and saddled up with reality and we should be honored to be following along in her life. In spite of the fact that I have not made much of a difference to her in all these weeks, I can only look on with concern and as much care as I can muster. Often, I am left with amusing myself in some way, as I can't seem to depart from this place. Now what is the explanation for this? Somehow I remain enchanted and therefore bound. Perhaps it will all come to me someday. But in the meantime, I am "making the best of it", as they often say on the flat-screened devices that grace these domiciles of the first century in this new millennium. I rather find these things a bit tedious, as I prefer observing humans and human activity in live, three-dimensionality. So last night, I ventured outside and followed along one of these Mardi Gras parades and found myself enamored with the festivities. All week long, I noticed the events cumulating. I watched several groups of people, families and individuals as they each prepared for a week of fun and frolicsome celebration.

I noticed that there was a group of young students changing into marching band uniforms and people slipping into festive costumes as much wine and spirits were shared among many. But I did not notice our Claire partaking in any of this preparation for the big week to come. In fact, she has been most dismal, at times, and fearfully studious. And not a cheerful as a young girl should be, quite frankly. I looked in on her mother and her brothers as they were preparing to walk out of their warm and cozy home to attend the very same parade of that evening, but they were to be in a different part of the area.

I could not help sternly observing her aloof mother, buttoning her sweater and looking at her young sons with a care she did not grant her daughter. What was she thinking? Didn't she realize how worried and even frightened our girl could become, having to brave it all and persist with her studies for fear of anyone knowing her shameful circumstances?

I also caught a glimpse of the old woman, Mrs. Gaynor, a mere house or two away. She was fast asleep in her lounger chair, the moving picture screen animating away as she snored. As I am usually keen on keeping watch of Claire, particularly at dusk and into the evening hours, our dear child happened to come upon the festive scene as she was leaving yet another employment inquiry—this time, at a pet care facility. Being that our capricious one had no prior experience, I could tell she was not going to be—as they say, a "fit"—thus the single tear that emitted from her eye as she left another dashed employment prospect. And sad to say, she walked with such a heavy heart. I wish I could say I pointed our girl to the celebratory event, but the music and cheers were enough to get anyone's attention. The fanciful torch flames leaping from tall poles being held by rows of mostly young boys of African descent who are now American, the brightly hued stringed lights and marching, rhythmical, music along with colorful beaded necklaces, the silver and copper coins flying in the night air to be captured by a merry and enthusiastic crowd certainly had my attention and soon enough, our Claire's. It excites me when I see her forget her troubles. And there she was, leaping in the night air with the rest of the crowd, grasping for trinkets and such.

I certainly enjoyed observing the floating caravans of movable papier-mache', over- sized dummies and gross personages from a theme having to do with Genghis Khan, I believe. They all vary. These parade festivities of the Mardi Gras. The day before, I caught one parade in which the theme was Napoleon's last stand and eventual flight to Elba. But this Genghis Khan theme had my attention.

I followed along as each of the decorated vehicles displayed, I suppose, portrayals of highlighted events in the history of the great Mongol's rule over Asia. I was enjoying the pageantry when the maskers on the transport depicting a period when the Great Wall of China was seized by the ruthless tyrant caught my attention.

As I gazed with an almost child like curiosity, I found myself transported to that very majestic site as an impromptu wish formulated itself within my thought-emotion being. At first, I felt immersed in an almost indescribable beauty. But I soon realized where my wish brought me. It must have been about early morning there, as all was hushed in a silent and dew like imperturbability. I could see that majestic, winding work of constructive mastery and genius snake itself in a most exquisite display amid a lush green and blue mountain range of which I have yet to witness and it occurred to me, readers, that when I was last human, I must have loved it so, and this must have something to do with why I now linger among you. That I was clear across the planet on mere impulse is a handy convenience for me, I must admit, but my wish right then was that I could transport our Claire to share such a sublime loftiness.

Yet as I roamed this Oriental maze awhile, our girl was still standing there in the street among the merry makers, waving her lovely sinewy hands in the night air, hoping to catch a string of beads to hang on her bedpost back at her humble living quarters, which may not be hers much longer. And it wasn't too long before I returned.

After the last of the marching bands and walking krewes made their final appearance, with the street cleaning machines soon following, I noticed a young man as he was striking up a conversation with Claire. I swiftly moved closer to the scene and spun around in circles in protest as he handed the child a notepaper with an announcement written on it. Now the young man happened to be handsome and all that and certainly had our girl's attention. I managed to get a glimpse of the message and it had something to do with a job where young women answer ringing telephones and say all sorts of sordid things to these callers for a fee. Then I read the advertisement he was handing her. It read:

Entertainment for the lonely and the desperate, and all you do is answer a phone and chat!! Commissions, 25%. Make $100.00 per four-hour shift!

I attempted to take the notice out of her slender hands, but to no avail. I shouted at the crafty young man to leave the girl alone, but it was no use. As she left him there under the street lamp, the last of the sweeping street cleaners passing by, I followed the innocent one as she walked the dark streets. I saw that she was thinking about the list of jobs she had looked into over the past few days, distressed that none would materialize.

So bogged down was she, her thoughts funneling through tight little channels of fear. Crinkled brow worries vexed her young spirit like disorderly bees in a queen-less hive.

Would the child be able to obtain employment at another tired, burger and fries establishment or perhaps, a simpleton telephone job she frantically applied for just the other day? And that, an innocuous one selling newspaper subscriptions or, perhaps, raising funds for a needy Fire Department's Spring Fair?

Oh, but this questionable telephone job where she would create fantasies in words and breathy coos to a rather sordid and dubious clientele. It was bad enough she saw this on the computer and I tried to obliterate that posting off the screen by rolling myself over it—but, again, to no avail. The twenty-five dollars an hour flashing neon colored digits were too inviting, especially for one so desperate. And now, this questionable character telling her that all she had to do was show up at five p.m. on Saturday?

As Claire skulked along, I noticed the rows of charming homes with their nearly bare, deciduous trees standing singularly amid vast lawns of the finest landscaping. It occurred to me only when she approached the lovely lane with the magnolia tree growing in the middle of it—the one where cars must drive around its massive trunk in order to continue on to its quaint and serene cul de sac—that I noticed she was going to pass by her former home. As she got closer, Claire walked quietly on the grass to the side windows of the great house, a soft, buttery glow emitting from inside. Her brothers and her mother were standing around in the foyer tossing beads and trinkets back and forth and laughing. Claire's lovely face was pressed to the cool glass of the parlor window as she looked in.

Claire smiled as Marcel whacked his older brother with a toy machete before the two of them broke into a light jog around the living room. For a moment, she and Phil locked stares. A slight grin formulated on the boy's face as he turned to see if their mother was about. Luckily, she had gone into the kitchen. The boy approached a crouching Claire as she squatted uncomfortably in the cool grass outside. He took out his metal calling device and pointed to it, mouthing, "same number!" An infuriated Rita suddenly appeared, pulling the boy by his ear, and shaking him

"Who's out there? Tell your friends to go home, Phillipe!"

Claire quickly moved away from the glass and flattened herself on the frigid grass holding her breath for fear she would be discovered. Rita gave her eldest son an incredulous look and briskly walked toward the window. Now, readers, I looked at this woman in the face as she peered outwardly. Her gaze fixed on a wall of blackness

71

outside. I studied the worry lines, the caked make up, the heavy brows and painted eyelids, the frosty pink lipstick she applied on her lips with such fastidious care, and I could get no read as to the condition of her soul as it scrutinized behind light hazel eyes. This puzzled me slightly, as I can usually get a sense of what's going on inside there, but with this woman, I cannot really tell. I can only see a selfish anger that's centered on a hardened hurt somewhere very much entombed within her convoluted, tightly wound little spirit. It reminds me of a small fist, this woman's soul. At the same time, I looked down on our translucent damsel, lying there still as a 'Sleeping Beauty' on the moist flower beds of late winter, looking up at a dazzling full moon, and I had to smile to myself as a shiver of pleasure pulsated within my orb–like being. For only an inner condition such as hers could create such radiance, luster and ripe beauty.

My, she looked so luminous and lovely; her sweet breath coming out in soft frets, her youthful virginal bosom swiftly cresting and falling as she rested there, gathering her thoughts.

Later, back in her gloomy little traveler's room, I dozed well that night. Yes, I do rest, curious readers. And it's while I lightly float above her tranquil body. There I gently pulsate and flicker not unlike a glow-worm newly escaped from a lofty summer's dream.

♦ ♦ ♦

The school courtyard was filing in with students as the first morning bell of the old convent rung out. The two girls sipped their cartons of orange juice; a banana, croissant and a half-eaten donut lay between them on the little bench. Claire took a bite of her soggy croissant and swung her mane of hair over her face. Her long black tresses hung lifeless and wild like the languid gray moss that swayed from the Spanish Oaks that graced the school grounds. Claire took out her wide wooden brush and attempted to stroke her mussed up locks. Darva Jean leaned over to her friend as she yawned.

"Girlfriend, you look like you had a really bad night. Like after somebody dragged in some furry feline, alley-cat's butt, you crawled your way in, lookin for a place to croak."

Taking a final sip of her juice, Darva continued to explain the complicated matter to her once again.

"My momma's just not lettin up, girlfriend. Says she needs to keep that spare room available for a tenant next month, but she's been sayin this b.s. for weeks. Ain't nobody movin in back there. I think she still believes my daddy's comin back, that's what I think. Huh. Like hell."

There were some other girls looking over at the two of them. They huddled in a small circle. An occasional hoot and giggle could be heard.

"Let 'em laugh all they want. They're stupid, most of them." Darva quipped. Then she announced to the little group.

"Hey, Come over here and say that! Ask her yourself, Prejean. And you too, Comisky!"

Before any of them had a chance to respond the group of girls suddenly fell silent and darted their gaze downward at their collective saddle oxfords, a possible sign that a nun was in the vicinity. And sure enough, Sister Mary Boniface silently tiptoed her way through the dew-soaked grass in her black track shoes, approaching Darva and Claire from behind.

"Well, good morning, girls!" Boniface squinted, arching her little hand over her brow as she faced the two of them.

Claire swung her mane of hair away from her face in a single, forceful wave. Darva Jean got up and pulled at her

73

sagging knee socks. Finally, Claire practically stood to attention as well.

"Mornin, Sister Mary Boniface!" they both said in unison.

The old woman smiled.

"I see you two seem to be doing well these days. Especially you, Darva Jean. Heard about your leading our team to a hearty victory the other night in our debate with *Saint Joseph's.*"

"Yes, Ma'am." Darva sheepishly replied.

"Now, Darva, you're mother and father must be proud. Let's see how we do with *Saint Bernard's* in two weeks, eh?"

It was at this moment that I noticed that Darva Jean blushed. I didn't realize that a person with such coffee-caramel skin could, but there she was, blushing all the same. It had a kind of creamy glow there on the cheek, yes it did.

Darva smiled. "Yes, Sister Boniface. I'm looking forward to it."

Boniface then tapped Claire lightly on the shoulder and leaned closer.

"Claire, could you come to my office right after lunch today? I need to talk to you about a little matter. "

A chilly blast of fear pulsated through Claire's young veins.

"Yes, Sister. Of course."

The diminutive sister flapped her tiny hand as she turned to walk away.

"Good bye now, girls. I know your first class is starting soon."

They both watched as Boniface hobbled across the red brick courtyard to greet some of the faculty as they talked among themselves in the breezeway.

Darva leaned over to her friend.

"Gosh damn, girl. I'm scared to death of that old nun. What you think she wants from you?"

Claire emitted a shrill sound, then quickly sat upright.

"Rita. It's about my *bag*, girlfriend, I can feel it."

◆ ◆ ◆

Rita tried to ignore them. The women she ran into in the smart shops and boutiques along Evangeline Way. She could feel their whispers and gossip pouring from their lips every time she'd run into any of the Runelle de la Houssaye crew, in particular, the higher echelon of the social elite of which Rita so unabashedly aspired. *It's that Anne Leblanc,* Rita hissed to herself, as she tried to distract her thoughts by roaming her hands through the Hermes scarves at *Lamar's*. She lifted each of the silky creations and running her fingers through them, occasionally checking the stately beveled mirror that flanked the great wall of that elegant boutique for any familiar face that might be walking through, hoping she would make it to lunch without having to take in the cold stares and pinched lips of her social club acquaintances.

And that's exactly what they were: *acquaintances,* including: *that Anne. She must be blabber mouthing away about my business. I knew I had too many of those vodka tonics that night at the club*, Rita thought.

Regretfully, she felt she had said too much. Now rumor had it that her daughter was pregnant and living in squalor with some handsome, wayward bohemian from Quebec. Actually, after getting wind of it so many times these days, her daughter was rumored to be living in sin while Rita didn't really give a damn, or so it seemed.

After all, there one would find her, shuffling cards with her bridge buddies, shrugging her shoulders, resigning herself of her recalcitrant, cigar puffing, teenage daughter. But there certainly was something too odd about it all, most of them would say. Claire Molyneaux was always at school, according to some whose daughters were fellow classmates and most heard that Claire was applying to colleges of music all over the country. Somehow, she was maintaining herself as a proper *Immaculate Heart* scholar that would make any parent proud, although she seemed tired and nervous most of the time. But who wouldn't be, given her cruel circumstances?

Rita was also getting some cold shoulder treatment at home. Her sons avoided talking to her at every turn, and after Rita snatched Phillipe's cell phone to scan his call record, he took to hanging out tutoring *Special Ed* students after school. One night, Rita cocked her ear to her sons' bedroom door and swore she heard Phil say her daughter's name. A sadness fell over her. Maybe she was too rough on the girl. Maybe she should pull on her coat and take the car out and search the college bars. She had heard her daughter was seen playing pool for money late one night, drinking cheap beer and yes, smoking *stogies,* as they were the only kind of cigar her daughter could afford.

But Rita stopped in her tracks as she was on her way to grab her things. She couldn't do it. She could not see herself bringing her daughter back in from the cold, harsh world. She was not going to think of it any further, either. Her mind was already made up. The decision was final. Claire had to learn what it's like to be on her own and to be without and see what she will do about it, yes. And Rita had to be strong in her stance with such a wild and difficult teenage daughter.

Well, Rita was not going to think about all that mess back there in her very own childhood, either.

What was done was done. Lord knows Hilaire tried to get her to talk more about the roots of her troubles years ago when the children were very young. That shrink, that funny looking man who tried to help them earlier in their marriage, when Rita and Hilaire sought help for her nightmares and phobias, he was just too slow for Rita, and actually, too stoical and methodical, asking all those silly, irrelevant questions. And so, Rita walked out on the two of them, Hilaire and Dr. Whatever-his-name-was, as they puffed a cigar and pipe respectively in a leather-rich, book-lined office one autumn evening so many years ago. *I just can't do that now*, Rita decided as she headed for her bedroom and softly closed the door. There she would linger in her chaise lounge and busy herself with crossword puzzles, needlepoint, anything to stave off any spooky thoughts of wrongdoing. And lately, it was getting worse.

Marcel and Phil were under strict instructions not to go into any of this with their father. In fact, she convinced Hilaire that now that he was taking on a fresh contracting position with a new company, to use that business's domain as his email address and disregard his former ones. Clever Rita. She has it all down, or at least, she believes she does.

Little does she know that Hilare has become rather tired of her and took on the spot in Dubai to get some real distance from the woman and actually, the once a week email between the two seemed to suit them both. Of course, he did miss the kids and wondered why they had only one family chat on the living room phone with just the boys, of course, and that it was a short and sweet one.

"Well, they're teens now, Hilaire, and you know all they got is their friends and other such nonsense on their minds" Rita would say when he would suggest another chat on the family phone with everyone included. And so far, this was working. And it's only been about five weeks now since he left. And about four and a half weeks since Claire was shown the door.

Rita would often repeat to herself: *She's just too much work, that girl. And sassy.* But Rita knew she had to be careful with her words to these gossipy women. Rita had to remind herself that it was always Claire who left. Not the other way 'round. And Rita was now wondering if she had let anything slip in the past few occasions when she mingled with her socialite, fair weather friends. She could not shake the look she got the week before when she ran into Anne Leblanc and Tiny Welles at the *Daughters of the Pre 1803 Society* luncheon. *Well, I might have said something.* What, Rita could not exactly recall. The matter had something to do with La La Bruno's telling them at the Bienville Club bar one evening about a niece sneaking out of the house late at night to meet friends down at some hub near the river bank, and Rita blurting, "Well, hell yeah, stuff like that and then some! That's why I kicked Claire out for good." Rita prayed she had not said it. She truly did.

But she did. And now she was going to have to deal with it. And she would. She would just say, next social occasion, *"Well, you know, it got to the point, Tiny, that we just couldn't stand it any longer. And I even saw the girl take out a cleaver from the kitchen drawer one night and I swear it, she was walking right behind me with the thing gleaming right at me. I kid you not".*

And as far as Claire's obsessive piano playing?

"She would get up at two am and start playing away like it was broad daylight. We were just at our wits end with the girl."

But none of this was true. Or if it any of it were true, Rita was distorting things, big time. Claire did take out the cleaver one night, but it was because Rita said that Consuelo, their Mexican cook/cleaning woman who came to the house three times a week, could not find it as she attempted to cut up a chicken for dinner the next day. Rita had asked Claire if she could find it, and she did. While Claire scrambled the pots and pans in the lower cabinets as she searched, Rita ranted about the girl's staying an extra hour or two to practice her piano playing at Mitch Logan's, her now defunct piano teacher. In the middle of egging her on about it, Claire waved the cleaver as she declared that nothing was right for Rita. That accepting that her heirloom piano be removed from the house was not good enough for her mother. And in typical fashion, Rita abruptly walked away from her daughter in a huff. Claire only followed her with the cleaver still in her hand as she tried to complete her point. It didn't take long for Rita to turn around abruptly and accuse her daughter of stalking her with the sharp object.Rita waved her hands in the air and shook a fist at her beautiful daughter, who was now crying, admonishing the child that her father would excise her out of their *will* if she continued to bug her about her confiscated instrument. But Claire was only trying to justify her lengthening her practice time at Mr. Logan's.

Yes, Rita is a pernicious one, all right. And if her husband knew she had made these sort of threats...well, Claire imagined, he wouldn't like it, that's for sure, and Rita knew this. Usually, after such harsh words, she would warn her daughter:

"One word to your father about this and you're outta here, you wretched little witch", she muttered through grinding, clenched teeth one night.

Claire would think back on these terse and fierce fights with her mother while she rested on her little bed in the rooming quarters down by the college bars.

Sometimes a tear would fall from her eye, rolling off her pretty face and landing on the little pillow. Often, though, it was more than a tear. In fact, there would be a leaky faucet of tears. And Rita, before retiring on her luxurious, satin covered bed, would immediately obliterate any thought of her daughter being in such a state. Actually, she was more concerned about how her *front* was holding up to her peer group and how bad a slip of the tongue she might have made more than any actual emotional, mental or physical suffering her daughter might be experiencing at the moment, and on this particular evening, Rita sat up in her fluffy covers and wondered if she had remembered to get her Oleg Cassini suit from the dry cleaners that morning.

♦ ♦ ♦

Sister Mary Boniface looked rather crisp and refreshed as she popped a peppermint candy in her mouth. Nodding to the girl, she announced, while parking the candy in her cheek,

"Well, now, Claire. I want to thank you for coming in here today. Make yourself comfortable. I'm just going to get a note-pad here. Don't look so frightened, young lady. Sit down. Please."

Claire nervously clenched the hem of her uniform skirt as she skulked over to the fancy silk chair that faced Sister Mary Boniface's great desk. She really tried to not show her trepidation. Her mind reeled with possible shocks that may spring unexpectedly from the ensuing conversation. Claire thought it might be good preparation if she were to imagine as many possible scenarios as she could: *" Your mother*

called and told me that she had you leave the premises." Or
" *I called Child Protective Services, even though you are
only a year's shy from being of legal age. It was all I could
do. They are coming here to take you away to a home for
girls like yourself downtown.*" "*We know about your
situation, young lady.*" "*Is it true that you are expecting a
child, dear girl?*" "*Do you know much about being a Foster
Child?*" *We have a list of interested parties that wish to
adopt you temporarily.*"

"Yooo hoo! Anybody home in there?"

The good nun was now snapping her fingers about an
inch from Claire's lovely face.

Claire came out of her frightening reverie.

"Oh, Gosh. I must have blanked out there for a
minute, Sister. Too much studying late at night, I guess."

The frisky nun quickly replied:

"I see. Is that what your doing with your free time?"

Claire straightened herself in the little chair.

"Yes. Sister. Of course."

Boniface bobbed her little old head.

"Ah…okay. Then tell me, how are things with you? "

Claire shrugged her shoulders.

"Great. Really good" .

Claire lied, but continued with a steady clip:

"Looking forward to *Gras* and seeing the results of
my college applications, Sister."

The good nun leaned back in her great chair and
nodded. Suddenly, she picked up the telephone receiver
and told her secretary to hold all her calls. Then she
looked back at the girl seated in front of her as she hung
up the phone.

"Well. I'll just get right to the point, then Claire."

Boniface paused for a moment then came straight out with a blunt:

"I know about your mother."

The very bones in Claire's young body froze. The soft, wispy hairs shivered down the smooth nape of her neck. All vertebrae stiffened as she became mummified right before their very eyes. In fact, she could feel herself turn to stone as the good sister continued to speak, that is, until she caught the tail end of the nun's lengthy sentence.

"…Come again, Sister?"

"Well…I think it's a shame that your mother doesn't seem to appreciate your capabilities. Taking away your piano like that. So I was going to offer you free use of one we have in our convent. Don't worry. We mind our business around here, and the piano is in a parlor we rarely use. So you will have your privacy. In fact, I'm giving you the key so you can lock the door when you practice."

Boniface swiveled herself from her chair and opened the lower drawer of her desk, fishing around for a set of keys.

Claire flushed with excitement.

"Wow. Sister. Thank you." Claire announced as she took the golden key from the nun's moist little palm.

There was a palpable tone of meekness, of actual gratitude that the good sister rarely encounters, especially these days, among such girls of privilege and pedigree, which makes up the majority of the student body at *Immaculate Heart*. Actually, so many are of spoiled temperament and haven't a clue as to the sweat of life, the struggle to earn a wage, like the tough times the good sister witnessed in her own family during the hard scrabble Depression years when she, herself, was a mere child. Rochelle Claire's sweet, humble tone also reminded Boniface of when she was a volunteer counselor at the

girls' quarters at *Juvenile Hall* when she was a young
novitiate, back in the late 1950's. Often the girls there
were so grateful to receive a compassionate listener to
their woeful tales of beatings, abandonment, and near
destitution at the hands of callous and malicious families
or other such grim situations and well, the good sister's
heart collapsed right there in her little old chest.

" Oh, come on…" with accompanying flapping hands,
" …it's no biggie. Good time is right after school, though.
We can give you two hours a day if you like."

Claire rapidly bobbed her head.

"Wow. Yeah. That's good."

Boniface then sat back in her great chair and looked
up at the girl and smiled.

"I hear you're very good. I have to tell you, though. I
never heard of a mother *not* wanting her child to practice
the piano".

Claire let out a nervous laugh. "Well…my
mom…she's just a character."

"Is she?"

Claire felt that she was digging herself into a little
hole with that one.

"Well. I dunno, quite frankly, Sister."

The old nun intently looked into the girl's warm,
obsidian eyes

"I dunno, either, Rochelle Claire. Everything okay at
home these days?"

Claire nervously shifted her lithe, thin body in its
quaint silk chair, sweat beginning to formulate on her
crinkled brow, a bumbling *Miss Muffet* spilling her
porridge.

"Sister, I don't want to be rude here, but I do need to
run to study hall."

The old lady leaned back and let out a yawn, tapping
her pen on her desk

"Alright, then. Run along. Hope you get some practice in today. Remember, ring the bell out front and somebody will show you the room. Don't forget the key."

Claire quickly shot up from her tufted silk seat and thanked the good sister for the third or fourth time and hot tailed it out of her office. Darva Jean was waiting for her just outside the library when she showed up, exasperated and out of breath. Claire flapped her hand at her sweating neck:

"I don't trust that old lady, girlfriend. She says I can play piano all I want after school in the convent. Then she kept hinting around about Rita. I think it's a trap. I'm not going near that place. Besides, I have to work. My piano playing days are over. At least, for now."

Darva fiddled with her book bag, and looked down at the floor, checking to see if there was a roaming saddle oxford or two sticking out from under the stacks. Darva turned and lowered her voice to a fierce whisper:

"How did that old *white*…"

Darva spread a spry, dimpled smile, which Claire returned.

" …*nun* know you had no piano?"

Claire quickly explained that Sister Boniface told her she had overheard this from another student in the hall one afternoon. But Darva assured Claire that her hunches were probably right. That old nun will end up asking her questions and sticking her nose into her business all the more if she were to show up and practice there. Surely, there had to be another way. Some place where Claire could hang her hat and also practice her piano. That would be the ideal. As Darva Jean and Claire walked the stacks of the library, they brainstormed on possible options. Could she call her old piano teacher and ask if he had a spare room? Claire could clean or something in return for practice time. Claire shook her head. She did not feel that was a possibility. It just felt weird.

Darva piped:

"I know, girlfriend. Your piano playin days ain't over. I got a cousin. Now, he's a little different. Actually, he's a real smart guy. He's like 36 years old. Maybe older. Related on my mom's side of the family. He teaches math at *Sophie Newcomb*. Real brainy.

He's considered a master at algorithms. But he's…well…he's an entertainer on the side. Let's just put it that way."

Claire looked at her friend very intensely:

"So what's the catch, Darva Jean?"

"He has a piano in his house. Got a nice sized place. Not so far from where you're living. He'll let you practice there. Maybe he even has a spare room. In fact, I know he's got an extra room."

Claire toyed with the key the nun gave her and sighed.

"It looks like there's gonna be a *catch*, either with those nuns or with your cousin. So what gives?"

Darva shrugged her shoulders. "Just lemme call him, then you'll go check it out for yourself."

◆　◆　◆

It seems our Claire is not alone in facing one perilous situation after another. If you believe that humans are the only ones with troubles, you might want to re-consider your precepts. I've been having some difficult times, myself, as of late. Of course, I do not want to pester you with my own woes, but here in the spirit realm we, too, have our issues. Is this the word? I overhear that word coming out of the big flat moving picture-talking screens quite often. Issues. As in: " Well, you have issues, then". "Oh, no", a news announcer speculates, this famous wealthy couple or whatever, " are having issues" about their marriage.

Or, this or that country "is having issues with this fractious group of rebels" or how about the universal: "But they do not understand our issues, you see?" It goes on and on, off into space, as the varying channels on the parlor screens of the world flicker back and forth, transmitting this information through fiber optic technologies as they bounce from satellite to transmitter to satellite.

Yes, as you can see, more new words pertaining to your modern world have been added to my list of discoveries. Now I ask, do you think much on these colossal floating machines out there in your orbit? If not, may I suggest that you take a look outside a jet aircraft window sometime during one of your overnight transports? Now, look at the black sky on the side of you. Cup your hands over your eyes and focus. The ballet of the satellites is performing so many miles above your collective heads. And there are hundreds of them. I go up there now and watch. But I only recently learned of these things. And what piqued my curiosity was this tune I overheard from the backyard of one of Claire's neighbors near her former dwelling place. A tune about satellites spinning in the sky filled the air and intrigued by this term, "satellite", I decided to investigate.

And just as that very idea registered with me, my thought-emotion being zoomed right past the Stratosphere and my... there is a wonder-world of intricate machinery, floating and waltzing right above your lovely planetary orb! They move and dance in a celestial lightness as they transmit billions of microscopic blips of compressed information: images, words, ideas, at an amazing speed. It seems to be a nervous kind of wiry energy. I must admit, I am not exactly fond of these giant dragonflies of metal with their spinning propellers and oddly shaped extensions and wings, if you will.

For me, it's like drifting into a low-emission, lightening field. I don't believe you humans understand the reality at work as you go about your digital business. Understand, I can appreciate the practical value of it all. But when you step away a bit and think about it, what does all this transmitted imagery and information contain but practical things at best? Is it prolific as say a bubbling brook? Is it as profound as the beauty of a sun setting? Is it transmitting the love that moves your soul into new territories of sentience and knowing? A knowing that can transform harshness to something woven out of love itself? No, it cannot do these things. Cannot render in this way, and perhaps, this is why I wanted to see for myself, if this little tune had any real meaning. But for this pop crooner, this Lou Reed, to fancy that an indifferent, cold piece of machinery could ever transmit a function of love, well, I thought, it is indeed, quite frivolous. But then again, it could be nice. Imagine such a thing. Which brings me to some further points.

Material living is a very different matter from spirit living. From a spirit's perspective, all of this becomes most interesting. Now, I mentioned my own troubles. Let there be no doubt, there are matters that pertain to us spirits. I have come across some strange beings. And of course, they are only visible to me.

They pass through on their way to somewhere. I am not so sure. In fact, I am not so sure I want to know where they drift. Some are angry and are looking to pounce on a human. I have remained still and unobtrusive, as I have observed their odd preoccupation with earthlings.

Right now, there are two entities that show up in Rita's affairs. They observe her as she pours herself a whiskey or when she is in the process of cheating someone in a card game, or when she's lying to her husband about how well their daughter is doing and that her busy little schedule often prevents her from coming to the phone to chat with faraway Pops. Well, this thuggish spirit who happened to be drawn to pernicious Rita's dark heart, gave me the once over and in so many words told me to bug off as I was checking in on the woman one evening. It's not my nature to hang around such distasteful creatures, so I bugged off. But I am wondering what sort of mess these unhappy beings could cause. So I am now watchful all the more in keeping these creatures away from my beautiful musician, my little composer, Claire. Did I tell you? When the opportunity arises for our girl to forget her survival woes, out pops a makeshift keyboard she has fastidiously drawn on a light wooden plank she keeps under her bed. There she takes her notebook and writes the music that pours forth from her lively little spirit. I watched her doing this and I heard the notes she was selecting and I even made some suggestions. And I must say, some of them were quite good.

And for a moment I thought: How could that be? How would I know the sound? How would I know the outcome of these musical suggestions? But there I was doing just that. Maybe it comes with being on this side of things. I am not so sure. Well, as she was finishing up her time composing, in popped this seedy little spirit, attempting to muss her pages.

I forced myself into a compact thrashing wind and got the bugger out of there, but I fear he may return with some companions. I say it's all I need. It's bad enough that I have no idea as to why I am here, but this sort of company pestering me? I am tempted to send the good nuns a message to pray for me. Yes. I will go there, and find sanctuary, and get this menacing spirit off my trail.

♦ ♦ ♦

Claire fell right in step with the St. Barnard *Marching Mayhem Band* on her way back to the hostel after yet another failed attempt at employment. This time, she brazenly walked out before anyone could tell her whether the job was right for her. And she simply didn't know if she cared anymore. What could be more dull than rolling dough and sprinkling toppings on limp, soggy, depressing pizza, anyway?

It was a messy, low-down way to earn a buck, that's for sure. And it was gross. When she got the condiments out of the refrigerator, Claire swore she saw weird things floating around in the little trays. An older guy and a fat lady just sat on the stools in front near the cash register, chatting away with customers while Claire did everything. She couldn't wait to get out of there, so she threw off her apron and left with the twenty-five dollars in cash they handed her.

In spite of yet another lousy job experience, there were some good signs in the air this evening. To run right into her favorite marching band just as she was crossing Evangeline Boulevard was a remarkably lucky sign for Claire. It had to mean something. She could just feel it. And as she watched the pageantry of yet another Mardi Gras parade pass by, everything suddenly felt transformed.

Claire stood there for a while near the languid oaks, watching the horn section pass. The polished instruments swaying from side to side as their gleaming brass reflected the colorful array of lights from the floats. Claire waited until she could follow in step with the awesome drummers that gave the *Mayhem* their renown.

Roughly, there are about fifty drummers in all, marching and strutting in neat rows, thumping and tapping and thumping and tapping and Claire jumped along side of them and strutted all the way past the intersection that leads to the hostel. The flambeaux carriers walked just outside of her. She waived at them as they twirled and spun the flamed torches in the night sky, the crowds around them growing wild, with their arms waving in the air. Claire let her worries slip, at least, for a while. This was one of the older, traditional Mardi Gras parades that line up into the weekend before Mardi Gras day itself. The realization of this gave her a start, the precariousness of her dismal living situation becoming more pronounced by the day. The management at the hostel had given her a special break as she cried and begged the owner, Mr. J.J., if she could just stretch her stay a tad longer. At first, he was resistant. It was, after all, the season where he could get three times the money she was paying. But Claire's lovely doe eyes welled up and the man, thinking of his own kids, gave in.

"But just two more days, ok?" He scratched his hairy belly under his sweatshirt, the weather being a bit cool on that particular evening.

Later, back at the hostel and as Claire finished up her homework, lounging about in her over sized flannel gown and fluffy pink slippers, she noticed a text message on her little phone; a notice from someone she did not recognize. It read:

"Got the wd. 'bout u. Meet me tom. @ 4 pm. 1040 Bijoux Blvd".

♦   ♦   ♦

As even the best of us are wont to do, these chilly days and nights of being on her own has brought Claire to ponder the rather creepy unfairness of it all. As far as she could tell, it's been business as usual for practically everyone she knows. Classmates who are now former neighbors still attend *The Convent* with the fresh scent of perfumed soap on their necks and their eyes are always bright and rested from sleeping in luxurious, 600+thread count, Egyptian cotton sheets most nights. Of course, their bellies are full from scrumptious servings of luscious, piping hot pancakes, fluffy hot biscuits and velvety scrambled eggs wiggling on fine china plates most mornings while Claire rummages the industrial sized bins of generic granola back at the hostel, thankful she has usage of the plastic dinnerware as it was one of the many conveniences not included in her going away cache. Certainly, she's not complaining. The free breakfasts are actually the highpoint of Claire's day. All you can drink *Sunny Delight* and 2% fat –free milk. It could be worse, but let's face it: the beautiful stately homes of Claire's former neighborhood couldn't appear more indifferent these past few weeks as the poor child has clawed her way to survive in the underworld of marginal, low-rent life and all that that it brings. It was as if there were now two versions of life for Claire: *pre*-Rita's expulsion and *post*-Rita's expulsion. To Claire's young mind and spirit, it was the yin and yang, the alpha and the omega of reality itself that seemed to toss her into torrential emotional whirlpools of which she felt she could never quite safely escape.

Perhaps, then, it's good to know that there are individuals who remain consistent and stable, no matter the vicissitudes that life brings.

So what if old lady Gaynor falls asleep at about eight in the evening in front of the television after a couple of tall glasses of cold gin and soda? She's got a good (though aging) heart and a spare room, and in times like these, that is a major plus for Claire. Actually, this could work. Claire could stay true to her study schedule, (which has actually not gone so badly these days), review her music pages in relative peace and quiet, and Mrs. Gaynor would most likely see to it that the girl remain healthy. Who cares if she serves the same old tired seafood gumbo or turtle soup night after freaking night? It's better than nothing, and besides, Mrs. Gaynor would be fast asleep while Claire could stroll out of the back door and through the winding footpaths that divide the quaint avenues of her old neighborhood, thus bypassing her former home, where she would be able to make it out to Evangeline Boulevard fairly safely and un-recognized. She would then be free to do whatever's allowed. Make it to a new after-school job or a game of pool at the college bars. Or how about a bit of piano practice at the old *River Road Bar* where most of the patrons are too drunk and too few to care? It most definitely could work. Claire could be living right back there in her old elite stomping grounds, right under Rita's nose and no one would ever know it. Except for her younger brothers, Phil and Marc, as they are known to meander about through the leafy pathways on their bikes and such.

And what of it? Yes, it was a teensy bit risky, but the boys know fully well how impossible Rita could be, and more than likely, they would be happy to run into their big sister, who was so unfairly treated and now living on her own. Surely, they would cheer her on and give her comfort.

Actually, it wasn't that long ago that Claire ran into Phil at the streetcar stop near the hostel where after big hugs, they both agreed to walk over to one of the local college hangouts to have a bite to eat.

Phil couldn't have been happier to see his older sister and even said she was lucky to be out of the house. Phil kept shaking his head and saying he was counting the days for high school to end and he would be free, a prisoner knocking off time, and for Phil, that meant three more years.

"And I'm going far away, Claire. I mean, maybe even Oregon. Someplace like that. Mom gives me the creeps. Oh, I emailed Dad. I just said that she was treating you unfairly. He wants you to contact him."

Claire sat there pensively. Mulling over her chilidog.

"Yeah. I'd like to, too. I don't want to upset Pops, though. I mean, he'd come back and all hell would break loose. Besides, I love my new life, Phil. Okay. I'm basically broke. But I'm making it. And all Dad would do is bring me back to live with Rita. Ya know?"

Phil nodded his head. "Yeah. She's railing on us now. Marcel caught her at my computer, so now I have a spy device in my screen saver. It's pretty cool. She can't go in there so easily anymore and now she's threatening to take the whole thing out. You aren't missing anything. Hey, do you ever wonder why Dad married her?"

Both of them laughed. Claire blurted, "I have no idea, Philly-boy. Whewee."

But this was about two weeks ago, and since then Claire made the unexpected visit to the house. Why she was out that night walking the streets, thinking about her latest composition and ending up at her former home, she could not say. Maybe she wanted to check and see how it might be to return there, even if she would be staying at old lady Gaynor's. The impromptu peek through the living room window was just that. She didn't realize that Rita and the boys would be hanging around. Usually, they are in their separate rooms: Rita reading or crocheting and the boys doing their homework, or maybe a little cyber-stuff. But it was *Gras* season and she should have known they would've gone out. Now Claire was wondering if she was putting off contacting her father for too long. Phil gave her their dad's new contact information that he pilfered from Rita's cell phone when she was in the living room hanging new paintings one Saturday afternoon.

Phil rolled his eyes.

"She's stupid, you know that? She really thinks she can stop us from contacting Dad. Like... duh...gee whiz...like I don't know the company he's working with and that I can't get his info in seconds on the Internet. I wonder sometimes what planet she's living on."

Claire realized that Phil was trying to help his big sis feel better about the situation. And she knew he would fork over any money he might have had if he had it. But being that Phil is all of fifteen that would be a tough one to accomplish. Before leaving, Phil got up and squeezed his sister's soft hands in his.

"Beware of those wolverine dudes, Sis. And call me if you want. Oh, Marc says 'hi'."

Claire watched her younger brother walk out of the restaurant and along the tree-lined side street that flanked the bustling university section of town. It was difficult to fight the tears that slid down her soft cheek. She missed her brothers. She missed her former life where she didn't have to worry about paying for a night's rest like a perpetual weary traveler in a strange land while she attended school by day as if nothing had ever happened. It was hard living this *Jekyll and Hyde* existence and maybe that was why she now found the idea of old Mrs. Gaynor appealing. Yes, she would call her and go there. And let the old lady play grandmother to her *Goldilocks* misfortune.

◆ ◆ ◆

I want you to know, good readers, that before I left for safer pastures (as it were), I transmitted mental suggestions to our Claire in a sort of telepathic, text message way. Perhaps as a compliment to your clever,

21st century technologies, although, if I could be so bold, my method may be a tad faster as it is instantaneous and does not require any transmission process from one point to the next and such in order for the message to arrive. Not that it matters. It was just the idea that, perhaps, her former neighbor, (the elderly lady who snores), might be a good shot and it seems our Claire is now considering the situation. However, I am not altogether convinced that my meditative transmissions or her sheer desperation were the cause for such a change of heart.

Alas. As I surmised, I have found sanctuary here in the old chapel among the cloistered ones. In fact, there's a sweet little nook I enjoy here. It is a most tranquil place for relaxing and finding a respite from those vexing presences.

My worries and troubles are diminished in the soft, luminescent, golden glow of this marvelous little place. I have been hanging around here waiting for the good sisters to return from their evening meal for a while now. The chapel candles have been lit some time ago and already, they are melting into disfigured lumps of wax dripping down the sides of these finely crafted alters of wrought iron.

There is one very old nun mumbling prayers, I believe in the old language, Latin, and fumbling her fine old liver-spotted fingers on the black beaded rosary she clasps in her other hand. She has been praying in front of the beautiful lady, the virgin, for some time now. I am soothed by the soft voice and its supplicant tone. I am at peace here, at least, for a while. I rather enjoy observing these cloistered ones, their lives of quiescent silence and seemingly boundless equanimity. Sometimes, I join in the vespers, and I enjoy the presence of the cool marble statues of angelic and saintly beings. It all feels so comforting to me.

Occasionally, I have seen fellow souls; actually, rather weepy spirits enter through the stain glass windows above. They peer in and find themselves spinning in circles, looking for clues, perhaps, not unlike myself. But they are harmless and they usually don't see me. I am not certain as to why except it seems they are so intent on finding a resting place, and I am of no relevance. Actually, right at this moment, I am wondering why the good sisters are taking an unusually long time to show up for their prayers. All seems so uncharacteristically silent.

◆ ◆ ◆

And silent it is, now that the truth has come forth. Of course, it all came as quite a surprise. Just as the good sisters were all making small talk around the dining room table with Boniface chatting about the Molyneaux girl coming to the convent to practice piano.

"Please be easy going with her. She's rather nervous. Actually, I'm wondering why she didn't show up the other day."

Sister Agnes suggested that maybe the girl's a bit taciturn. But it was then that Sister Pauline mentioned that she could have sworn she saw the girl wiping off tables at *Luigi's Pizza* one afternoon.

"It looks like she works after school, Boniface."

Boniface flapped her old hands.

"Nonsense, the girl's well off. Ah....listen to me...her family is. Her mother's always at that *Bienville Club* with the society elite. Those old glasses of yours need replacing, Pauline."

Somehow, in the midst of such frivolous chatter she said it. Which was unusual, as Sister Mary Boniface is almost always of the utmost fastidiousness and certainly, disciplined in what she chooses to conceal or reveal to her fellow sisters.

In between the servings of the crusty French bread and the passing around of Antoinetta's gravy bowl of a piquant and rather zesty marinara sauce—ladle askew—somehow the news about being flat broke was the side dish no one expected. Understand, for all of these months, Sister Mary Boniface mentioned that there were problems, that some things were taking longer to pay off, but being in the negative to the degree that they now were just never seemed possible. In all the years that the goings on of the convent has remained intact, their world was beginning to crumble. Sister Pauline let out a tiny yelp. Sister Agnes held back tears. Mary Boniface waved her hands nervously, lifting her spry frame from her seat.

"Now, now, we will be all right. Something always comes through. You all know this. We just aren't exactly *in style* anymore. The alumna is no longer in sync with our cause. They watch the PBS stations during their clever fund drives and give to this Indian physician and this other Buddhist organization, the *Zen Center*. I recently learned it's not even here. It's in Bogalusa, of all places. Why, I do not know. There are only old lumberyards and paper mills in Bogalusa. Nothing happens there."

"Maybe they need it, though," Sister Agnes blurted. " I mean, if they're a depressed community as you imply."

"Well, Sister, you should know. It's not that far from here. You've at least driven through Bogalusa sometime in your lifetime, I'm sure."

The good sister sat back down in her chair and quietly picked at her plate. The others followed suit and there it has remained for quite some time. Only the scraping of forks, an occasional cough and the pouring of hot tea and de caf coffee could be heard for the rest of their dinner hour.

Finally, Pauline spoke up.

"I think if we have to give bake sales, and write letters to our biggest donors—many we haven't heard from in years, we'll find a solution to this mess, Boniface. I just know it. Now I am off to get Gertrude. You know how she ends up falling asleep in the chapel. Besides, we were all due there twenty minutes ago for *Vespers*. We are off schedule. And maybe we need to just pray a little harder tonight. To *Our Lady*. I think this might be a good start to solving this mess"

Boniface took her napkin from her lap and gingerly wiped her mouth.

" I agree. Why don't you all run along without me? Antoinetta and I are going to have a brief meeting. I'll be with you soon."

The other sisters began to clear the dining room table, gathering their things and heading out the swiveled dining room door. The two nuns waited for the last of them to leave. Boniface finally leaned over and tapped Antoinetta on the knee.

" Ha. You know what I'm thinking, kiddo. It's going to take more than a bake sale. And I'm going: on a flight out tomorrow night. I may not be back for *Gras,* so you're in charge. I'll be okay. You just stick to the story. *Got a meeting out west with a promising donor.* Lips sealed tight. Understand me?"

◆ ◆ ◆

Once upon a not so distant time Claire lived amid trivial concerns that seemed of the utmost importance. In what now appears to be a far off place, on the other side of life's rainbow, where pompoms and cheerleading shakers grace the lilac bookshelves in a bedroom so removed from the realities of human suffering outside, Claire once ruminated on such *luxury* problems as which flats best matched her newest pair of leggings. The very idea that she would be preoccupied with such frivolities as when her next pedicure appointment would be or whether any of her classmates had remembered to download the latest *Cold Play* CD onto their *MP3 players* to file-share now seemed a tad juvenile. Never mind that this was the exact conversation Claire overheard as she rushed through the old convent courtyard, tardy for her second class on this brisk, late winter morning. There were more important things on her mind and Becca Prejean and Andrea Paternostro seemed so *adolescent* and downright shallow, standing there under the old courtyard archway complaining about their respective *"bags"* and having not a spare credit card to *max-out* for their next shopping splurge. *Poor little creeps.*

But Claire wasn't thinking this. Actually, Claire was counting her lucky stars that she managed to stay one last night in the hostel before being awakened this very morning by one of the maids who held a master lock and hammer in her hands as she watched the nervous seventeen year old gather all of her belongings to be placed in storage-hold (for a fee of two dollars a day) until she finds new living arrangements.

This was the exact order posted to the maintenance office bulletin board and there were to be no exceptions. The occupant in room number 28 had to leave the premises, no exceptions. Claire had reached her limit and there were travelers willing to pay triple her daily fee waiting in the lobby.

As Claire gathered every piece of her belongings, her mind raced wildly as she still had not exactly established a new place to crash. Her only choice seemed to be Mrs. Gaynor and our fancy-free gal braced herself for the inevitable phone call. Last night, before packing her things Darva *texted* that she nix the call and just show up at the old woman's in person and rap her knuckles on the back door instead of the front entrance in case Rita was around. Lord knows Claire didn't need any *scenes* to offset her transition from being a coed gal about the college area of town to genteel and demure guest of some wealthy, withering octogenarian with a spare room and warm kitchen. Claire had to get real and adopt a meek and grateful attitude… and fast. And no whining and complaining about her former freedoms, either. More than likely she could shack up for free and that was a relief right there.

Just as she was about to race into her nine-forty-five World Lit class with Mr. Gruber, Darva Jean stopped her friend in her tracks.

"Wow. What's up with you—dizzy-chicky? Girlfriend, you look white. I mean, really *white*. Like a *White Castle* on its annual *Let's bleach everything down* day—What on earth is goin' on with you?"

Claire let out a weak laugh.

"Well…I missed my first class, *Advanced Cal*. You know that's going to be reported right to Boniface's office. So I am nailed right there. But what the heck? I had my hide on the line back at the hostel. They had a padlock ready to fix on the door in case I tried any slick moves. I felt like a criminal…oh, Hi, Mr. Gruber, coming right in."

Claire waved Darva off as a handsome, rather dandy-ish man of about forty ushered Claire into the classroom, swiftly closing the door behind her. The teacher leaned in closer to Claire, wagging his index finger in her lovely, but ashen face.

"You and Miss Mobray…always up to stuff, aren't you? The two of you. Get in here, Molyneaux. We have a test today. And before you traipse back there with the others, drop your cell phone right here in this box".

Slightly breaking away from her, Mr. Gruber piped up, announcing to the rest of the class, "That means all of you!" Gruber gestured that they form a line, holding a cardboard box as the students reluctantly took out their electronic, potential *cheat sheets* for surrender.

" Give 'em up. Right now. Park those puppies right in here—you won't get them back until you turn in your papers."

A chorus of sighs rushed through the room.

" Oh, *tissy… thing…"* one of the students muttered to her group of friends in the back as she dramatically rustled her hair, her free arm held akimbo at her hip. Soft giggles wafted under the rustle of papers and the snapping of purse and book bag clasps. Claire watched as Gruber wrote out the one essay question on the board while gently propping the box on his desk. Louder cries and sighs could be heard.

Gruber spun on his heel.

"Quiet down, you brats. Either you know this material or you've been *e-Cliff-noting* your way through it. Well, now we shall see."

Claire spent a good extra fifteen minutes completing the essay question, which was on Rabelais' *Gargantua* and *Pantagruel.* The girls were to discuss either of these works. Claire decided to cover both—which was why it was taking her so long to finish. Although Claire padded her essay with some repetition, she was relieved that she could actually discuss these colossal works of French Renaissance fiction, at least, to some degree. Most of the girls left after writing only two or three pages, and Claire was the last one remaining, scribbling away in the very rear of the classroom. She knew it was of the utmost importance that she perform well in this class. The idea of college loomed large in her mind and, admittedly, Claire's grades weren't exactly stellar. Darva Jean had about a 3.7 GPA while Claire's dragged at a lowly 2.8.

The problem wasn't so much that Claire lacked intelligence. Throughout her young life teachers have remarked on Claire's natural smarts, some even noting a glimpse of genius sparkling from her lively dark eyes.

You could see it in her gaze, many a former teacher would say as they took note of the girl in unexpected moments of pointed inquiry. Actually, Claire was quite capable of being an exemplary student, but truly, any mental energy she had was spent building a psychological fortress as a buffer against the constant rush of Rita's mental and emotional onslaughts. It seemed much of Claire's attention was focused on the difficult and delicate task of warding off these psychic negatives born and carried out in the very crux of heart and home. Add the hideous shame she kept well hidden and you have a vastly preoccupied and worried child. Claire knew it was something she couldn't easily resolve. It was all she could do to survive. It's good to note, however, that one of the odd treasures Claire has discovered in her newfound freedom since Rita's expulsion a few weeks ago is a latent ability of unfettered concentration. Odd, given that the physical challenges of taking adult responsibility for her own subsistence has proved to be the easier task. Imagine!

Each evening, as Claire settled down back at the hostel, and after reminding herself that she had made it through another day, studying never seemed more appealing. Understand, there were no more doors slamming, knives or cleavers glistening under intense kitchen light fixtures, or the sound of her mother barking orders through the corridors. And let's not forget the sliding of serving trays on soft neutral toned hallway carpets preceding the light tap on Claire's closed bedroom door come dinner hour. Essay writing and reading the plethora of books she was assigned seemed easy now that she had her "*bag*" off her back. Claire was beginning to enjoy her studies and the improvement was showing. Of course, now there is the question of whether her recent academic resurgence has come too late. Would Claire's current high marks make up for all those bland C's and lowly B-minuses from her life back at chez Molyneaux?

Hugh Gruber certainly didn't seem all that interested in his student's fate, that's for sure. While Claire wrote, he impatiently drummed his thin, elegant fingers on his desk as he caught up with reading emails on his laptop. Claire continued to focus on her task and after writing out fifteen cursive pages she smartly rose from her seat, slapping the stack of papers onto her teacher's smooth oak desk. Gruber looked up, a wandering eye noting the substantive pages as he handed Claire her phone—it being the last one remaining in his silly cardboard box. Of course, Gruber delivered one of his signature, stinging remarks as his gaze remained fixed on his laptop-screen.

"Okay. Get going, Molyneaux. But do keep in mind—trying to impress me will not get you anywhere, much less into the college of your choice. That is, if any of them would have you."

♦　♦　♦

As when one is caught unawares, I ask that you pardon my mess, loyal, attentive readers. I am gathering my seemingly amorphous, thought-emotion being into a more compact and orderly fashion, as I have just been unraveled—let us just call it that—by some news from an unexpected "visitor".

Of course, as I was flitting from one end of the room to the other—a punctured, ethereal ping-pong ball of sorts—I happened to catch the tail-end of this wry, acerbic remark coming from the pursed lips of that fellow, the little instructor our girl must get on with as she is still bound to the convent school 'til that long-awaited commencement day.

I looked down at him as he briskly shut his fancy briefcase while our girl sauntered out of the door, a perceptible icy shiver tingling up her young, supple spine. I immediately mentally "messaged" to her troubled spirit: "Not to worry my lovely Young Talent, I'll be keeping my spirit's eye on him". But I am not so sure she got this. I watched her brisk away, her long, glossy hair in its pony tail glistening in the late morning sun- a dark green satin ribbon tied in a sweet bow. The sight of this gave me a slight sigh, I admit.

And so tantalizingly distracting, least I forget my telling you of my surprise guest. As you can imagine, he was a spirit similar to myself; my "visitor", that is. Another incorporeal being drifting about in the vast ocean of this ethereal realm, made separate and imperceptible from your world only by mere elements of chemical fact. Unbeknownst to you, dear, fastidious readers, we exist right in your midst. (Of course, I realize that I informed you of this a few pages back, as most of you recall. Just to let you know, I, too, will come up with the occasional "pop quiz' to see if any stray reader hasn't kept pace with the facts—of course, sans the pedagogy in the likes of that punctilious, Mr. Gruber!)

My traveling pilgrim in the spirit world was a curious sphere of sparkly lights bouncing about, searching for clues and connection with fellow beings, most of them lost souls such as myself. Or so it seemed. Just when I thought I was completely safe and sound in the solitude of my favorite chapel as I awaited those tardy nuns, in popped this new visitor. Rolling his way right through my favorite stain glass window. "He" certainly seemed to recognize me. The interest and engagement was all his. I did not really recognize "him".

In fact, I didn't recall knowing this creature at all. But his thought-emotion being circled about in festive hues— brightly shining, and singing that he was so glad to finally come across someone he once knew. "Hey." He exclaimed. " How are you, dear old soul? Seen any other "Cossacks" about?"

I was alarmed at this fresh spirit, ingratiating me and brushing against my orb as if we were the best of chums. I hadn't a clue, and I grew leery of this 'fellow'. I shivered and shimmied, in an attempt to escape—but I admit, I was curious, readers. I wanted to hear more of what he had to say, I finally blurted that I had no idea of what he spoke. So I asked:

"Were we from the great, vast land to the east, Russia?"

He laughed, as only a spirit could laugh and spun in rather expressive circles and curlicues of light.

"No! But we liked their winter fur chapeaus and ours were always of the richest sable—big round crowns of fur. It was how we could identify each other."

"We?"

"Don't you remember…in the cafes? The discussions that went on for hours?"

I shook and shimmied some more. Then his orb lost its shimmer and shrunk to the size of a child's marble. I take it he wasn't pleased. So again, I asked:

"Could you tell me more? Maybe if you could elaborate, it would start to come back to me."

He gingerly replied:

"I am so sorry you don't remember. I am not sure where I could begin to prompt your memory. But we knew each other for many years. There were a few of us in our circle."

"What did " we" do, exactly?"

Dear readers, it was right then that my "visitor" began to blur. And he started to do the strangest things. His orb began to grow larger and larger, then collapsed, spreading itself out into a flattened form of sheer luminosity. I don't believe I had ever witnessed anything quite like it, but he clearly wanted to continue communicating with me. Finally, he spoke again:

"I am getting an interference. Do you see the large white rays coming toward us?"

I admitted that I saw no such phenomena. Then I became very lonely and afraid. But he continued to speak to me, and re-configuring himself back into a sphere shape, he said:

"The Big Beings are indicating to me that I can't tell you anymore. I have been instructed that you dwell here because of something not resolved and that the facts are that you will discover this in your own time. They are saying this to me now. Do you see them? They are in our very midst—they are within this shaft of light that has come between us. My, they sure are pretty. "

For what existence my orb-like being constitutes, I did not perceive these beings. I could only see the fellow creature before me. No clues as to this "light" came to me.

He continued:

"Well...they're standing in our midst and now they want me to go. So sorry. They are telling me that before I leave you, I can reveal only one clue. But all I can think of is—Do you remember, the passageway that began in the basement? The one we called 'fiddlers' row'? We once had a problem with a certain piano?"

Again, I was stumped. And my "visitor" continued to inform me:

"There...Now the Big Beings are gently ushering me away...at least, for now...maybe again, sometime, we will meet?"

It was then and there that I attempted to un-do myself, attentive readers. Suddenly I became loose strings of wiry light flashing bizarre and dismal colors. The shades of panic, I must say. Round and round I went, loosening myself to the universe like the unraveling of a great cosmic spool of a celestial spider's thread. But it didn't seem to matter. I could not change myself. But I tried. For I believed, at least momentarily, that if I could change my form maybe I would pop myself out of this very troublesome reality and the pestering questions:

"What brought me here?" or "Why am I here?"

Yet never having the slightest hunch and now this entity leaves me with a riddle as a means to my ever reaching a slither of a clue as to who I might have been. Ah, to be blissfully unawares! Actually, it is instances such as these when I so wish I were a mere blip skipping across one of your flat screens in a state of sheer, unconscious, puppet-cyber obedience.

♦　♦　♦

While life's cool indifference continues to toss her delicate, petrified (despite a brave front) daughter from one end of near despair to the other (not unlike a rag doll in the jaws of the most savage beast) nothing of the sort is ruffling the feathers of Rita's lofty, bon-bon world these days. She's been quite the busy bee with her social schedule, attending various soirees and fundraising venues for the myriad charities that come to call. True, the boys haven't been all that communicative, and lately, Rita has thought about disconnecting their Internet service so they would spend more time studying or maybe visiting with mom during their after dinner-hour, instead of pretending to study while surfing these silly online chat-rooms.

Sites like *Teen 'Twaddle* or *Tit for tat, or whatever they are,* Rita mused. It hasn't been easy trying to explain her position. Either her sons walk away, cupping their hands to their ears whenever Rita would mention Claire's wayward ways, or they protest in unison, both saying they missed their big sis, that what their mother did was plain *god-awful*.

Rita would try to explain that the girl became impossible, that it was her own undoing. And, well, the boys weren't falling for it. *Too bad, it's my house now,* Rita thought, dismissing the memory of her husband's goodbye kiss as he was on his way out of the front door and to the airport for his assignment in far-away Dubai.

Yes indeed, it sure seemed to be Rita's household now. And the boys had better watch their lips if they intended to enjoy their Carnival holiday, that's for sure. Rita didn't feel they were old enough to pal around on their own with their friends and has already made darn sure they would be supervised. Odd. Given that her daughter was only a few years older, there were no doubts to Rita's way of thinking. That her daughter could be stranded and in need did not even cross her shallow mind. In fact, Rita had a big weekend coming up and she certainly wasn't going to worry about such untidy matters as her wayward teenage daughter. *Claire was practically packed and ready to leave the house anyway, and she's pretty enough—she'll do all right with that college guy I heard about. Let him take care of her,* Rita thought, as she slipped into her pearl gray, eel-skin flats. Rita remembered to stop by the hallway mirror one last time before leaving the house, as she was now running late for a luncheon at the Bienville Club.

Rita gazed into the great mirror. She just couldn't get used to these bangs her hairdresser, Totums, insisted on cutting and fluffing to give her that desired seven years younger look. "Okay, maybe it's more like *five* years", Totums remarked as he swiveled Rita around in one of his fancy salon chairs. Rita fluffed the strands of blondish hair with her comb and smiled slightly, rehearsing her manner in case she ran into Anne Leblanc and Ruenelle de la Houssaye.

"Well, girls, I admit, it's quiet around here, but what can I do? My daughter has gone completely hog-wild for this fellow and there's nuthin' I can do about it!"

Rita lied to herself, applying another coating of the frosty lipstick she picked up the other day at the neighborhood *Rexall Drugs*. The image of her puckering her pink, frosted lips beheld a strange, freckled refraction in the late morning sunlight. For a moment, Rita paused and looked toward the hallway windows, noting the streams of light pouring in. *Well, the hell I care about those phony, high society bitches,* Rita scoffed, returning to the kitchen briskly to spike her still-warm coffee with last night's leftover brandy sitting by the sink. *What the hell*, she muttered, and emptied the snifter right into her coffee mug. Rita straightened her skirt and reached for her bag—which was vibrating and slightly shaking—wondering who might be calling on her cell. She retrieved the smooth, soap-sized object and held it to her ear.

"Hey-ya! Rita here!"

A slightly audible female voice came through,

"Hello, Mrs. Molineaux."

"And this is?"

"Oh, I am not so sure I want to get into that just yet. Let's just say, we know about Claire. We know and we think you're due for prison."

"Who is this?"

"Like I said, doesn't matter. You stink."

The phone went dead.

Rita pinched her cheeks, feeling the blood draining from her head. She grabbed one of the stools at the kitchen bar and sat down, slightly trembling. She looked at the call record on her cell, "private number", it read. *Maybe I shouldn't go to the club*, she thought. *Maybe I should just stay here. Or go to the mall, or downtown.* Suddenly, she got up from the stool, announcing to the kitchen cupboards and walls:

"She's seventeen years old! She's not a child. She can deal with it. There's a lotta girls out there who didn't have what Claire had, and it was time for her to flee the coop!"

Rita briskly walked back into the living room and pulled on her coat. *Nobody's goin' to threaten me!* But as Rita backed her SUV out of the driveway, she looked both ways to the side of her to see if there were any suspicious looking characters lurking about her lavish lawn. She studied the lush Spanish oaks with their mossy entrails, checking for anything unusual moving about. Then she put the car in *park*, and re-checked the back seat. Slowly, she backed the vehicle into the street. A loud horn could be heard as Rita proceeded down Beaumont Drive. Rita checked her rearview mirror and noticed old Mrs. Gaynor dragging a suitcase on rollers as she stepped into a Mercedes sedan. Rita paused for a moment, and almost wanted to back up the vehicle and approach Mrs. Gaynor, but noting the stooped shoulders and the frail, sheepish manner the elderly woman seemed to have with her driver, Rita quickly changed her mind.

There's just no way that cute little lady would know anything, Rita figured. *Besides, she never speaks in that manner. Not sweet Mrs. Gaynor.* As she drove along, Rita tried to forget the disturbing call. *Pranks. Maybe it was her daughter herself, attempting to disguise her voice.*

◆　◆　◆

There are those unfortunates whose constant leitmotif is the very unknown and all that it brings. Of course, this has become the norm for Claire since her expulsion into the raw world so many weeks ago. While at times exhilarating, the mysteries as to whether she would have a job or a bed to sleep in by day's end is Claire's latest source of anxiety. Would she make it to old lady Gaynor's? Or would she be able to sneak in at Darva Jean's and hunker down through Ash Wednesday morn, at least?

Claire ruminated on these dire matters as she trotted off the streetcar to the Bijoux Boulevard address she received via text message the previous evening. Claire looked up at each address on the houses as she paced the sidewalk, remembering to occasionally look down and check the pavement for jagged fissures and bumpy cracks lest she fall and break an ankle or two. *Darn, cheap, saddle oxfords*, Claire murmured, stopping to tie her shoe. Claire continued to examine each address on the myriad clapboard houses as she crept along. She slowed her pace and furrowed her dark brows: *Was it the job inquiry I made, or is it the cousin Darva Jean told me about? The relative who has a spare room and piano on which I might be able to practice?*

Claire wasn't so sure, recalling the odd text message she received with only an address and time for which to meet.

Deciding she would be on the lookout for clues in their forthcoming interview, Claire thought of her bundle of belongings in the storage closet back at the hostel, still unsure as to whether she would succeed with Mrs. Gaynor. One can only imagine the nervousness and sweaty hope Claire was carrying to her four o'clock appointment.

A lean dark figure waved from a screened in porch. Claire squinted her eyes in the late afternoon sun. A trim, African American man of about thirty-five signaled for her to come inside, swinging a squeaky screen door open. An exhausted Claire gave a weak smile as she climbed the stairs leading to the entrance to the great house.

"Honey, come on in here and did you bring the material I asked for?"

Claire gave him a blank look, noticing the slender wisp of a mustache above his full upper lip. He reminded her of old 1950's photos she'd seen of *Little Richard,* the famous rock 'n roll singer/composer.

"I'm sorry?" she squinted

"Come on in here and tell me all about yo self. The agency only informed me yesterday—you read music, right?"

Agency? A job in entertainment? Claire decided to play along. She piped up without hesitation:

"Yes!"

"And you are versatile in your music selections as the venues in which you play, young..lady..er…Miss…?"

"Molyneaux. Of course!"

"And I see from your list of credentials here that they faxed over…or somebody sent over…that you are seeking a course of study in music with an emphasis in composition…well…how familiar are with being a "dresser". You know, for theatrical performances? I pay extra for that in addition to the twenty-five dollar an hour wage"

Claire sailed along, bobbing her head. "Sure…er…", trying not to show too much excitement.

The African American man gave her a blank stare that soon transformed into a warm grin. Extending his hand now, adding:

"Where are my manners? I'm Winnie. Also known as Wilfred La Rousse. Will during the week—Winnie on weekends and after four pm…" the young man glanced at a brass wall clock that graced the foyer, "…which it now most definitely is, being four fifteen."

Claire smiled back, remembering the tidbit Darva gave to her the other day in the library: "Oh, gosh, you' also teach math, right?"

The man wrinkled his forehead, adjusting his reading glasses a bit, "Well…now I am not so sure whatchew talking about there, honey, but as far as you're concerned, I'm *Winnie the Wonder*, the performer, and that's all you need to know."

Claire looked down at her lap in an attempt to quell the excitement that was rising up within the bowels of her being. Imagine! *A real job where she'll be a working musician.* And the money! Yes, Claire decided, it would be best to not even mention her bud, Darva Jean. She couldn't mess this one up. She'll be darned sure to get everything lined up at Mrs. Gaynor's.

"Just tell me when and where to show up!"

"Well…it's not that simple, you know. We have just oodles of applications here. I'll need you to take these" the young man handed Claire a stack of sheet music, "practice some of these classic show tunes, jazz pieces…and come by in three weeks' time or so and we'll have you do an audition. How's about one in the afternoon—say last Saturday of the month?

Claire's mind raced. Where could she practice all this stuff? *Audition? Wow. A real job!*

It's important to keep in mind that Claire never actually *worked* as a musician. Though she had been asked to perform for a church Sunday service or at the occasional debutante gathering, or to even tutor younger students, Claire would get the inevitable frown from her mother, along with a wagging of her cool, finely manicured and polished index finger, or perhaps a sigh, followed by: "*You get an allowance from your father, Dear. You don't have to worry yourself about some low paying, measly job playing tunes for the elderly or the retarded at some home, God forbid.*" Odd that Rita said this to her daughter on so many occasions, yet rarely did she offer much money to her daughter to spend should she need it.

As far as an *allowance*, that really didn't manifest on a regular basis. It was more of a catch as catch can scenario. Many a dinner hour, when Hilaire was actually having supper with the family, Claire would clear her throat and humbly ask for an extra ten or maybe twenty-dollar bill from the family till. True, Claire did have a low-ceiling credit card, but it was for emergency use only. Hilaire insisted on it if she were ever in a bind. (And now that that *bind* has come to pass, she has maxed it out! All three hundred and fifty dollars' worth!)

When Rita was around, it was always best to start with a low figure, with maybe a remote possibility that Claire could up the ante a bit, depending on the general mood of the day or hour.

And usually Claire had to state her case quickly—and preferably, while her mother left the table to refill the crystal pitcher of iced tea or fetch another loaf of French bread from the oven. Dad, Hilaire, was always more amenable, and actually generous. Odd, given that Hilaire was the sole moneymaker in the family, while his wife sat back, reaping the many benefits of being a post-feminist-age, house-frau enjoying the luxuries of an upper middle class subsistence. Hilaire was nary a one to be stingy with his children, though he was wont to not over do it. Always sensible, Hilaire, would offer money when needed...except for the time when Rita unexpectedly returned to fetch the butter tray for a fresh stick whilst remembering the warming loaf in the oven.

"What are you giving her now, Hilaire?" Rita bellowed, while her husband fished a one hundred-dollar bill from his wallet.

"She needs it to buy some sheet music and to get the new pair of saddle oxfords you've promised her since mid-September. She's got like six months left of school. Whaddya want her to walk around in, her socks?"

Rita quipped:

"She can get those at the *Thrift-Mart* nowadays. It's not like it was years ago. They make all that stuff out of plastic—they actually look like real leather—made for next to nuthin in China. Give her a twenty."

Hilaire shook his head while Claire hung hers, a lock or two dangling off her lovely face and barely missing the rim of her plate of *Shrimp Scampi* served in the finest bone china. A tear or two emitted from her eye, splashing now into her plate joining the dangling locks.

Claire murmured softly into her tea glass:

"I don't care. Dad. It's okay."

It was later that evening that Hilaire slipped four more twenties into Claire's book-bag while she lay sleeping, as an unbeknownst Rita showered away in her steamy, marbled bath. It was rather dreadful, these scenes, and often Claire wondered how she could find a way to subsist on her own, so much so that she would never have to rely on anyone's money, but to finally get a chance to actually work as a musician? Well, this was the opportunity from God. Yes it was. And Claire was not going to ruin her chance.

"Just load 'em up there, on that table, I'll memorize and play anything you want." She told Winnie.

Claire gathered herself, stuffing the sheet music into her massive, tattered canvas book bag as she shook Winnie's cool, lean hand. Racing down the front steps, Claire mused: *If I have to return to the nuns' practice room, I will. Will it really matter if they hear ' St Louis Blues' instead of 'Fur Elise'? After all, Sister's offer still stands.* Claire was all set to beeline for the nun's piano parlor when she suddenly halted in her tracks—a clunky, *Payless* oxford just missing a jutting piece of broken concrete in the sidewalk. *Mrs. Gaynor!* Claire pulled out her phone and keyed in her number, and after several rings, an old lady's chirpy voice came through. But it wasn't the usual warm greeting of which Claire was accustomed and wanted so badly to hear just now.

Actually, it wasn't a live voice at all, but a metallic recorded version of Mrs. Gaynor speaking on her answering machine, stating that she'll be away for a week and would be delighted to call back as soon as she returns. Claire didn't bother waiting for the beep.

♦ ♦ ♦

Boniface had to remember—it was *she* who invited Father Ignatius, principle of *St. Jerome's School for Boys*, into her office one afternoon late last week—*For a little friendly chat about things.* Perhaps it was a good move. She wanted to show the man that she was well aware of their interest in merging the two schools. There she laid out the situation for him, but did she really reveal all of those details? Ah, then she had to remember: they did have a couple of beers.

Yes, Boniface enjoys her refreshments as any good nun would, but did she really nervously pick at the straggly, two-inch silver hair that jutted from her soft aging chin?

Especially when they got down to the actual figures? She thought that might have been a bad sign. *Forgetting herself* and all that. Usually, she would reserve such personal things when she was alone and reading over the ledgers and spreadsheets on her own free time, but in front of that nosy Jesuit? Maybe she really was beginning to "*lose it*" as the girls often say to each other—but often, that's when they're talking about their parents, but yes, occasionally, the nuns. (such as absent-minded Constantine, bless her heart).

The flight attendant pushed the cart up the aisle closer to where Boniface was sitting. The old woman curled up in her small cramped space, attempting to calm her nerves by fixing her stare out of the tiny airplane window. Finally, the flight attendant chirped a greeting her way, leaning over the aisle seat, asking if she cared for another cocktail. Boniface turned her gaze to the attendant (yes, she enjoyed her refreshments as any good nun would), handing the gal her plastic cup and empty beer can.

"Another *Heineken*, ma'am?"

Boniface, looking so prim and grandmotherly, nodded.

"Okee-dokee, then." The flight attendant handed the good nun her frosty can and a fresh cup.

"That'll be five dollars, ma'am."

Boniface caught that vague flicker of uncertainty in the flight attendant's eye. A look that simply said "*I thought your type usually abstains.*"

As we know all know by now, Boniface dresses modestly and plainly, and not in the once identifiable *habit* as in the days of old when nuns were so immediately recognizable. Instead, she seemed like so many an elderly woman in a simple smock and cardigan, with a silver cross dangling over her lace buttoned-to-the-gills collar. She could have been anyone's *Amish* or *Mennonite* grandmother. Boniface handed her the bill quickly, as if by doing so, it would assuage the tinge of guilt blipping through her aging veins. After all, she was using the nuns' money for this little self-appointed junket to that Mecca of decadence, that desert-haven of money-lust as a last-ditch effort to save the *Convent of the Immaculate Heart School.* Yes, Sister Mary Boniface seems to be a risk taker of the most brash kind; an old, *ace in the hole*, dice-pitching, devil-may-care, unabashed *gambler. Yes—indeed-y*, as she is wont to say. And you know she'd have to be a pretty darn good one by taking such a chance.

Well, yes and no. Boniface certainly has seen her share of better days. But it was the horse races where she excelled, and given that she had been spotted on so many occasions by key student body parents at the New Orleans' *Magnolia Downs*, it was some time ago that Boniface decided to just go for the big time and try her luck in far-away Nevada.

Craps, Roulette, Black Jack. She knew these games well. It all started some fifteen years ago when Boniface happened to be walking through one of the casinos with her nephew and his wife who live in Southern California, deciding that maybe a drive through the Mojave and on to Vegas would be a treat for the old gal, and trying her hand at the roulette wheel, winning a walloping $50,000, on a whimsy. (*I got that old roof tarred, new kitchen equipment for the cafeteria, and cracked marble repairs done in the old chapel for that money,* Boniface recalled.)

You could say, Boniface has been hooked ever since—although she has tapered down her junkets to a once every two or three year affair, and aiming to give it up altogether for fear of being discovered as she brushed against one of the more moneyed parents of an

Immaculate Heart student few years ago. Boniface tried to remember what she told the startled couple as they crossed the lobby of *Nero's Pyros* on their way to the casino bar, "Just here, visiting my nephew," she remarked, only she realized too late that she was carrying a win ticket to cash out at the cashier. Boniface recalled that she swiftly tucked the item in her skirt pocket nervously flashing her graying pearlies like an old grinning cheetah, while the handsome couple collectively nodded their heads, with shocked, frozen smiles. Of course, Boniface stayed clear out of the Vegas scene for a few years after that unfortunate encounter.

But here she is again, aiming to try her hand in a desperate move to prevent her Convent school for girls from going co-ed—the wave of the 21st century. And she is a bit worried. It's one thing if the risk will work, quite another if Boniface looses her till. The old woman rechecked her duffel bag that nestled at her crouched feet—it all seemed to still be there—all five thousand dollars. Boniface took another swill of her beer. She was now recalling that conversation last week, as the late winter sun began its descent across the fine, polished oak library shelves that graced Boniface's handsome old office. Father Ignatius gleaned over the reports and nodded his head, saying:

"Yep. I figure we have no more than another year before we make the announcement, Boniface. It's the times we're in. Parents are finding it difficult to donate—it's not just attitudinal changes, although I have my en-absentia mass attendees—but that's been going on for decades. Actually, ever since that Maharishi Yogi came out with that autobiography and the Beatles dropped acid and wrote that dastardly song about a Mother Superior being some kind of junkie..."

Boniface held her soft tiny hand up a bit and blurted:

"All right, 'Nate. We don't need to go into that one. I had so many students guffawing behind my back "whenever they announced for the Mother Superior, which I was at that time, over the PA during those years. Please. It's different today. We have more competition, let's just put it that way. Our graduates have grown up to watch all this stuff on the PBS channels, that Indian physician and this cross-eyed Tibetan scholar. It's ridiculous. I wish they would bring back Sister Wendy."

Father Ignatius interjected:

"But she's *Anglican*, Boniface. That doesn't really do us any good. Imagine, an English, *Anglican* nun posing as an art critic. She actually inspires people to waste their money on Wayne Thiebaud paintings for their designer kitchens."

Their conversation went on this way as dusk gradually appeared and then the room fell silent. The mossy entrails that hung from the Spanish oaks outside her office window gently wafted in the early evening breeze. The lean and spry Jesuit cracked his knuckles and stretched his arms a bit. Then they both smiled. It was useless for Boniface to argue with the man. He had a point. Actually, she was grateful that 'Nate seemed to understand her feelings. It was important to her to maintain the integrity of her school, that education for females and males remain separate to ensure stronger, individualized development. But the good father, a mere sixty-two compared to sister's seventy-six, was wrong in thinking Boniface would simply need a little time and gentle persuasion. He had no idea just how passionately she held these opinions and beliefs and actually, just how far the good sister would go to keep everything as is.

Boniface pulled herself away from her thoughts, distracted by the little red lights flashing on the plastic boards above the passenger seats. It was a reminder that this wasn't a dream. That she had actually gotten up the nerve to gather her things and gallantly attempt a rescue in the midst of all this chaos and fiduciary turmoil.

She reached for the smooth strap and fastened the metal clasp on her lap. The plane was about to begin its descent into Las Vegas.

◆　◆　◆

And what a distant place that bayou capital now seemed. Back in the town of *laissez le bon temps rouler,* or as the *locals* call it—*the city that care forgot*—everyone was preparing for a big Mardi Gras weekend. Although Claire had nary a place to call home, she, too, felt the excitement stirring in the early evening air as she made her way back to the hostel to collect some of her things from the storage area.

Claire hoped her favorite desk clerk, the young man she encountered the first night she had moved into the hostel, would be there, and sure enough, Claire noticed his familiar, Adonis-gorgeous self standing near the front counter – all six foot two, wavy brown locks and sparkly blue eyes of him.Everyone knew that Gabe was a student at Tulane and had a looker girlfriend who would come by and sit at the counter with him, poring over her books while stroking his luscious, wavy brown hair with her fine, French manicured nails. The two of them were often seated at the front desk, their arms propped up and wound together in complicated configurations like some crazy sculpture. But the girlfriend wasn't there tonight and Gabe had that frisky look on his face: *Gabe was game*. He rather enjoyed seeing beautiful, innocent, lying-her-ass-off-Claire and would actually miss her now that she was no longer going to be a resident at the hostel. Gabe flashed a

Cheshire cat grin as Claire sauntered her way into the lobby. Gabe leaned over the counter, beckoning Claire to come closer, which she did, an inch or two at a time, looking coy and deliciously fretful.

"Stuff's still here…Gotta couple of towels for ya, too. The boss is out—so relax, you can take a shower and change, if you want. No problem."

Claire bobbed her head in relieved gratitude, attempting to hold back fresh tears. Gabe, as if on cue, quickly snapped a tissue from the decorative box on the counter top and offered it to her, along with some soothing words.

But he had to ask:

"Hey—why on earth are you in a Catholic girls' high school uniform today?"

Claire flushed scarlet. *Gosh. How could I forget to change? I managed to keep my act going all this time and here I walk in, forgetting to change into my street clothes like the most idiotic of fools?* She asked herself, but still she managed to quip:

"Oh, *this*… It's for a skit I was in today. I have a cousin here in high school. They needed a quick fill in."

Almost instantaneously, Gabe winked, friskily adding:

"Yeah. Well. You can't go out in the streets that way for the parades. There are perverts who really get off on the *school girl look*, ya know."

"Oh, yeah?" Claire raised a brow.

Gabe then quipped:

"Yeah…like thugs, sailors, or maybe a stray priest or two?"

Claire flipped her long black locks over her perfectly aligned shoulders and snapped:

"You're warped. But that's kind of what intrigues me about you."

Gabe smiled away while reaching under the counter to hand her two large fluffy towels.

"Here. Get your stuff. And go have yourself a relaxing shower. If you need anything, I'll be in the boss' office next to the *taxidermy display* we have there on the walls."

Wow a 'Psycho' fan! Claire mused, wagging a wry finger at him before helping herself to the towels and key, her svelte, young body quickening its pace as she made her way down the hall.

While Claire enjoyed these few jocular moments with the *honey* at the counter, little did she know there was trouble brewing just a few blocks away. And damned if Darva Jean could do anything about it! For it was while her brother, Dan, finished up the final details on his feathered Indian headdress —their mother steaming his costume in the kitchen—that Darva made her final plea. Lucy Darlene seemed nonplussed, but Darva drove her point home anyway, in her best debate fashion, of course.

"Ma, it's critical. I don't know how I can ameliorate my argument with you by simply saying, my friend needs emergency asylum. She's tryin' the best she can. She has barely any money, but she stays up nights studying her butt off anyway. She has no piano, so what she do? She makes one with all eighty-eight keys on a plank of balsa wood, and has this tiny flute by her side in case she needs help in remembering exactly how a note sounds. She's trying to be a musician. Think of those Jazz dudes. Hell. They didn't have any money. And they kept tryin'. My friend needs a break, a bed to lie on just through *Gras*—so she doesn't panic. Don't make her go over and stay with some gin and tonic guzzlin' old lady. And she's a really *white* old lady. Got all this white hair when she don't leave that rinse in too long—then it's periwinkle blue."

Lucinda Darlene silently slid the steaming iron over the pearl-toned satin pants and sequined vest of her son's marching Indian costume. She wanted Dan to look like he had arrived. He had become a real Marching Indian and had the feathered headdress to prove it.

And was it a beauty: three and a half glorious feet of the most beautiful plumes, all in rich shades of gold, white and emerald green, with purple and gold sequins flecked throughout.

"Darva Jean, for the last time, your friend's hardly a struggling jazz musician. Okay? She's from that uppity, *Pre-whatever it is Society* part of town. And I don't want anything to do with that, ok?"

Darva snapped:

"What that have to do with anything? She's not in that part of town now. In fact, she's in no part of town 'cuz she lost the only roof over her head. It's not right. That mother of hers is more like a wicked witch, Ma. And it's not right".

Lucy Darlene Mobray paused for a moment, fixing her attention on a loose sequin before resuming her ironing, her tortoise-rimmed glasses sliding down her nose.

"All the more reason, we need to let that girl alone, Darva, dear. She'll be all right, I tell ya. That wealthy old white woman will take care of her. You know how many rich, drunken, old white ladies your *Tante Marie* work for? As a matter of fact, one of 'em left her some money cuz she was good to her. She put that old white drunk to bed every night and at sixty-two, your *Tante Marie* got to see the world. Even Africa. Besides, with all that rappin you did about that girl and her mama the other night, an mixin' that all up with that caterpillar-eye-browed movie star, Joan Crawford, I'd have to be outta my mind letting that girl in—woman's liable to come to pieces right here in front of our house. Maybe carryin' one of those butcher knives up to our front porch. I don't want her coming over here, poking her nose in our business, draggin' her child out by her hair and into the streets. Bad enough the neighbors around here know so much as it is. Let's leave "well enough alone, Darva Jean. Now that's it. Besides, I gotta surprise for you. "

It was right about this time that Claire was bringing an inordinately long session under a deluxe showerhead to a close. It was a rare luxury to wash with a super- message nozzle and only one shower had such a convenience—but the stall that housed it was almost always unavailable. There was always a line most evenings, while many a hostel-dweller was willing to wait quite a while for it, too. But it looked like most everyone was out and enjoying the pre-Gras celebrations, and the showers were all empty. Yes, everyone seemed to be out having fun. Everyone except Claire, who somehow managed to keep her spirits up while hot water poured over her young, soapy, supple body, brainstorming on every possible avenue available to her. Could she manage to slip into the back cottage at Darva Jean's? It would have to work simply because there was nary a room available in the whole city. Not this weekend. Forget the money issue.

Claire gingerly stepped out of the shower and as she quickly dried herself off, a slight buzzing sound could be heard from under the heap of clothing that lay on the shower bench. It was her cell phone. Claire clasped her hand on the towel rack as she heard the voice on the other end chatter away. Anxiety flushed through her body. It was her bud, Darva Jean, speaking staccato, in between gasps of air:

"My *bag's* driven me baffo, girlfriend. Hey…what size are you?"

"About a nine, a nine *tall*." Claire managed to say as she patted herself dry.

Darva was slightly relieved, realizing they were about the same size.

"Okay…that's good…I think I have something here that'll work. Meet me at the *Cozy Chat Cafe* in about forty-five minutes. It's the only way we're goin' to be able to do this one, girl."

Claire Ange

♦ ♦ ♦

I am almost certain that you believe that I regretted making that parting remark during our last encounter on these pages. But I need to tell you: a blip skipping across one of your flat screens wasn't such a bad experience after all. I'm giddy and woozy; woozy with a whirring attraction to the little figures I encountered in my brief cyberspace adventure. Perhaps, you believed that my last wish might have ended in a mess? Well... if it was a mess, then it was a marvelous mess. And I admit, I insouciantly blipped myself into a waltz of the algorithms, and it was surprisingly educational as well as fun. I got to know a few more things about your digital world, dear readers, and I rather enjoyed myself as my orb-self blipped with the best of them.

Of course, I sobered up in time to realize that I had to have better things to do with my thought-emotion being than to amuse myself with your flat screens. As you might imagine, I reminisced about my earlier encounter with that charming and clever display of metamorphosing shapes and designs. You know, the one I felt some kind of kinship with in an earlier cyber encounter. But as I disengaged, I realized this was merely a way to stay occupied while I wander in a larger maze I've yet to resolve. And I should know that anything I utter—be it a wish or a desire or an impulse—will become an actuality.

The key is: knowing. But since I do not have information enough to satisfy, then I can't really visit any place or time that might give me the clues I need. So I make the best of it. Or is it: make the best of things—that saying I always hear coming from your plasma and desk screens, and now the little palm screens. That and, "take care", or "have a nice day". Or "Awesome. Gosh, that's

*totally awesome, dude." My. I am still a bit dazzled by
your world and its outpouring of copious information at
your fingertips! I can't help but think this is bound to
become problematic. I can see it formulating: your central
nervous systems on overdrive, or overload because of an
unquenchable thirst for information. Soon, you will have
short-circuited humans on cyber-info overload entering
special units of withdrawal therapy in your hospital
emergency rooms. This, you may see. Might want to tame
these things while you can.*

*But, of course, this is such a frivolous matter when I
realize how I have wondered about my "visitor" who tried
to assist in my ongoing exploration of who and what I was
at one time, when I last roamed your earth in physical
form. And it is too painful for me to recall his trying to
assist me. I wish "him" well.*

*Now I tried exploring the few things my "visitor"
mentioned a wee bit further. For instance, as far as his
remark about this "fiddlers' row", the only possible clue
that came to me was when I blipped into a dark alley
outside a quaint little pub also by the name, "Fiddlers'
Row" in Covent Garden, London. It was a quaint and cozy
enough establishment, but as I entered the premises and
looked around, nothing came to me.*

*I eavesdropped a bit on conversations here and there,
mainly at the bar, but nothing registered.*

*Then I soon found myself in a charming millinery
shop in Vilnius, Lithuania—where I observed a woman who
was trying on full crowned, fur chapeaus to match her
luxurious sable coat. I was a bit miffed by this little venture
until I realized my thought-emotion being considered the
term: "Cossack", and the hats my "visitor" seem to recall
us wearing. I remained there awhile, observing the patrons
sauntering in and out as a light snow fell outside the shop's
frosty windows. I warmed myself near the little stove in the
corner of the room and watched some lovely women play*

about with fur wrappings, muffs, mittens, and of course, the abundant sumptuous hats and hair pieces the shop had to offer.

I left and soon found myself among the ballet of the satellites. I often zoom my orb-like self up there, in your earth's outer atmosphere, when my thought-emotion being is unhappy. Usually, I do this as a way to distract myself from the slightest self-pity. It often amuses me to observe your technical, orbital instruments. And I was fancied by some data transmissions coming in from the Republic of the Congo to a small island in the South Pacific. They were selling money ventures that didn't seem very sound. This being a welcomed distraction, as I simply can't seem to ascertain any of this information my "visitor" was attempting to tell me.

Except there was another place where I did find myself wandering about—back on your planet. The best I can say is it seems to be a music school of some kind in Budapest, Hungary. I have taken a liking to this place and in particular, one of its practice rooms. Yes. I felt a warmth there as I observed a young man practicing some lovely tunes, I would imagine for an upcoming performance of some kind, but I could not be so sure. However, I wasn't just intrigued by the music, lovely though it was. I was entranced by the very instrument, itself.

It was an exquisite parlor grand piano—the size, the loving way in which it was built, the sweet curves of its body, the rich woods, the gold leaf designs in its crest, the tender touches built in each detail; the fine old, ivory keys. It almost reminded me of the one that once belonged to our ravishing Claire—back in that swampy, humid and damp city in the New World—'Nouveau' Orleans. My home as of late, I should say.

And do you know, my dear good readers, as soon as I had that sparkly "eureka!" moment, I found myself in the very storage room where Claire's lovely antique relic sits? Under a grey quilted cover, it silently waits to be rescued. Which I know it will be someday, dear readers. But I had to take a peek—and as far as I could tell, there is a similarity between the two instruments. I must say, a spooky similarity. As soon as I checked, I zipped back to that young man who was still practicing in that Budapest music schoolroom, and I could swear that the two are of a similar make and constitution.

Yes. Now I can only wonder if there's an answer in it for me somehow. For it seems to be so. However, I could be mistaken. I could have felt that warm, friendly feeling when I first recognized Claire's piano's twin because I was so fond of hers, or could it possibly be the other way 'round? Oh, my. How could I ever know for certain? More importantly, dear readers, what could it all mean?

◆ ◆ ◆

Warren Leblanc lifted himself from his cozy perch and extended his great mitt of a hand to hi-five his buddy, Squires, as he sat down on one of the lounge chairs on Warren's cozy veranda. Warren enjoyed inviting his cronies over for conversation, a beer or two, and maybe a little music.

Squires is a regular, showing up at least every other week or so, as he lives nearby and is always ready to play some tunes on his trumpet which he would often bring along. Sometimes Warren would have his saxophone resting nearby in case he and his guests wanted to break into a few tunes, and it being Gras season, he was up for a few late afternoon sessions. Warren's wife, Anne, didn't mind. Usually she would be out with her friends, or at a card game and the kids, now in college, were probably out at the parades, if they were visiting. Squires Montgomery was a good friend to Warren over many years of crossing paths in the corridors of justice as he was also an attorney. A criminal lawyer, as a matter of fact, and Warren, a trial attorney. Both men were well known in their respective fields. Warren leaned over, lifting a sandwich from a tray, and taking a hearty bite.

" Yeah, glad you could come by, my man. Get yourself a beer in the kitchen, why doncha? And while you're at it, grab some meat in the fridge and fix yourself a sandwich."

Warren's a very sharp and shrewd practitioner of the law, make no mistake. Everyone knows he's one of the city's finest, but his origins were humble. And often, it showed in his speech and manner. It was very 'South Mariny', as they say. Warren Leblanc had to study very hard when he was growing up and making his way through the corridors of higher learning at the famed Jesuit, *Saint Jerome School for Boys* back in the late 1960's. He remembered the cold mornings when he'd have to leave the shotgun house down in the lower *Faubourg* to take the city bus that would eventually ride through the French Quarter and on to Canal street where he would then connect on the streetcar line where he'd ride all the way to the luxurious Evangeline Way with its sleepy Antebellum mansions set back on great lawns that spanned the old uptown neighborhood.

Usually, he'd have to catch up with the previous evening's homework, actually savoring those quiet times to himself when he had all of about an hour and half to prepare for another school day. Warren was a scholarship student and was reminded of that everyday. He was frightened of ever failing, of ever missing his chance at getting into a good college and hopefully, on to law school—where he envisioned a mighty future. If he didn't hold fast he might end up like his father, Ed. Not that Ed wasn't anyone to admire. Ed Leblanc was a decent family man, doing what he could on a bartender's salary. Of course, one had to remember that Ed wasn't just any old bartender at any old hole in the wall. Ed Leblanc had to change into a smart black jacket, crisp, starched white shirt with an equally stiff collar, shiny stud cufflinks in his starched white sleeves.

Ed was head bartender at *Chez De Roche,* the famous old New Orleans restaurant where the crème de la crème hung out. Day in, day out. Winter-spring-summer...Ed Leblanc would come home, slap the sock of coins and rolls of bills on the kitchen table and wiping his brow with his forearm, laughing, eager to tell his wife and kids the latest goings on with the DA's office or which well known lawyer was having an affair and with *whom,* and all the other tidbits and *ear-fulls* (depending on the shift) he would end up taking in, depending on those who stayed around long enough to wrap their legs around *Chez De Roche's* brassy bar stools, hunched over and very willing to loosen their lips on the latest gossip.

Later in the evening, when he was lounging in the den, watching *The Jackie Gleason Show*, he'd yell out to Warren as he was finishing up his homework on the dining room table: "Hey dare, Tiger. Tell me ya not goin to end up like the old man, kid. Come on over here, and tell me you're goin to become one of dose big shot downtown lawyers, eh?" Ed would usually break into laughter for a while, simmering down to a sigh or two. "Better not. It's a drag. Don't end up like the old man, ok? I shudda stuck it out at old *St. Anthony's* and got my high school diploma.", he'd mumble to the little goldfish swimming around in their little bowl in the corner of the parlor, sprinkling fish food into the water.

Warren, being sensitive toward his dad, would always shout back that he better stop talking to the fish and flip on their favorite show. And just as soon as he'd finish up his homework, Warren would skip into the living room and sit next to his dad on the couch. No matter that the program was a bit late for an eleven year old, they would both sit back and watch *Perry Mason*. Every weeknight. The re-runs. It was their show, all right, but it was also part of young Warren's education. Ed didn't care if the kid was drowsy in the morning, he could always nap in the afternoon for an hour if he needed to. *Perry Mason* was boss and little Warren was going to grow up to be a lawyer just like him.

Now some forty years later, Warren Leblanc metamorphosed into that big lawyer. Whether it was in the fashion of that *Early Days of Television* icon, Warren could not say. But what he was, at age fifty-two, would have to do. Sometimes Warren would reminisce on those days back in the old neighborhood, and sometimes he'd be in a stupor thinking back on those old TV episodes. How clever they were. For the time period and all.

Warren reached over the coffee table, scooping the sour cream dip with a broken potato chip. Squires reappeared with a cold bottle of beer, taking a seat on the sofa opposite his friend. Warren looked over at Squires. What a great guy he is. For some ten years or so, they had become tight friends. Actually, Squires had a similar background to Warren's. He didn't grow up all that far away from the *Mariny*, just a bit deeper into the old, industrial part of town downriver, known as the *Lower Crescent*. And Squires, too, had to study hard. Probably a bit more fastidiously than his friend had, and his alma mater was the equally stellar *Aquinas Academy*. Squires was a wee bit older than his buddy, Warren, and many a citizen who knew of him (being a sought after attorney, himself) were aware that he was one of the few African Americans to not only be admitted to that upper crust high school, but to have received a full scholarship. Never mind that Squires went on to bigger and better pastures. In fact, Squires usually maintains a low-keyed front with his fellows.

Actually, it was at the annual black-tie, Bannister's Club fundraiser where just about every local lawyer and judge would drop in, that one of the attorneys there—in between sips of champagne and a stuffed mushroom or two—looked up at Squires and asked where he had obtained his JD. " Oh, that was when I was in prison." Squires flatly told him. The other attorneys sitting nearby, overhearing his remark, leaned in closer, with a momentary, puzzled look.

"I drop that once in a while just to mess around a bit. But there's always the inevitable deer in the headlights reaction. I mean, for at least five seconds. Then they thaw and smile. Finally, *getting it*, you know. Oh, here's a brother taking a stab at the *white* man. Ya know?"

Squires said this to Warren, a frisky smile formulating on his lips, as they sat looking out the screened porch, the late afternoon sun casting a golden light over the soft green lawns.

"I try to keep things real smooth." Squires has said on many an occasion. "That way, people don't know what I'm up to."

"Well," Warren said, munching another potato chip. "Yeah, gotta maintain that inscrutable air, my man. Keep 'em guessing. Tell me about your recent trip, eh?"

"You mean, to the West Coast? Just visiting some old friends. I tell ya though, they sure know how to live out there. So serene. Now, talk about keeping one's cool. Not a worry in the world. Of course, most of the people I know there are wealthy. Living in Malibu and Marina del Ray. And it's not that they have it made, man, they have the Buddha."

Warren raised a brow,

"The Buddha? What do you mean?"

Squires continued:

"Well. It's like this. You walk into these luxurious ocean front homes—say in Santa Barbara? And you're going through the house, with its impeccable interior design, gorgeous views, and soft, plush carpeting, and there, amid the fronds, near a rock or waterfall, or maybe in a quiet little room off in a corner, there you'll see it: a Buddha statuette. Nestled there amid lush foliage and overgrown ferns. Looking so serene. I tell ya, the dude digs wealthy people. Actually, favors them. It's the rich man's religion, really. Think of all those celebrities."

Warren paused.

"Living tranquilly with the Buddha, eh?"

Squires just leaned back and grinned.

"Yeah. And when I think about it, it's not just the Buddha. It's a mixed bag, actually. It's all these eastern dudes. Like the Hindu, Sri Ramakrishna. Now he was the ultimate cool cat. He's an Indian saint who lived back in the eighteen hundreds in rural India. Ugly mutha. But he was enlightened. He also re-founded Hinduism. Called it, *The Vedanta*, which means, *the end of the Vedas*. You know the first question he'd ask his novitiates, privately, before he would work with them?"

Warren shook his great head, a slight grin formulating.

"Well...he'd say: how do you perceive God? Would that be *with* or *without* form?"

Grabbing another chip from the bowl, Warren leaned back, thinking about what his friend just said, and added:

" Yeah. Okay. Are you seeing God as a bearded old dude or some vast, amazing, indefinable ...Okay."

"Yea. Exactly. The idea was getting clear—first off, in where a person was in understanding what we call 'God'. Now that's smart."

Squires took a swill from his cold beer, Warren mused aloud:

"*With or without form...yeah...*a kind of *"hold the pickles, hold the lettuce, special orders don't upset us"* way of approaching the question. Yeah. I like that."

Squires emitted a slow grin.

"Yeah. Okay, the old *Burger King* commercial. I dig. He was the ultimate, cool, have-it-your way-dude, that Ramakrishna. I suppose you could put it like that. Well anyway, while I was visiting, I was invited by someone I know who's in the Vedanta Society to attend a special event. It was quite an affair. The swamis, swathed in their orange and white robed finery and sandals stood around among the beautiful people there for a reception after they all gave speeches about various things. Some of them were actually funny dudes. Like good stand-up comedy and all. Well, one unforgettable thing that happened..."

Squires shook his head, grinning,

"...was... later at the reception, when I found myself standing behind this highly respected, old Indian swami. Real skinny guy in his orange and white toga get-up and in front of him were two or three people—obviously Indian—two women dressed in the traditional saris and one man. The three of them greeted, and then immediately "prostrated themselves in front of the old guy. Understand, man, I just happened to be standing right in back of the elder swami. And the place was packed, so I couldn't move. Well, just as they were waving their arms and bending down in abject devotion to this holy man, the swami lowered his gleaming, bald head in pious acknowledgement, all the while, and of course, unbeknownst to them, he's scratching his ass. And I'm right there getting the full view."

The two break out laughing. Squires grinned some more, as he leaned forward helping himself to a handful of chips from the bowl.

"Yeah. These people were just waving their arms and dropping flowers and rose petals at his feet, and the guy's bowing his head while he's going about the task at hand, you know. I couldn't think of a more clarifying moment. And laid out before me? Why, *reverence and realization*. Right there."

"A moment of clarity". Warren chimed.

"Indeed." Squires winked.

Just then, Anne walked in on the two of them. For a moment, Warren's lovely wife of over twenty years looked wane and a bit piqued. Warren glanced her way,

"What are you up to, you bad girl? You have that cat 'n the canary look all over your face, Annie. Please tell me you haven't made any more of those sneaky calls to our favorite neighbor."

◆　◆　◆

Rita drove through the busy, old French Market section of the Quarter, looking for a place to park the SUV. She had spent most of the afternoon browsing at some of the antique shops, looking for some new items to add to her lovely home. She felt she had made a wise decision to forgo the club this morning, after that strange phone call earlier. What she needed was some frivolous distraction. Ah, the life of the devil-may-care, housewife, with teenage sons and a daughter who is now free and on her own. Rita couldn't be more pleased. In fact, in these past few weeks she has become all the more resolute in her decision. A beautiful, skilled girl like her daughter could do well and boyfriends are always out there to be had. They would take care of Claire and lead her into the life that's waiting for her.

Rita figured that not many girls her daughter's age had the opportunity to get out and venture into the world—it would add a spark to her daughter's blithe, young spirit. Now whoever that caller was earlier that day—obviously, it was just some prank. Maybe one of Claire's friends who probably had to take her daughter in for a while. *Too bad. My life was difficult. I had my hardscrabble parents to deal with; they practically threw me away when times were rough, but I learned. I went to work after school. I paid for Miss Josie's Charm School, so I could learn about the finer things in life. I did that with my own money, too.* Rita proudly recalled as she slid the SUV into a spot just blocks from the market area. But as she was adjusting her rearview mirror, and applying another coat of lipstick, Rita noticed a young girl in the same plaid grey, white and green skirt worn by the girls at the old *Convent* school, a long ponytail swaying to and fro— similar to the way her daughter ties her hair on most schooldays, always with a satin ribbon in either of the colors that match her uniform skirt.

Rita's fingers and arms tingled. Butterflies scurried about in her stomach. A flush of guilt coursed through her veins. *Is that my baby girl? Oh, God. I hope she's okay*, Rita sighed, her heart pounding a bit.

Rita stepped out of the SUV and stared at the figure, her back still to her, walking ahead, a heavy book bag on her back, carrying what looked like stack of portfolio files, the kind her daughter would use to carry her sheet music.

Rita wanted to call out to her, but just as the figure was about to turn the corner, Rita noted that the profile was hardly indicative of her child's lovely countenance. She also remembered that Claire's hair was much longer and of a glossier, finer black hue than this girl's. *Maybe a classmate of hers,'* Rita sighed. Thus the struggle again resurfaced.

Am I really angry with Hilaire for going off for the next... how many months? Is he seeing some other woman? Did he take her with him? Now Rita found herself in a mental maze. She would stop in at the little quaint café near the outdoor French Market and have herself a wine or two. Yes, that and people-watch a bit as this is always the season for doing so, with early Mardi Gras revelers bounding afoot in the Vieux Carré.

As Rita settled in at a table next to a window, she noticed two women chatting clear across the room. Rita adjusted her bifocals. Yes, it was Tiny Welles all right. Sitting with a woman Rita did not recognize. Should she wave a hello? Rita wasn't so sure. Tiny made her uncomfortable. In fact, it was only the other night at the Bienville Club, during Rita's usual card game session with Anne and the Knowletons that she got an earful about an acquaintance of Tiny's neighbor who was abducted after an evening studying at the university library? It wasn't just the news about this incident that got to the little hovel Anne and Rita happened upon as they were on their way to their table to set up their bridge game. It was the way Tiny, Lala and Ruenelle all looked up at Rita just as Tiny blared the headline that the coed was now fighting for her life in the intensive care ward at *Beauregard General.*

It was a chilling moment; the three of them momentarily staring into Rita's glassy eyes, a micro jury of her peers.

"Well...that is just god-awful!" Rita announced, swilling the remains of her wine, wincing a bit as there was a terrible guilt hovering over her heart.

But Rita persevered and drove her points home.

"Why, I worry about my darling Claire all the time—being out there on her own. But what can I do? She's headstrong. But I pray to God's heavenly angels to keep her, I do." Rita announced in her empty glass, waving to Fred the bartender for another refill.

Now so many days later, Rita sat quietly alone, looking out on the street as she picked at her hands, her nasty habit recurring. *Maybe it wouldn't be a good idea to have a glass of wine*, Rita thought, looking slightly over at the two women chatting away at the table across the room. Rita jumped up suddenly, and grabbed her things, slipping out of the patio door, hoping to escape Tiny's inevitable gaze. *Woman's got eyes like a friggin hawk*, Rita murmured to herself as she walked back to her vehicle.

It was only a few hours later in the day and just about a mile upriver from where Rita wandered the quaint streets of the French Market, thinking about how everyone seems to be looking at her in that cool, askance way these days, that Claire and Darva Jean were having a time of it. Try as she might, things just didn't seem to be working out as Darva Jean had hoped. Claire tried to apply the glittery makeup and mask but it wasn't exactly working. Darva shook her head, while Claire stood still as a scarecrow, a limp, over-sized costume draping her slender body.

Darva worked her way around Claire, straight pins sticking in a pincushion affixed with a Velcro strip near her shoulder, something she borrowed from her *Na Nan*, her grandmother. Darva fussed and chatted nonstop.

"Well, I can always just put a pillowcase over your head while I sneak you into the cottage outback. Just rustle you up with blankets and things. But maybe it won't matter. My *bag's* goin to her women's group tonight anyway. As I overheard her say to one of her friends the other night, they'll be discussin' ways to resurrect the lost Isis symbol so they can bring down the male sky god. In case you didn't know, for millennia, God's always been some dude. I get her point. But if ya ask me, my *bag's* lost it. All she needs to do is just get it off her chest about my Dad. Ya know? Runnin back up to Kalamazoo. Instead, she's got to turn this into some kind of event with these women so they can run around some Maypole come spring and chant this *bs* to Isis. Why they go through all this trouble, God only knows. But to my *bag,* I should make that *Goddess*. Turn around. Let me see how that mask looks now."

Claire did look a bit disproportionate. Whatever, the disguise was not doing the job. In fact, it seemed to be making things worse. The costume and cape were a bit large, and all Darva could do was tighten things with some oversized safety pins.

The orange feathered mask looked more appropriate for Halloween than *Mardi Gras*. Darva threw up her hands.

"What the hell…go ahead and wear it anyway. Might take a little while to get used to, but by Sunday night, my mom's goin to be plastered on that crazy punch my Tante Suzette makes every year, she'll be dancing with everybody. She's got *Lundi* Gras off, too. So I have a double whammy dealing with her. We just got to make sure she stays away from you. You know? In case she "starts axin' you questions while you're breathin' there underneath all this stuff."

Darva Jean truly appreciated her bud, Claire. Lord knows she's going out of her way to provide emergency shelter for her. But if you asked her why she would go through so much trouble, she'd just shrug and say: *a bud's a bud*. The two have been tight since they shared homeroom back in freshman year. Darva Jean couldn't exactly say when the two became friends, but a turning point occurred when a group of girls were overheard saying some nasty things about Darva Jean debating down the old nun who once taught Civics.

These girls believed that Darva was one of those *sisters* with an *attitude*. That she probably had posters of Malcolm X and Connie Chambers all over her bedroom walls. That she probably supported radical underground groups that planned to overthrow the government. But mainly, they were jealous. Darva Jean's smart and not afraid to show it, and these little sessions would always occur right after this particular class, where Darva Jean excelled so much so that it got the attention of Sister Mary Boniface to get the young freshman on the junior debate team. Usually, the same group of girls—Becca Prejean, Jenna Muledeaux, Andrea Paternostro—would huddle together and collectively hiss and sneer as Darva Jean would saunter out of the classroom, still discussing her point about some missed chance of an amendment that might have made a significant difference to the way things are governed even in today's times. Just as Darva stepped into the hallway, one of them called out:

"The only thing you're missing, girl, is your mind."

"You're making the class a real drag, *Miss Smart Ass*. Why don't *you people* just stop bitchin' about what's wrong with everything. Besides—*you* people didn't write "that Constitution. You should consider your ancestors lucky to have been dragged over here in the first place—" another quipped.

And then there was the bit Andrea Paternostro added:

"…Yeah, be thankful *you* people were brought over here, otherwise, you'd be sittin' in some hut over on the east coast of Africa weaving baskets right now."

It was at that very moment that a voice could be heard from behind an opened metal locker door—the one that had a missing hinge and squeaked a bit when moved. With only a pair of long pale legs and drooping white knee socks in cheap, dirty saddle oxfords showing from below, one couldn't exactly say who bellowed:

"Hey! Dumb-dumb, Paternostro! If you bothered to actually know anything, it's *west* coast of Africa."

The squeaky metal locker door swung shut. A pretty white girl with long black hair and dark sparkly eyes smiled and glanced over at Darva Jean just as she was bending down to slide her notebooks into her backpack. Darva looked up and rolled her eyes at Claire, simply mouthing a *thank you*.

A day or so later, Claire and Darva Jean ran into each other again, right after that class, at first, just smiling and waving a hello. This went on awhile until they began to run into each other during lunchtime hour. That was over *three* years ago, an inordinately long time in the life of a teenager. Gradually, as they became more acquainted, the two revealed further details about the goings on in their respective lives, and at first, Claire talked in bits and pieces about her strange situation with her mother. Usually, Claire would just shrug her shoulders and remark on how *baffo* Rita was until she mentioned the night her mother appeared in her bedroom while she lay sleeping.

On that particular evening, Claire roused herself out of her slumber momentarily when she realized Rita was standing over her, holding a pair of shears as she attempted to cut off her lovely, long locks. A sliver of moonlight peered through the filmy, diaphanous curtains, lending Claire a better view as to what was about to take place.

Darva nervously fanned her face with her notebook.

"Shi-yut..girl…what'd you do? My heart would've spilt right outta my chest right then and there. Whoa, Jesus. That's some scary shit."

But Claire remained unabashed.

"Aw, that wasn't anything. She was drunk, that's all. She'd done this one before when I was about twelve…and she actually *did* cut my hair off. I woke up screaming in the bathroom mirror, my bangs practically up to my hairline. "

Darva Jean would listen to her friend with rapt attention, thinking to herself that white people surely seemed weird. True, Darva Jean didn't exactly *know* a lot of white people, but still, they did seem a bit peculiar. Now, black people could be kind a off-kilter, too, Darva would sometimes remind herself on her after-school bus rides home. Everybody's messed up, one way or another, and her family wasn't exactly stellar, either. She had a father who was proving to be a slick trickster on the one hand, or maybe just another black man profiling the old *Papa Was a Rolling Stone* prototype. Of course, a bit updated and fitting along more with today's world. But gosh damn if Dad wasn't driving everybody nuts. And his latest run up to Kalamazoo seemed to be the last straw.

One day, Darva explained to Claire some of her own prickly issues.

"Sometimes I get it from my own people—especially, my kin. Not my mom, of course. She's all set to get me in the best college possible. So she's up my back constantly with keeping the GPA as perfect as I can get it, girlfriend. But it's my other kin, my aunties and cousins. They really don't like it if I speak in complex sentences. I have to remember to ease up on the six syllable words, otherwise they snub me. So I keep all that under wraps until I do a formal debate. And that's when I can kick back and just be myself. But it's strange. I hope I can get the hell out of here, too. I'm hopin' to be up in Chicago or maybe Boston—Git out'a here for my advanced education, ya know?"

But right now, Darva had other, more pressing needs to attend and Claire's disguise was turning into a failed plan.

Darva sighed,

"Okay. This is all wrong. But I have another idea. And I got this stuff back at the house. Don't worry. I can git you in the cottage tonight. But tell me, girlfriend, have you ever wanted to be a real Mardi Gras Indian? You know, with an elaborate three foot high headpiece of plumage and all?"

◆ ◆ ◆

Sister Mary Boniface hesitated to return to the gambling tables downstairs. She had already won a walloping, fifty-five thousand dollars playing *Roulette*, and now she was wondering if she would be pushing things too far if she were to try her hand at her favorite, *Craps*.

Yes, she could try for an even one hundred thousand, but she would have to cross that section again, the one where there's a dealer who seems to look her way whenever Boniface makes a beeline across the room. *Who is this ruddy, large-boned woman, the one with a tattoo on her forearm and silver cuff bracelet on the other?* Boniface tried to cull any memory from her ancient mind. After ruminating awhile, Boniface surmised: *Oh, I'm just worked up over nothing. I don't know who that person is. Maybe she saw my win while the wheel was rolling away, and was wondering if I'd make a round at her table. Maybe she's on to my win, that's all.*

Boniface stood in front of the mirror, musing to herself as she adjusted her crisp white collar, gliding the silver chain that held her beloved silver cross to lie at the center of her chest. Boniface thought: *I should be shouting for joy*. But she wasn't. Actually, the good sister was feeling a tad guilty. She had to keep reminding herself that she was gambling to save her beloved *Immaculate Heart*. In fact, it took quite a resolve for her not to call Antionetta to tell her the good news. That if she wins again, she could come home a day earlier. But that might jinx her luck. *Better to mums the word for now.*

The good nun sat back on the motel room bed and wondered if she should eat in, rather than dine downstairs—or at some other over-kill, restaurant environment in every Vegas hotel you run into. Maybe she would be more conspicuous, being an older woman alone, in simple clothes, while wads of bills from a series of Roulette wins sit in her room safe upstairs. Maybe she would be on the Management *watch–list*, as she had heard about such things when one wins so precipitously. Boniface grinned and grabbed the phone. *I just can't help my lucky streak, that's all,* she thought, as she dialed for Room Service.

After finishing up a bowl of chili and bland chef salad, Boniface decided that a walk downstairs might do her some good. If she felt like playing a few rounds, then so be it. She would remember to keep the bets modest, so as to not bring unwanted attention. She would be doing it for fun. Boniface rather enjoyed people-watching in such a milieu. The variety, the excitement of the tables, the happy looks on the winner's faces, and of course, the sadness that befall those less fortunate. Boniface amused herself as she waltzed around the various game tables, becoming engrossed in some of the plays. It took her by surprise when she felt someone lightly tapping her on her shoulder.

Boniface turned around, looked up and smiled,

"Yes?"

A big-boned, ruddy complexioned, middle-aged woman with barely any make-up, and cropped red curls sticking out from what looked like a black baseball cap beamed,

"Sister Boniface? It's me. Kate."

The woman grinned.

Boniface's mouth was suddenly drained of all moisture. Her tongue was as dry as the desert this electric city was built on. Even though she couldn't exactly pinpoint the name, clearly, she was at a loss as to what to say or do. So many emotions ran through her inner circuitry all in a matter of seconds.

But the sheer feeling that predominated, and the one that seemed to overtake the old woman was fear. Just plain, naked, flat-out, *now-everyone-is-going-to-find-out-about-me*—fear. The ruddy woman's jowls relaxed and softened as she reached out for the good nun's arm, as she was afraid the old woman would lose her balance.

Then, in a low voice, the big boned woman pulled Boniface closer, assuring her:

" Now, Take it easy, there, old girl. It was about fifteen years ago when I left. Had to. Wasn't being honest with myself. I'm a *certain way*, Boniface, and now I'm a dealer here at the casino. I also have a partner in my life. I'm happy. Truth is good. Ya know? I mean, when I was *Mary Katherine*, I wasn't happy. You remember. Besides, we all think we got our secrets. Sheeeesh! Are we wrong about that one! Hah, everybody knows about your gamblin', Boniface."

◆　◆　◆

Well...it looks like I wasn't the only one aiming to give a light tap on the old nun's shoulder, that's for certain. But it seems that, in your world, I am always at a disadvantage and someone or something always beats me to it. My way of persuading any one of you requires much too much work. It seems my mental suggestions can't penetrate your vibrations. Your world is too dense and heavy to receive my light and wispy spirit. Perhaps if I could configure myself in some way on the back of one of your text messages or email transports, I could possibly succeed, but I don't believe that would work, either.

I was just about to mentally suggest to the old woman with the soft, purple aura, that another gaming table awaited her in bringing her to her financial goal. But the big-boned woman distracting her is making my work all the more difficult. She is still chatting away with the old woman and is now walking her over to a cocktail lounge of some sort where they can slip into a dark, leather-upholstered booth in the corner of the room.

Apparently, this woman has something to get off her chest, as you say, and the old woman is none too pleased. She is telling Boniface her life story since she left the convent and came to a realization that she was in love with another woman. It was the librarian at another school nearby. The old woman is nodding her head agreeably, lightly drumming her fingers on the table as she resists the slightest smirk, the two of them now having frothy beers." Kate" is happy to be working in a casino these past few years. Loves the hours, the benefits. Still prays for her fellow sisters. But the old woman is looking very nervous. Her companion assures her that it's good that she is aiming to help the school in whatever way she can. Who cares if the others talk? The "others" being the community of nuns. Kate emphatically states that it's really juicier gossip among the cloistered ones when one learns that one has a certain sexual leniency than any proclivity towards gambling.

"Gads. That isn't really all that exciting. Look at the times we're in?" the ex-sister asks her, "No one practices their faith like they used to. And no one donates anymore. So what choice do we really have?"

The old nun's eyes are slightly tearing now. But it could be the beers. Boniface just ordered her third. She had had another earlier, while she was roaming the casino floors. The ex-sister assures her that she intends to make a contribution to her old convent, to assist in saving their school. "Now you better not call that hush money. I'm proud to be who I am today," Kate tells her. Boniface emits a weak smile. I'm slipping inside of her old mind now, dear readers and her inner thoughts seem to be saying: "Gee... don't I have all the luck? The one hotel I land in to do the dirty deed, to make a few swift bucks and this crazy girl, our beloved, conflicted Sister Mary Katherine, who is now shacking up with a woman, happens to notice me in my simple frock as incognito as any nun could ever be, and here I am, stuck—because she's on to me, and I have to endure it, like it or not".

And at this moment, just to make sure, Boniface announces:

"Well, Kate. I'm sure the girls think well of you, too, and my lips are sealed as far as out little encounter. I mean... I certainly would hope we both stay low about our little meeting here. Hmm?"

Kate doesn't look so assured.

" Honey. I mean, Boniface, dear, I hate to tell you, but see, see this woman here before you? I have absolutely nuthin' to be ashamed of. It took me a long while to git where I am today. I understand what you're saying, but dear, speak for yourself. Relax about your old secret hobby...Nah. Git. Git on back out there an show 'em. It's what ya came here for."

Well, you must admit, for being a woman in her elder years, feisty Sister Boniface sure seems to maintain her composure. As I observe the grinning old cheetah as she wipes her lips on a napkin after finishing her mug of beer I am certain she'll soon let this encounter slip past her memory, for she truly has far more important things to attend.

◆　◆　◆

But in that boggy, swampy terrain, as opposite from the arid Nevada desert as you will ever find, there is another wheel of fortune at work. In fact, its symbolic manifestation could not be more present than in the invisible stars that are guiding Claire through this perilous time of seeking safe harbor. For three days now, she has rested calmly and serenely in the leafy-sequestered cottage of which Darva Jean has so tirelessly secured for her.

Claire Ange

At times, Claire's eyes have swelled with tears of gratitude in being spared a sleeping bag-under-a-Spanish-Oak scene over in *Deschamps Park,* a favorite of street bums and meandering *meth* fiends alike. There have been moments where Claire imagined herself in some lofty future a recognized composer, offering her friend, Darva Jean, an all expense paid trip to…well…anywhere she'd like, yes, or maybe a purchase of a condo in the city of her choice. But maybe that would follow after even more success. Yes! And still that can only be expected for the help her friend has so unselfishly granted.

While Darva Jean's mom has entertained her friends, kin and neighbors these past few pre-*Gra*s days, Claire has remained under the radar by staying in the outback cottage, writing music, pining for college and with school being out for the extended weekend, sneaking out only in the evening, (which came early as it was still early March) to practice piano at the *River Road Bar* during the dead hour as most patrons were out enjoying the parades 'til about ten pm. It has been so easy to slip back into the little cottage late at night and Lucy Darlene remains unawares. Only once had Claire shown up at the convent late one afternoon to play some Gershwin and early R&B tunes. The nuns looked refreshed when Claire walked out after two hours of fastidious practice, inquiring if Claire were preparing for a performance somewhere. Claire only shrugged her shoulders and remained deferential and very quiet. *Such a kind child,* Antionetta thought as she was preparing the dining room for the nuns' supper, asking if Claire wished to join them. Although Darva Jean had brought her friend smuggled helpings of the best fried catfish and hushpuppies, salad and hot rolls she could ever find, it was usually on a catch as catch can basis as Darva was wary of stirring any suspicion from her ever-watchful mom. But Claire declined the nun's offer fearing she would be subject to an array of uncomfortable questions. She was betting that

Darva would show up at the cottage at some point with some munchies. And sure enough, later that evening, around ten pm, Darva lightly tapped her nail on the window holding a paper bag of goodies hot from the stove.

That Darva Jean! Make that, *Saint Darva,* as Claire is calling her these days. It wasn't such a bad arrangement, either. Claire found the enclave to be quite cozy and didn't mind holing up, poring over her books and music, taking breaks to daydream about being ensconced in a fancy conservatory, writing music, attending classes with brilliant professors and musicologists some day.

Claire welcomed the privacy and seclusion, having some free time to reflect on it all. Has it been almost two months since Rita's expulsion? Did she miss her mom? Yes and no. One thing Claire couldn't help observing was the way Darva and Lucy Darlene seemed to get along so well. For being mother and daughter, it almost seemed alien when she overheard a conversation they were having in the driveway the other night. Claire was amazed at how Lucy reached out and embraced her daughter as she congratulated her on her latest debate team preparation session or just how she expressed her appreciation for Darva's understanding when Lucy's schedule got tight.

Actually, it made Claire a bit woozy to be in the vicinity of such normal relations. She had only to recall the few, scant moments when her own mother ever gave her praise. *Let's see*, Claire mused, there was the occasion when Claire deftly *crazy-glued* a *Wedgwood* dish Phil accidentally dropped, and another when Claire ran out in the rain one blistery night to tie a loose garbage bag that was spilling refuse all over their perfect front lawn. Rarely did Rita give the slightest compliment to her daughter's musical abilities or the way she tirelessly helped her younger brothers with school projects and the like. Or who could forget the way Rita neglected to ever make the slightest compliment on her daughter's lovely countenance and how modest and humble she seemed to be about it all. It was as if Rita harbored some kind of jealousy against her own daughter, and often the feeling sent shivers down Claire's lovely, supple spine. Yes, Claire surely had a different life from her friend's, that's for certain, but she didn't let it bother her. In fact, Claire felt grateful this crisp wintry Mardi Gras morning and could hardly wait to try out the costume gear Darva left for her on the lounge chair near the fold-out sofa on which she slumbered these past few evenings.

Over the years Claire has only intermittently seen the marching African American groups known fondly for their remarkable, colorful costumes. *The Mardi Gras Indians* were an institution in itself with some groups going back to the 1800's when they first formed to honor the unique friendship between the Chickasaw Indians and escaped slaves who sought their welcomed assistance and asylum. For about one hundred and fifty years these groups of African Americans would sew and create the most elaborate of Indian costumes to honor that special bond between the two peoples. Plumes and headdresses of such elaborate detail and colors and plumage in such an abundance that it becomes an impossibility to determine any troupe that outshines the other. These were by no means mere costumes created on a whimsy. Rather, they are so detailed, so lovingly created that each tribe tries to out-do the other in sheer flamboyance and decadent luxury of color, sparkles and feathers so elaborate that the average costume takes a good year or two, and a few thousand dollars to create.

Darva Jean is quite familiar with the scene as she has accompanied her cousins in previous years and now her twin by marching this year. Many of the men in her family have so regularly participated in stitching and threading, embroidering and sewing together so many marching Indian costumes there must be about three closets full of them—between Lucy Darlene's cache and her kin's, no one would realize what might be missing and from what year worn any given year. So Darva had not a worry picking out an outfit that would suit her friend. Darva would be selecting one for herself, too, although everyone knows that the vast costume makers and marchers are almost always exclusively male. Darva didn't care. She'd dress up anyway, and sometimes putting on so much glitter and being weighed so much by the plumes and oversized satin costumes, no one could really tell if she were a girl or a guy. So she had it all down. She and Claire would both join in the *Bijoux Renegade Revellers*, the "tribe" Darva's family has marched in for decades.

Claire would wear something Darva's cousin, Jamal, wore many moons ago, and as Darva so well remembered, a satin covering was worn over his mouth to render a certain, *Arabian Nights* mystique. All Darva had to do was add a face mask, some white cotton gloves and no one would ever know there's a white girl marching and struttin' in their midst. Well, maybe the two of them wouldn't join up too chummy-chummy. Claire and Darva could stray a bit and have their own fun in the crowds, especially when the time comes for the tribes to do their competitions.

While Lucy Darlene went over to her women's group late Saturday afternoon, Darva ran back to the cottage and dragged her friend outside so they could practice the strut. Claire had to get that one down and Darva showed her all the moves.

"If somebody speaks to you, just bob your head. I'll tell them you have laryngitis or something. Don't worry. You'll be fine. Later, we'll meet some people I know down in the Fauborg. You just sit tight and no one will pay you any mind."

But Claire had her doubts. She wondered how long a person could just sit there and not say anything. Claire tried not to think so far ahead and stay focused on the good fortune that has been set before her. It was only an hour or so earlier that Darva roused her up, giving Claire instructions as to when and where to meet her and the marching troupe. Claire carefully read over the instructions Darva wrote out for her before sneaking out of the house. Claire read the note:

Girl, I also left a post-it for my mom on my bathroom mirror. She'll have a fit 'cuz she wants me to hang out with her awhile, but I got to check things out, first. Just get on the bus in your costume and look for the address. I'll see you soon.

Claire looked over the costume as she spread it across the entire length of the couch. The plumes themselves were so high she knew she could not put the headpiece on inside the cottage or wear it on a bus—and gosh knows where the city transit system buses were to be re-routed today. She would have to carry the feathered headdress and just make the best of it. Somehow she would find a way to make it all work.

Claire stepped into the smooth, satin costume pants and pulled on the accompanying jacket, heavy with sequins and colorful, faux jewels. She then placed a purple satin scarf around her head, wrapping it like a turban so she could cover all of her hair—which was wound tightly in a bun. Claire then took the colorful mask and applied it to her face, a bright green silk cloth wrapped nicely across the mask, covering her mouth right down to her chest. Tiny shivers ran through her body while butterflies frittered away in her belly. *Wow. This might just work,* Claire mused, pulling on the white gloves Darva left for her.

While Claire hummed away, checking the bus schedules and then gathering her coin purse and effects, the cottage door unexpectedly opened. Assuming it would be Darva Jean returning to give her a few more tips and reminders, Claire was stunned by the figure looming before her. Lucy Darlene, looking as serious as a drill sergeant, her arms held akimbo, stepped into the little doorway.

"What in the heck are you doin back here? I've been searchin' all over for you, Darva Jean. Well, look at you! Let me see. Turn around. Well. Ok. You're lookin' pretty *Gras,* girlie."

Waving her arms in the air as she turns back toward the idling vehicle puffing exhaust in the driveway, Lucy shouts back to the costumed figure now hesitating in the doorway:

" Go on, now—git yourself in the car. At least I got one of you. I gotta check the house again. Maybe I'll find your brother in there."

◆　◆　◆

Sister Mary Boniface was delighted she made another winning, in spite of the strange and unexpected encounter she had the night before. She quietly rose the next morning to lightly tread the casino carpets, making her rounds to her favorite gambling tables and quietly amassed a killing, as they say, even though it was a Sunday, *God forbid.* Sister mumbled her prayers to herself as she tried to hide her excitement. Word got around about the little gray haired lady and many a gambler at the other tables raised a brow or two and talked about the smart and clever old woman with her unmistakable sleight of hand.

"Where in the hell did she come from?" A middle-aged man remarked to his wife, as they counted their measly chips and debated whether they should continue to wear out their dwindling luck. The woman, throwing the chips on the felt clothed gaming table, announced to her husband:

"Let's go, Jake. We need to go."

Later, while the good sister was enjoying a light breakfast and coffee in the hotel café, the couple appeared at the counter, the woman sliding herself on a stool next to Mary Boniface, remarking a bit breathlessly:

"How 'd'ya do it, honey? I mean—you just don't look like the type. Does she, Jake? Gonna put your great grandchildren through college, is that it?" the younger woman laughed.

Sister Mary Boniface spread a sheepish grin, her dentures flashing, her small head bobbing.

"Well actually…why…yes! You could say I am going to be paying for *my girls'* education. And quite a few at that!" Sister chuckled.

Admittedly, it was a bit strange having the hotel security escort the good sister, looking her bland, incognito, Mennonite, old lady persona best as they walked with her to the curb to flag her a taxi straight to the airport. But Boniface didn't mind. She felt triumphant, actually. For now, her troubles had come to an end. She would put the winnings to good use. It's not nearly the total amount the *Convent* needs, but it's a hefty start. Did she feel a tad penitent? Of course she did. But deep down, Sister knew it was all for a good cause. She was really making a sacrifice on behalf of her beloved institution and to hell with those dominating, overbearing *Jesuits*. The *Convent* will stay an all girls' independent school as long as she remains *vertical*, as they say.

When Boniface returned to her humble living quarters, looking tired and haggard in the early, wee morning hours of *Lundi* Gras, she quietly creaked upstairs to her cozy room, hoping no one would hear her. As she approached the upper landing—the tiny wheels of her bag squeaking down the newly polished parquet wooden floors—Antoinetta, her hair tucked in a simple linen bonnet, greeted her with wringing, moist hands.

"Well?"

Boniface retorted with a harsh whisper:

"What do you mean, *"Well"*? I already told you everything as it is. It's four am. Why are you up?"

"Can't sleep. Can I at least see it?"

Boniface shook her old weary head.

"Not all of it is in cash, Antoinetta! We'll chat in a day or so. See you then."

And with that, Boniface quietly shut her bedroom door. *See it?* Boniface chortled to herself. *What is going on with that crazy Antoinetta these days?* She mused as she put her bags on her bed, humming softly while she unpacked her things.

Boniface took the earnings and carefully put them away thinking that she would later decide how she would divide the money and into which accounts come the following business day.

She would not be doing any errands or much of anything else until *Ash Wednesday*—after Mass and morning prayers, of course. She also had no plans for celebrating any of the Carnival festivities. What she needed was rest and quiet. She figured all would be well come that first day of the Lenten Season. For now, she was going to take a long, late winter's nap.

✦ ✦ ✦

As I was about to update you on the latest goings on of my meandering existence, it occurred to me that I have not been very courteous toward you, dear readers. Here you are, following along and patiently keeping up with the random activities of these curious humans, and with all the attention that must entail, I then barge into these very pages with my woebegone laments about a life I can't even remember. That, and my wandering about your planet: from its myriad, chain-fenced, upper strata orbital satellites to its electrified desert oases. Yet, somehow, you always seem so patient and willing. You take in my reports and findings and serenely allow me to state my case. And now I must ask:

Are you, good readers, enjoying your time here on earth? Hmm? Are you "making the best of it", as the people speaking from your flat screens often ask? Or is it: "Have you set aside enough for your retirement years?" I also hear that one a lot. Usually, there's a grand-fatherly-looking man with silvery hair putting a small white ball on a soft, rolling green lawn, talking directly to the viewer. And what of this stream of announcements (that always include the phrase: "ask your doctor about..."), pertaining to a vast array of pharmacological substances, be they powders, liquids or pills? There's much fanfare in these little flat-screen skits, with laughing, happy people, seemingly overjoyed with the results of these remedies.

Actually, I find these modern elixirs rather dubious as their manufacturers seem to be asking you, dear readers, to be their middleman, yet, I don't believe these medicinal manufacturers are sharing any of the proceeds with you, now are they? Yet again, they are asking you to get your doctor to write a prescription for their products. You.

*Bringing it up to **your** doctor. And I hear nothing about a profit sharing allowance or tip, for that matter. Not even a discount. Your flat screens show a multitude of these pill, tonic and tincture announcements and curiously, each culminates with a list of the possible horrid effects that can occur if you **do** take them up on their offer. Which, to me, tends to cancel their premise. Now I would think most of you would change your minds, but this is not the data that's pouring in. I get a very queasy feeling about it all (and I wouldn't be surprised if they have a dubious remedy for that!)*

I see that this sort of transaction would not go well in my ethereal domain. Such practitioners would be part of a very dismal order, wandering around the spirit world not unlike the lowly critters that scrounge around for the slightest edible morsel deeply nestled in your ocean floors. It seems, if you are "making the best of it", you might want to avoid these advertisements, therefore increasing your chances of staying well.

Otherwise, you have these medicine manufacturers earning all this money off of you and then making things worse by their disclaimers, almost guaranteeing an early and a most unpleasant demise. A clear sign that one did not "make the best of it" on your fair planet, after all.

In case you're wondering, my orb-like, thought-emotion being is gently resting up here near the ceiling of the little room belonging to our Lady-luck, Sister Boniface. I've toned things down to a soft golden glow as I have transformed myself into a sort of imperceptible nightlight awaiting her arrival.

Tardy, though she is, as I've been waiting here in the good nun's bedroom since about 2 am. Her plane was delayed so I amused myself with Sister Antoinetta's insomnia and observing her as she restlessly twisted herself silly in her bed sheets down the hall. After flopping and flailing her aging body like a newly caught flounder atop a tired, sagging mattress, Antoinetta rose to take out her deck of cards for a few rounds of Solitaire. It seems this was a final attempt to lull away the hours in the hopes of tiring herself to ensure some much-needed rest.

Alas! It occurs to me that I've yet to fill you in on my new decision. It's a wonder I have my wits about me at all. Over the past few days—even while I was following Sister Boniface about on the gambling floors of that casino—I developed an idea of sorts.

All right, so she made off with the money. And I feel, along with most of you, dear readers, that the earnings were justified. I tried to encourage a few more rounds, but I don't believe my telepathic suggestions did much good. However, I take full credit for inferring that she try her luck that early morning after she, too, tussled to and fro in her hotel bed sheets most of the evening after that unexpected encounter with the former sister, Mary Katherine. "Kate", as she now calls herself. It was the least I could do. And I am glad for her success. But was it entirely hers alone? Yes it most certainly was. I've wondered if my mental, telepathic abilities are improving, the more attempts I make. I am never quite sure. And it has only been recently that I have come to the conclusion that in these wee early hours before dawn, as soon as Sister Mary Boniface enters a deep sleep, I am going to boldly slip into her consciousness and make an appearance. I must. It's all I can do to state my case. I feel she may be the one to help me, as I am desperate for information.

Ah, I see the door is creaking a ways, and I'm now looking down on the good nun as she quietly slinks into her cozy chambers, the wheels of her luggage bag squeaking slightly as they roll on the waxy wooden floor.

I can see her soft purple aura humming at lo-flame. While she brushes her dentures and places them aside for the night, I am going to ruminate on exactly what I need to suggest. Readers, I ask that you pray for me, a lost miserable soul from somewhere, from some mysterious time, as I ease my way into this old woman's spiritual bosom as she blissfully snores deep into the night. Wish me luck.

♦　♦　♦

The early morning sunlight beamed mightily on the windshield as Lucy Darlene took an occasional sip from her travel mug smoking next to her in its little caddy. Traffic was already beginning to pile up on this frosty Mardi Gras morning. She continued to tell the still, quiet figure sitting next to her of her latest ordeal at work. It was going to be a hectic Mardi Gras Day, that's all she could say.

"…Well. Honey, you know what I told her? Hmm. You can bet…what on earth is that driver doin now?"

Lucy Darlene chattered nonstop as the masked and fully costumed figure bobbed her head in the passenger seat, wondering how she was going to keep her cover.

"You sure are quiet today, Darva Jean. I thought you'd be practicing your rappin'. Whew. Need I say, I'm a bit relieved."

Claire nervously pointed her gloved hand to her throat. Lucy Darlene momentarily glanced her way.

"What? Coming down with a cold or somethin'? Well, now. Tante Suzette will give you a remedy for that. Just hang in there. I gotta see where your brother is. Maybe he's there already, I dunno. Anyways—as I was telling you, that boss of mine is a real pill. I know I need to keep

161

"this job to put food on the table but I am about to crack under that woman's whip. And she's a sister, too. You'd think they'd be some solidarity around that place with so few women in charge and so few black women, I should say. You think I should invite that bitch to my women's group? Oh, that's right…you got yourself a sore throat, just nod your head then. Nod away, darlin' and hold on while I swerve my way around this butthead. There ya go! Flip him the finger, honey. He's just another arrogant a-hole musclin' his big butt through traffic."

Claire held up her other gloved hand, the middle finger resting against the passenger window. Lucy sped down the busy Claremont Blvd, racing her way to a good side street she remembered to get her down to the *Faubourg* more quickly.

Lucy continued:

"Well, now I just wanted to tell you, Darva Jean, that after some really good talks over the past couple of weeks or so, your dad is going to be visiting with us sometime tonight. Now he's going to stay back there in the old cottage. In fact, that's one of the reasons I wanted to check on things back there; make sure we have some sheets and stuff. Takes a while to talk things through, so I am not askin' your daddy to stay in the house just yet. But I know my prayers have been answered. He loves you, Darva Jean. He really does. I know he misses us, too."

It was then, at a stoplight that seemed interminable, that Claire felt she had to make a decision and fast. She placed her trembling gloved right hand on the door handle and pushed up the lock with the other as she remembered to grab all of her things before making a run for it.

A flicker of movement caught Lucy's eye.

"Darva, honey, what on earth…"

But before Lucy barely realized what the costumed figure next to her was about to do, she shouted,

"Now, Darva, honey, I know it's been a while since you last saw your daddy…let's just talk about it. What on earth..?"

Claire slid out of the passenger door and made a run for it. She didn't think, she just let her legs carry her and actually, she could not recall running this fast in all of her seventeen years. Even when it was her very own stocking-footed mother giving her chase. But she gunned down the heavily tree lined street as fast as her legs could carry her lean body, cumbersome headdress (weighing quite a few pounds) and a duffle bag of random things. Afraid the grey SUV would come after her, Claire ducked into the nearest alley and crouched behind a cluster of smelly garbage cans.

◆ ◆ ◆

Rita stood transfixed in front of her ornate bedroom mirror, another antique relic Hilaire bought for her as a gift so many years earlier when they were traveling through the Carolinas. Rita was costumed in a faux leopard skin get up—a feline mask covering her eyes while a simulated tail dragged on the carpet behind her. Her son, Marcel, was standing outside her closed and locked bedroom door, pleading with her that he be allowed to hang out with his older brother, Phil and his buds, and not having to go with his mother to Rita's faux friends' on Evangeline Avenue—an enviable residence where one had a front-row seat view of all the Mardi Gras parades from ten am to early evening. To Marcel, that was a boring and a fake way to enjoy Gras. The action was in the *'Quarter* and that's clearly where he wanted to be. The thought of having to hang out with mom and the crowd of shallow acquaintances turned his tummy a tad sour. Surprised that the lock somehow gave way, Marc leaned his lanky, slender body against the doorframe.

"Ma, I'm old enough to hang around with Phil. I'm not ten, you know!"

"Marc…" Rita barked, as she continued to stare at herself in her treasured wardrobe mirror, "I think you're still too young to hang out with those boys…the only reason Phil's down there today is that he and his friends are being supervised by some adults, but you're still too young for that scene with all…those…people.. down there……you're with me today. You can hang out with the other kids *there*".

If the truth be known, Rita was feeling a tad insecure and did not wish to attend the annual gathering at the de Rosier's lavish home alone. She also didn't want to face the barrage of questions that would most likely come up— questions about her wayward daughter and Hilaire's station in the Middle East. Marc would have to stick it out with her, or maybe he, too, would be out on the streets. *I'm just not putting up with these rotten kids anymore,* Rita hissed to herself as she affixed the fake, exaggerated cat whiskers above her upper lip on each side of her face, one set sliding downward as she fussed.

"Marc…I told you the terms. Now live with it or you'll end up like your sister."

Marc brightened and quipped: "Oh, *really*, Ma? That'll be fine with me. When can I leave?"

Rita scoffed back:

"Keep talking like that, young man, and you'll be grounded big time."

Marc responded:

"Ooooooooo. You really scare me, Ma. Like what are you goin' to do to me, especially after I clue Dad in on what you really did to Claire, our beloved and sadly missed big sister."

Rita flung her bedroom door open and shook a cool lean manicured finger at her son:

"You will do no such thing. I will take away all of your things: your I-*puddy* or whatever you call it, your computer, your games, your CDs…your…whatever it is you do… now hush and fetch me a teensy drink from the bottle on the bar. Go ahead. Just a bitsy shot. Your daddy's *Noah's Mill Bourbon*, Marc."

Rita handed Marcel a crystal whiskey sour glass. Apparently, Rita got an early start to the *Gras* celebrations by having a shot with her morning coffee. Perhaps it was more than a mere shot, as there seemed to be smudges and lipstick marks on the rim.

The boy grimaced:

" Ma, this needs washing out…"

Marc slid past his mom and headed for the bathroom sink. He pulled the hot water lever and placed the glass in the sink bowl. He could hear his mother chattering away in the next room. Marc didn't hesitate at the sudden flash of insight that came over him. He swiftly opened the medicine cabinet, looking for a possible way to get out of his little predicament. There were myriad plastic bottles for a variety of ailments. Pain pills, along with medicine to help one sleep. Marc lifted the sleeping pill bottle and nervously shook out two tablets. *This should do it,* he thought to himself, slipping the pills in his pants pockets while tossing the newly washed glass in the air as he stepped back into the hallway, heading for the stairs.

At about the very moment younger brother, Marc, hit the smooth wooden floors of the bar to fetch the requested shot of the prized bourbon, big sis, Claire slipped out of her hiding place and gunned down a busy uptown side street, still masked—the silk scarf flapping, the three foot high headdress tucked under her arm, feathers wafting gracefully in the morning breeze behind her. Claire hoped Darva's mom was still pretty much locked at that tight intersection, on the far left lane, making it difficult for Lucy to swerve over to the other lanes to successfully trail her. After racing down several blocks, Claire stopped at a house that seemed to have enough trees and shrubbery where she could shield herself from Lucy's SUV in case she succeeded in her pursuit. Claire imagined Darva's mom, neck craned, waving her arm in the air as it jutted out of the driver's window as she aimed to fetch what she thought was her runaway daughter. But of course, she was not her daughter. And this disguise business was making Claire all the more uneasy as she crouched deeper beneath the shrubbery and closer to the clapboard house that seemed miraculously vacated.

Claire leaned back against the outer wall, hoping her hunches were correct. It seemed its inhabitants had already left for the Mardi Gras celebrations as the driveway was bereft of a single car. Sensing that enough time had lapsed, Claire took off the mask and scarf that covered her face down to the sternum. She breathed with relief and rested there for a good twenty minutes before she felt the coast was clear. But her thoughts were now spinning out of control. Claire wasn't sure where she was. She was also uncertain of the whereabouts of her bud, Darva Jean. But Claire closed her eyes in relief, taking deep breaths as she attempted to quell any anxiety.

Even though she loved her bud for coming to the rescue, she knew this idea was a crazy one. It would prove to be too much. *The idea that I could pass off for a Mardi Gras Indian*! Claire thought, holding her white gloves in her hand, nervously flopping them against her thigh. Claire wasn't ready to make any decisions. She knew she had to contact Darva soon. But she was too scared at the thought of her knowing what had happened so unexpectedly. Claire sat in a stupor, unwilling to move, mainly for fear that Darva's mother might be driving around looking for her to scoop back into the car.

Claire remained still as the trees that enshrouded her, noticing a quaint statue of a Virgin Mary perched nearby. Her little arms were slightly outstretched, her porcelain bare feet standing on a shiny green orb. These were common adornments gracing many a lawn in the old neighborhoods of the city. Claire rather liked the 1950's kitsch charm of it all. It reminded her of old Mrs. Gaynor—her kindly neighbor who still housed the many garbage bags filled with Claire's belongings. How she longed for her kind grandmotherly manner, her soups and soft bed in her charming guest room that awaited her. Claire felt an urge to call the old lady's house but remembered that she would still be away.

For a moment, Claire had a crazy thought to call her dad in far away Dubai, but of course, she had no such capability on her little phone. But Claire was curious if he had ever asked about her. Was he wondering why he hadn't spoken to her all these weeks and what, pray tell, was Rita telling him? Claire shuddered at the possibility that Rita might have said she's shacking up with a college guy, as rumors had it. But if her mom did say that, more than likely her dad would return. Maybe Rita was still making up excuses. Lost cell-phones, bad Internet service, or discontinued Internet service because of necessary punishment for the boys' lackadaisical, if not ornery, attitudes. Sure enough, Rita probably cooked up fresh excuses every week.

Claire tried not to worry about her situation. She hoped that she could call Mrs. Gaynor by Ash Wednesday evening. Claire surely didn't think she would be able to continue staying in the outback cottage—especially if what Darva's mom was saying were true. This made her especially anxious. Slowly, Claire managed to turn her thoughts to a melody she had playing in her head the other evening. She even tried out a few bars on the piano at the old river road bar when she went there to practice the other night. She developed it a little more in her mind as she stared into space memorizing the notes to jot down later. It might make a good piece for my audition, she thought. Audition at any music school that would have her. That is, if she were to go a bit further in the application process.

Claire felt that familiar, warm buzzing sensation in the soft satin pocket of her costume pants. It was her cell phone in vibrating mode, and on impulse, believing it to be Darva Jean, Claire immediately spoke up:

"Look—I am a-ok, but your mom thought I was you—don't worry: I was covered head to toe—and she practically cattle-prodded me into the SUV—I acted like I was you with laryngitis. So don't worry, She doesn't know. I ran out the car, though. Now I don't know where I am. Don't kill me. Okay?"

A voice chimed in just as Claire finished speaking.

"Okay, darlin. I'll consider that. But looky here: my piano player's too skunked to make it in today and my next replacement decided to do *Gras* at the last minute and I need a substitute, *fast*. I interviewed you last week or so, right?"

Claire was a bit taken aback by the not-so-recognizable voice.

"This is?"

"Wilfred La Rousse. But for *Gras*, girl, I'm all Winnie. So. Tell me, feel like makin' some good money today?"

♦ ♦ ♦

Marc stood at the bar in the living room, pouring a short shot of the prized, mellow-aged Kentucky bourbon and felt the weight of whether to add a tincture of newly crushed sleeping meds into the richly brown, fragrant liquor square on his frail, teenage shoulders. It wouldn't be an easy decision. On the one hand, Marc very well knew he had no idea how much his Ma might have imbibed earlier, and two, being interested in chemistry, he had no real idea what two crushed sleeping pills might do. *What if she ends up in a coma?*

For a moment, he horned in on a memory of fluffed blankets and Ma cooing to his four year old, footed pajama clad self, newly fresh from a warm bubble bath. Jeez. Catching a brief flicker of his own image in the smoky beveled glass mirror flanking the wall of the bar area of the living room caught him by surprise. Then the siren call from the top of the stairwell,

"Where's my drink, Marcel?"

While Marc continued to mull over the crushed meds nestling in his moist fist, neighbor and Mom's bridge buddy, Anne Leblanc, just happened to be taking a general survey of things through hubby, Warren's, ultra-grade, high powered binoculars. Anne was only so many yards away, on her porch, standing there, already dressed for the big day, and waiting on her husband to finish dumping bags of clear ice cubes into their favorite ice chest that sits in the red wagon they always pull along on their miles long strut with their Mardi Gras marching *krewe*—the *Bergeron Avenue Steppers*. Anne was pleasantly surprised that she could actually see into the large window on the side of the great house. Not that she intended to aim directly for the living room interior of the Molyneaux household, but she somehow landed there, as the silk taffeta curtains were fully drawn open. She could vaguely make out a figure moving around. Certainly, Anne felt a tad guilty. She had been a regular card playing mate to Rita for a while now, but with all the talk going around in their respective social circles, she could no longer afford too much camaraderie with her old bridge buddy.

There was talk that Rita had sent her daughter off somewhere secret—while she continued to go to school at the convent. Some strange arrangement made under dubious circumstances. But Rita claimed it was the girl who left in a huff one chilly school-day afternoon. So far, there didn't seem to be much evidence of a Canadian boyfriend. That is, to justify Claire's supposed waywardness. However, there were random scenes of Claire playing pool late at night at some of the college hangouts in order to rustle up rent money for a flophouse kind of boarding room near the universities. Young Claire was also spotted crossing Evangeline Boulevard late on a school night, carrying a portfolio of some kind and entering the old *River Road Bar*.

Little did they realize that Claire was spending her spare evenings practicing at the 100 year old, Neufeld piano in the back of the bar. But there was also talk that old lady Gaynor was giving the young gal a hand—yet the old lady hadn't been seen the past few days. Whatever the situation, Anne had a bad feeling about it all and that's why she made the prank call to Rita's cell the other day, blocking her number so Rita wouldn't know who was calling. Anne just knew there was something not right about the picture Rita painted when she met with her for cards so many weeks ago.

But today was *Gras*, and Anne felt that curiosity creeping up. It's not that Anne hadn't anything better to do. Warren was fidgeting around in the kitchen, the sound of ice cubes pouring into ice chests could be heard from where she stood. Anne figured she had a moment to steal a few quick glances over at her neighbors'. After all, she was already dressed and ready for the Mardi Gras festivities she and Warren were to attend. She didn't know how they were going to do all that marching all the way down to the French Quarter with their favorite marching *krewe,* and then later meet up for some parties after the big day was done with.

The front door shut unexpectedly. Anne slightly twitched, tucking the binoculars back on the shelf space near her knee as she registered Warren's familiar patter on to the porch. Anne spoke up,

"Didn't you say you saw old lady Gaynor the other day putting out large bags of trash?"

Warren resounded,

"I'm not so sure it was *trash*. It looked more like loot stolen from the back of a Salvation Army donation truck. But it wasn't the other day. It was weeks ago, Annie. I told ya this, already. It was big bags of stuff and the girl was helping her. The cute girl who luckily ran away from that bitch friend you keep spyin' on. Come on—cough 'em up. I know you got 'em hidden somewhere. Gimme my binocs. ya bad ass. Those are for my games…if I were you and needed a spy, I'd hire one."

Warren gently tickled Anne's soft cheek, "Hey…Want me ta spank ya now, or do you want that later…in the bedroom, huh, you bad-girlie, you?"

Anne shooed hubby away.

"Oh *stop*, you silly…"

Warren stepped back, taking a lean survey of his wife, all a costumed.

"I don't know if I like you dressed up as a martyred nun from the eighteen-hundreds… I'm thinking you look a little too sexy all covered up that way."

171

A lean, coffee-toned man appeared just outside the screened-in veranda, lightly tapping his knuckles on the door. Warren hesitated for a moment, then realized the figure before him was none-other than his band mate and friend, Squires.

"Hey, my man. Didn't know who in the heck that was out there, come on in. Yeah, you're looking pretty authentic there, boss. Your glasses and... check out that beard."

Squires stepped in, nodding to Anne,

"Now, this is what I call a fine Mardi Gras Day."

Anne piped:

"Fine it is, Squires. How'r'you?"

Squires turned back to face Warren, arms outstretched.

"So you know who it is, then. Who I'm supposed to be an all."

Although it was a bit brisk this Mardi Gras morning, Squires was bare-chested save for a few strands of wildly colored beads. Warren's buddy pranced onto the porch, donning white pantaloons, cropped at the thigh and somehow puffed and draped in an elaborate swirl; a coiled sheet rode up his back, crisscrossing his torso. His get-up looked like a giant diaper held together with a sash. His socked feet squished a bit in old, crinkly leather strapped sandals. Squires paused, sliding his wire-framed glasses up the smooth line of his elegant, slightly aquiline nose, his trumpet resting at his thigh.

Warren looked him over:

"Yeah...*Gandhi,* right?"

Squires, looking disappointed, quipped

"No man. I'm *Ramakrishna*. Remember?"

Warren took a good step back, and surveyed his friend.

"Oh that's right. He was a *saint*, wasn't he? *Saints*, that's what we're goin' as...Right?"

Back at chez Molineaux, Marc dutifully brought his mother her shot of whiskey, and nervously awaited the results.

♦ ♦ ♦

Claire stayed in complete costume for all of Mardi Gras day, warm and uncomfortable as that was being she was stuck in a crowded, decadent, gay bar tucked away in the lower French Quarter. But how could she complain? Winnie greeted her at her dressing room door, almost two hours after her initial call, but it was still only ten or so in the morning. Claire was out of breath as she practically walked the entire way, due to traffic.

In the back of her mind, Claire wondered if Winnie even remembered that she hadn't officially auditioned for her. That she was in line to do so and had been furiously practicing for that special afternoon. But Claire soon felt she had nothing to worry about. When Claire finally arrived, Winnie only nodded to her, casually pointing to the coffee and spread of pastries on a tray outside her dressing room. Claire was handed a stack of sheet music to review, nodding to Winnie each time she asked if she knew a tune by rote or not. This made Claire a tad uneasy. Actually, the idea of whether she could play a tune from memory didn't seem to pester Claire as much as her being able to remain fully costumed, right down to her gloves. She was under-age, and her only hope was this crazy Indian costume get-up. Winnie remarked that it was silly to have such a concern on *Gras* day as she herself was about to be fully costumed in a tight fitting gown and a bejeweled face.

"Hunny, we all have or little secrets. Go on, girl, I like that get-up of yours, yes I do. Especially that *Arabian Nights* scarf over your mask there…Just don't let any of that get in the way of your playin, aha."

Then Winnie added:

"I'm goin to pay you in cash—that a problem?"

As if cash could ever be a problem, Claire mused, then blurted:

"No! Cash is never a problem for me!"

Claire grinned to herself as she traipsed behind Winnie as they walked back to the interior of the club to fetch more sheet music. Winnie reminded Claire that the drummer and base player would be arriving a few minutes before show time—which was just about an hour or two away. Claire tried to remain calm and nonchalant, to her mind, the way a professional would act if being offered mere cash instead of a check. But being part of a trio? *A real ensemble*? Now that's something Claire hadn't had much experience doing. Actually, Claire grew even more excited as she entered Winnie's personal nook, and looked around, charmed by the rather garish, glittering costumes and feathered boas, strings of faux pearls and gemstones adorning Winnie's wardrobe. It reminded her of a scene from the old musical, *Gypsy*, the famous Broadway show about famed stripper, Gypsy Rose Lee. The scene where the young ingénue is shown the ropes by her new burlesque chums came to mind.   Okay. So it wasn't exactly the big time. But it sure was a start. Life as a real money-earning musician, getting prepped for the big show! Who cares if it was in a hole-in-the-wall- drag, gay club in the bowels of the French Quarter?

Claire looked around Winnie's dressing room, and dutifully followed Winnie's instructions. After all, that's her new boss—even if it were just for one day. One big *Mardi Gras* day, that is. When Winnie announced that she was going to pay Claire a walloping twenty-five dollars an hour, plus a share in the tips, Claire nearly lost her balance right there as she stood next to one of those wardrobe dummy models adorning a tight-fitting spandex gown crawling with gold and silver sequins.

"Yes, ma'am."

Claire humbly replied, wondering to herself if this were the correct form of address. She looked up and eyed the figure flaunting a vibrant red silk kimono and figured she was right on the money with that one. Claire sat in the corner of the room and pored over the sheet music, nodding her head, knowing she'd ace the job.

She could do these in her sleep. Or rather, in her monstrously huge feathered and bejeweled Indian headdress and mask with its emerald green silk, Scheherazade silk scarf draping right down to the sternum. Yes, indeed, it was going to be bright sunny *Gras* day, after all. Claire smiled to herself—crouching behind shrubs and bushes now seemed like a far-away dream. On a shelf space nearby Claire noticed stacks of notebooks, taking a sideway glance as Winnie applied her lavish makeup.

"Don't touch, now. Those are my homework assignments from my students. Algorithms. You good at math, Claire?"

Claire shrugged her shoulders.

"To a point…but that's only because of my musical training."

"Aha. I see… you a straight-A student, then."

Claire laughed:

"Oh, I didn't say exactly that!"

Glancing back to the *Diana Ross* face that was gradually formulating thanks to a skilled hand and eye when it comes to the art of *drag* cosmetology, Winnie winked:

"You ever need any help with those math problems, you come see Winnie, now. Or maybe I should say, Wilfred. That's Doctor Wilfred La Rousse, the mathematics professor. What I do in my day-job.

"Right now, right here, I'm Winnie, the sexiest thing this side of the Mississippi. Yes, I am."

Winnie puckered her full lips in the mirror and swiped them with a luscious, frosty pink color. A fascinated Claire continued to observe Winnie as she studied her reflection, wondering why she still had that slight pencil thin mustache there, though barely visible. As if reading her mind, Winnie looked up,

"Hunny…the crazy people that are goin to be in here today? They be so skunked they ain't goin to notice a darn thing about Winnie's little upper lip…besides, some of 'em kinda like that."

Winnie's reflection winked at Claire, who caught her gaze and quickly darted her eyes to the floor. Winnie shook her great wigged head and outstretched her lean bangle bracelet adorned arms as she basked in her reflection, the rows of bright stage bulbs framing the mirror gleaming, as she announced:

"Whoa! Dorothy-girl! You best believe you *is* not in Kansas anymo'. Welcome to my bad-ass crazy world!"

◆ ◆ ◆

Please make no mind as I tippy-toe my way into the slightest corner of our girl's latest adventure. I am here merely as an observer and I could use the break. Actually, being in the world of woken, ambulatory humans as they frolic about on this decadent day of mischief is quite refreshing to me as I've recently managed to pull myself away and out of the inner world of our favorite snoozing nun, Sister Mary Boniface. I admit, it was a phantasmagorical journey, swimming in the interior of a human's unconscious night life—the one domain we spirits feel is most like our own—that filmy world of slippery, liminal subsistence.

And do you know, dear readers, that I enjoyed the risk without knowing the consequences? I intercepted the good nun's dreams and stated my case as best I could. I spliced myself, actually, into a succession of scenes—flippant scenarios culled from the spool of unsorted human experience that is the very nature of your dream life and now I await the results. But still, she sleeps and it is already some thirty-odd hours since she first rested her old, weary head atop plump, downy pillows. What's a loose spirit upon your world to do but thrust its thought-emotion being forward into the big celebratory day?

As is customary, I felt I had to check up on our Claire and I realize you must be transfixed with awe and amusement as you follow our girl into her latest den of initiation. Yes, I know you are, dear readers, but you know my situation since I first laid my thought-emotion being's "eye" on her. I must see to it that she is safe, foremost, and admittedly, I am a bit concerned. This debauchery may overtake her, lead her into deeper, darker terrains she may not be equipped to take on. Just in case, I am here on standby.

Alas, as you might say: perchance I dream? Well…perhaps. I have the sneaking suspicion that with all my practice at studying your technologies I may be able to eventually "crack the code" as they say. The idea that I could possibly show up in one of your text messages thrills me, I must say. But still, I test and await the results. In the meantime, I'm fondly observing our Claire as she flips through the pile of sheet music that sits in her lap. I look on with her, not recognizing a single tune.

Certainly, this in itself could be a sure sign. I could have lived at a time well before such music came to my attention or experience. Perhaps, I should meditate on this. But only for a moment as I am watching the two of them gather their things.

The costumed Winnie, now spangled up and aglow with glittery makeup adorning her powdered and buffed copper-brown face, her hair a cascade of curls accented with bejeweled adornments like some great Nubian goddess slowly prancing her way out of the dressing room and into the cool, cavernous space where she is to perform. They are now going to do a rehearsal before any reveler is allowed through the cavern doors. Our girl slides onto to the piano bench, her flamboyant and elaborately feathered headdress resting in a chair nearby, her lovely dark tresses tucked neatly in a turban piece, her face completely masked. Is it any wonder she can breathe under all this paraphernalia?

The two accompanying gentleman musicians have arrived and are now having a shot at the bar with their coffee, both masked, the bassist in a pirate get-up, patch over one eye; the drummer dressed as a court-jester of sorts, a colorful, joker cap atop his head, glittery stars pasted on his bearded face. Both looking rather gleeful on this festive morning, I must say. And now they are glancing over at our Claire, with thumbs hitchhiking in her direction, as one of them asks:

"What's with the Injun pianist, Winnie?"

Our performer waves the two off,

"Never mind. She's a composition student".

The two look at each other,

"She?"

Walking like a pageant contestant down the length of the bar, Winnie glares at the two of them while aiming a pointy pump's toe at nubby fingers drumming on the bar.

Winnie quips:

"Now you be nice and take it slow. She needs to practice a bit mo' so shush yourselves, the both of you."

Our performer gently wafts her feathery boa in their faces as she slinks herself down the length of the bar—which is narrow. But she walks it like the sleekest of feline creatures outstretching her lean, copper glittered arms as they gracefully drip brassy, bangle bracelets. Winnie coos a breathy tune, sashaying back down the bar to give our Claire finer points of instruction: increasing the tempo here, slowing things there. The accompanying, off-duty musicians, still lingering at the bar, both smirk and shake their silly, foppery-capped heads. Sensing their disapproving gaze, Winnie sends a sharp, scouring look their way. The two break up laughing. I have to admit, dear readers, it is rather amusing. But the poor girl is becoming quite fidgety, as she pulls at her sleeves, and perspires under her black and gold mask. Winnie swings herself down from the bar to give Claire more suggestions. After she's done, Winnie gently gives Claire an affectionate squeeze.

"Now, darlin, you are doin' just fine. Those two oafs over there are just having some early Gras brandy with their coffee and they're acting silly. Pay no mind to them. They nice guys, you'll see. You are good, girl. So polished. Now let's try that tune one mo' time."

Winnie shoots another dagger look their way. The two straighten up and walk over to their stations, the joker-drummer now setting up his drums. The bassist, now polishing his great instrument with a soft cloth, remains silent. Claire resumes playing. Winnie reassuringly shouts,

"Alright—that's a nice touch you got there, ahmm. That's the way Winnie likes it. Aha."

As long as we're getting the 'ok' from our diva duchess here, I might as well rest myself near the tin-plated ceiling high above while our Claire is fastidiously playing each tune as the clock nears the noon hour when, already, there's a mob forming outside. The costumes and plumage, the debauchery going on so soon in the day—and these two older, more experienced musicians. I fear for my little one here, so innocent, so young, so fresh, yet so gifted in her fingering of the piano keys, never missing a note. She is growing into quite the pianist, yes she is, and miraculously, on her very own. Sneak-out time at the River Road Bar to practice on a badly tuned back room piano has paid off, apparently.

Oh, my, as if we don't already have enough with which to contend, now we have two very young men showing up shirtless, in tight fitting satin short pants and devilishly decadent facial masks as patrons will soon be lining up to slip folded crisp bills into the elastic bands of their colorful briefs. Male entertainers, is what I believe they are called. The image of sweating, muscled gladiators and semi-nude disc-throwing games in Nero's Rome comes to me. Now how would I know this? I check my inner, thought-emotion being, scanning any possibility as to a personal reference and nothing appears. This doesn't give me much hope—but there are more experiences of which to draw, hmm? Winnie is obviously the chief performer here as she shoos away the brief boys, insisting they stay in their places as she sashays in her glimmering tight-fitting gown, colorful feathered boas flouncing the air about her.

Finally, Winnie announces to a stocky, balding gentleman near the sound system.

"Okay, Randy-girl, you can let'em in now. We is ready-teddy."

♦   ♦   ♦

Darva Jean arrived in time to help out her Tante Suzette with getting everything set up for the big day. She was certainly glad she bypassed most of the traffic as she left barely after sunrise, high tailing it to the bus stop. She only hoped and prayed that her friend would follow her instructions and slip out of the cottage in time. The two had not really communicated, though, and her mom would more than likely want to stop somewhere and load up on even more goodies to bring along, delaying things as usual. Of course, Darva didn't know that Lucy left the house in haste, forgetting her wallet and a few other items. It was when Lucy returned to fetch those things that she decided to check the back cottage. An hour or so later, Darva began to get some strange text messages from her friend—"*tell M. costume died. It just died & hd to b replcd*" Darva Jean huffed and puffed as she took hold of nearly everyone milling about the backyard of Tante Suzette's house.

"If my mom says anything about me being in a white satin Indian costume, tell her, I had to come here and change, ya'll understand? I done split my pants and got axel grease on the sleeves as I was helping Charlie here with his busted carburetor and I had to plumb completely change, ya understand me?"

Most of her family members shrugged their collective shoulders and raised a brow or two wondering what had gotten Darva Jean into such a tizzy. A rather rotund figure in a turquoise and marine blue feathered headdress, broke from the crowd, approaching Darva Jean who was sweating profusely in the morning sunlight.

"Why doncha relax, Darva-girl and come smoke some herb with us out back in the alley and have yo'self some of this rum Jen and I brought with us," her cousin Ray suggested to her. His girlfriend, Jennifer, walked up to Darva Jean, playfully twirling the fringe on her costume,

"Come on with us and just relax, you nervous *Nellie*."

But Darva turned away from them. What did they know of this crazy situation she got herself into? Darva Jean knew when her butt was on the line with her mother, so she had better have the story straight, and drinking rum this early in the day didn't look like the way to go about things. So Darva stationed herself to screen and check every costumed figure that walked through the side gate and up the walkway to the backyard of Tante Suzette's charming shotgun house. The torrent of text messages Claire sent were so frantic and barely decipherable, so over-loaded with mysterious abbreviations and obscure codes that it all looked more like Egyptian hieroglyphics than the basic text lingo of which she and every other teenager were accustomed. Darva Jean finally had to call Claire. And the attempts were many until her friend finally picked up the call. Slow and breezy base notes and soft drumming could be heard in the background, a breathy voice singing the Supremes' "Someday, We'll be Together" softly rose to the accompanying music.

"Where in the heck are you at, girlfriend?" Darva whispered as she walked back to the side of the house.

Darva Jean listened with full attention as Claire described every bit of information pertaining to her current situation. Actually, it was a stroke of divine luck that Claire was so swiftly rescued from what could have become a most uncomfortable situation. At any moment, Darva Jean knew her mother would be showing up, expecting some fast talk as to why the costumed figure she presumed to be her daughter escaped so unexpectedly. Darva cupped her hand over her mouth as she spoke into her phone:

"Gosh-damn, girl, that's my cousin you're with. Hey! Maybe I can pull myself away and come down there and meet up with you."

Darva then asked for the name of the bar where Claire and her cousin were performing, wondering how she was going to slip away from the family scene. It was probably the best idea she had all morning. And right at that very moment, Lucy turned a sharp corner, carrying Tupperware containers full of food.

"Where's Darva Jean?"

Her mother could be heard asking as she greeted everyone. Darva lifted her arm and waved to her mom, still listening to Claire who was now laughing as she described the den of decadence she was now ensconced.

"You have to come down here, girlfriend. It's a hoot. There are people clamoring at the door. I think it's goin to be a stampede. Your cousin's having a hissy fit keepin' that wig on."

Darva Jean smiled and turned away, her mother's face now squarely peering into hers.

" …Well that's kicks. I gotta go! See you in a few…"

Darva clicked her phone shut.

Lucy Darlene was in no mood for a tussle with her daughter. She let out a weary sigh, boring into her daughter, frustrated with her apparent evasiveness.

"And, what, pray tell, was that stunt you pulled? You know how late I am because of you? Where's your brother? And what happened to the costume you had on?"

♦ ♦ ♦

Marc re-read the prescription label. Just in case he had it wrong. Rita had fallen fast asleep on the couch in her bedroom by the time he took a shower, patted himself dry in that fastidious teenage way, and retreated back into his bedroom to make a few phone calls and change into his costume. At first, he was a tad alarmed that his mother was not answering his knock at her bedroom door. Especially so soon after he gave her the tainted shot of bourbon. Marc briskly trotted to his mother's side. At first, his mom was a silent as a baby kitten. This made Marc a bit nervous. What if that means she's going into some kind of coma, he thought. After a few minutes, though, Rita sighed and turned her body to her other side. She even cried out:

" I'm just resting up a bit here, Marc. We'll go in a few…"

But soon, she was snoring away. And deeply so. *Rip Van Winkle,* see-you-in-twenty-years, so. Is this okay? Would everything be all right if his Ma were left there, sleeping it off most of Mardi Gras Day while he took the chance of joining his brother and his friends for the parades? Or should he hang out a while longer?

Marc mulled over these things carefully before deciding to make any calls to his brother. Of course, every sleeping pill prescription says about the same thing: *don't mix with alcohol.* Marc dialed the corner *Rexall.* Just to make sure. The pharmacist came on the line, reminding the boy that they close at noon for Gras. Marc read out the milligram amount of the pills, the brand, and asked what could happen if one had a couple of drinks. The pharmacist sighed and said it should be ok, but that the person would be out like a light—for at least a few hours. But two pills wouldn't do much. Then there was the inevitable:

"Why do you ask?"

Marc cleared his throat and attempted to sound mature:

" Well…my brother had a few shots of whiskey and impulsively took the pills. Now he's snoring."

"Okay. That's about all that'll happen. Let him snooze."

Let 'em snooze, Marc amusingly echoed the pharmacist's wise words of counsel to himself as he walked back to his bedroom to finish up his costume-get up. Odd, though, that he was dressed as a red devil. Marc studied his reflection and decided to wear the Darth Vader costume instead.

But when he checked himself again in the mirror, he grew frightened. The idea of stripping down everything and dressing *Goth*, instead, didn't help. Marc sat on his bed in his underwear, wondering what his next move should be. Finally, he dialed his brother's phone. But he didn't seem to be answering. What if I'm stuck here all day? He wondered aloud as he paced the floor in his dread boots and briefs. Finally his cell rang. It was his brother. Marc immediately went into his spiel about Mom being too tired to make Gras and so whether big brother, Phil liked it or not, he would be meeting the gang in a few downtown.

Phil quipped:

"No way, José…we're already neck deep in crowds…we're just following the floats…we don't even know where we are, it's so crowded. I don't know how you'd catch up with us. Just go over to Mom's friends' house…it won't be so bad…we may be able to work our way back up your way and meet you there."

But Marc didn't like the idea of mingling with debutantes and snooty kids his age and older, who were bound to be at the de Rosiers. Marc walked back to his mother's room and approached the sleeping figure once more. His phone still nestled in his moist palm, an idea slowly occurred to him. Was he watching too many of these cop shows where meticulous scenes of crime investigations take the viewer to great lengths in evidence gathering?

Perhaps so, but Marc raced down the stairs and grabbed the bottle of bourbon by its slender neck and returned to his mother's boudoir, placing the bottle on the table next to his mother's resting head. He quickly arranged the whiskey glass and gently rearranged the mask askew for greater effect. He backed up slightly and pulled out his phone, nervously taking a few snapshots of his inebriated, sleeping mom, not exactly sure why he decided to do so.

Marc returned to his red devil costume and stepped into the satin pants, re-attaching the smooth satin tail before lifting the black pitchfork from its perch. He walked over to his bedroom mirror and carefully covered his entire face with theatrical red makeup. After waiting a bit for it to dry, Marc fastidiously applied the goatee and mustache, sprinkling glittery rhinestones all over his red face, waiting a few more minutes before finally placing the pointed red cap and pointy ears atop his head. Faintly, ever so faintly, he could hear someone tapping on the front door. Marc quietly walked down the stairs and sneakily tiptoed to the side window to get a glimpse at who could have possibly come calling. A woman in a nun's habit, a fellow with arrows sticking out of his chest and back, wearing a halo, and a skinny, copper-brown dude with a long bristly, goatee dressed in what appeared to be a giant white diaper and sandals stood on the porch.

"Who in the heck are these people?" Marc wondered to himself. The knock came again, this time, louder.

The woman's voice announced:

"Rita! We just wanted to check and see if ya'll wanna come with us!"

Marc stood there frozen in his tracks. He realized his mom's SUV was still in the driveway, and more than likely these people might get suspicious if Rita fails to answer their call.

The door squeaked open,

"Yeah?" Marc asked…

The three of them stepped back, and pointed, announcing practically in unison like a chorus:

"Well…Now. What in the heck do we have here?"

Then the threesome broke out in laughter.Anne, in her nun get-up, inched a bit closer to the red-deviled figure, conspiratorially elbowing, adding:

"Hey! Look at you! You're our come-uppance! No accident we're dressed like *saints*. You're just the right touch to join in the fun!"

◆ ◆ ◆

It was much later in the day that Boniface finally sat up in her bed. It had been almost thirty-four hours since she first laid down to rest. Her aching bones, her sore muscles, especially in the upper arms from all that dice throwing (she laughed to herself) were in need of a good hot soak.

All was still and silent in the convent as most of the nuns had already set out for the day to enjoy the parades from the archbishop's mansion on Evangeline Boulevard. It was a tradition the nuns held dear, as it was also a grand occasion to visit with other cloistered folk from the Catholic community at large. Usually, there are good eats and punch (sometimes spiked) and convivial fun for all. But Boniface was not to join in the celebrations this year. Actually, she rather enjoyed the quiet of the great house for a change.

It would be a good day to contemplate her next moves. She would have to meet with 'Nate again later in the week for another round of discussions, but she was not daunted. In fact, Boniface felt rather energized and confident that she would be able to forestall any further efforts on the part of that prickly-backed Jesuit in *absorbing* (a term he used) her beloved *Immaculate Heart*. It sounded so corporate and masculine.

How dare he, as if he's some Wall Street big shot, swallowing up everything! Keeping in mind that hubris is a tad sinful Boniface bent her head down in pious contemplation and said a quiet prayer to assuage any further ill feelings towards the man. After all, he's only doing his take-over, masculine duty, Boniface mused, with a barely perceptible smile.

Somehow, though, and much to her surprise, Boniface found herself thinking about Claire Molyneaux. Had she been to the convent to practice? *After all, I gave her the only key*, Boniface mused, still in her white cotton kerchief. For some undetermined reason, Boniface felt a sense of uneasiness about the child; that the young girl might be in need of some care and guidance. Boniface wondered if young Claire had a spiritual life, a meditative practice of some kind.

Without thinking of stepping into her soft plush slippers, Boniface leapt off her bed and walked over to the great bookcase that held her personal favorite reads. She perused the shelves. Was there something she could recommend to her? Something that would give her encouragement for whatever ill that may be plaguing her young spirit?

But Boniface shook her head and thought that what the girl really needed was just some good, old-fashioned, *TLC*, as they say. *I'll make sure I have a chat with her after the holiday*, mused Boniface. *Maybe I'll get a better sense of things if I have a little face-to-face.*

Boniface sat back down on her bed and stared at her old alarm clock on her nightstand. What possessed her to sleep so darn long—and without interruption to get up even once to use the bathroom? And what's with the strange dreams she had? Something about being in some vast, barren and cold land like Bulgaria or was it somewhere in Russia or Poland? There was a storage room of some kind and someone shaking out old rugs from a balcony in what seemed to be an old city like Budapest while a rich and beautiful tune from a piano could be heard from a building across the way?

Then she remembered a group of men donning big black fur Cossack hats, and heavy, almost military style black coats, walking and laughing in a flurry of snow. The group of men were leaping and dancing in front of some great building, a conservatory or perhaps, a museum of some kind. Slowly, the fuzzy memory of being in a great hall resurfaced.

There were musicians rigorously playing, rows of violinists vigorously rehearsing. And eventually, a performance of some kind, but the attendees didn't appear very jubilant or healthy, for that matter. But maybe that was because of a severe and incessant snowstorm that seemed to be going on outside of this great, dark arena? *Now why would I dream these things?* Then Boniface remembered: there seemed to be a figure there, in her dreams, watching her.

Yes! A shadowy spirit of some kind wanting directions through Boniface's own interior maze of collected experience, talking in a coded language she couldn't quite grasp. It was all so elusive. The only thing that came to mind was the Molyneaux girl. *Was that her, lurking around in the corridors of my dreams? I hope that child isn't in any danger*, Boniface thought.

The old woman remained still as one of the many religious statues one finds stationed amid the great lawns of the convent school. There she sat motionless on her plush little bed. Several minutes passed before she rose very slowly and like some somnambulant figure walked over to the antique porcelain, claw-footed tub, leaning over to release the old faucets. As she was about to undress, there was a light tap at her door

Boniface barked:

"Not decent—won't be for a while. Is that you, Antoinetta?"

"Who else?" a chirpy voice replied.

"Well…I will see you downstairs in a few…all right with you?"

"Okeee dokeee, then…"

A question flashed through Boniface's mind, and as she impulsively grabbed her robe, and briskly walked back into her bedroom, she called out to her fellow sister behind her bedroom door.

"Why aren't you at the parades? Okay...don't answer that, I know what you want and you can't see it all just yet. Tomorrow we'll get a wheelbarrow and take it all to the bank together. Sounds like something you feel like doin', girlie? Hold it...I want to ask you something..."

Boniface swung her bedroom door open, her old head thrusting outward.

"Do you know anything about dream analysis?"

◆ ◆ ◆

Claire tried to forget the beads of sweat that now colonized her face as it hid itself underneath its ornate, faux-Indian-*Scheherazade*-disguise. After all, she had a job to do. She fastidiously fingered each number on the keyboard, trying earnestly to keep time with her accompanying bassist and drummer, who now seemed to have adjusted to her presence.

"Chill, baby", the drummer kept telling her in between songs. But the little Bourbon Street bar was so thick with wall-to-wall revelers that he had to shout,

"We realize you're new at this. But you really shouldn't be so uptight. No one really cares about how great we sound. Not today, at least. Winnie, there, almost got pulled off her perch a few times already. Take a good look. She's just a mess...spaghetti straps droopin, wig sliding off that crazy head... Did anybody really notice? So relax. Nuthin matters today...not in *this* place."

True, Claire felt she had entered a new world; a sort of wonderland she had yet to experience. And it really was exhilarating, and so not like any adventure her school chums had ever indulged, that's for sure. A *Never-Never-land,* indeed. While most of her lackluster classmates were with their beaus and equally lame cronies catching beads and trinkets off wholesome, family-friendly flat-trucks, here was Claire in a den of luscious decadence, amid bare-chested males, torsos sleek and ripple-muscled, wearing barely anything but scant bikini briefs and lustrous feathered masks of outrageous hues: screaming orange, vibrant reds, bodacious blues.

Three barely dressed youths were positioned at various posts on the winding and curving bar, dancing and grinding away while Winnie wove herself around them, her frosty pink lips practically kissing her hand-held mike as she bellowed Diana Ross tunes from the 1960's—an era well before Claire's time. By mid-afternoon, dollar bills were being thrown at the dancing boys by the handfuls, while the masked crowd cooed and cheered. Yes, Claire sure wasn't *in Kansas anymore,* and the world she found herself in was miles away from her wholesome and profoundly limited experience. Never had she seen so much openly supple sexiness. And yes, it wasn't exactly your run of the mill, *hetero* debauchery (which you could get at the other bars, further up Bourbon Street, and on balconies throughout the *Vieux Carre* where college coeds flashed their chests for the chance of being on *Raunch TV,*) but it was pretty randy. So many hands groping, making blind explorations of smooth, sinewy bodies, while usually reserved for quiet dark corners on most ordinary days (and nights)—were now in full view and extending out of the bar's doorways and into the streets. But that wasn't all. No, not even close. There were lips and tongues wiggling and flashing not unlike the sexy denizens of Hell depicted in the great Renaissance prints, the ones Claire recalled when perusing the back pages of Grandma Molyneaux's great old *Marian Bible.*

As children, she and brother, Phil, would marvel over the old treasure where there were colorful plates of fallen humans with remarkably sensuous bodies, scantily dressed, as Satan appeared in the background, pitchfork in tow. Yes, these were the portrayals of souls who found themselves in Hell.

Though they were children when they relished this secret pleasure, Hell sure looked more interesting (and enjoyable) than their Catholic imaginations conjured while listening to their weekly lectures at Catechism class, that's for sure. Relieved to get a break, Claire got up from her perch to amble about this strange den of decadence, still fully costumed as people stroked her multi colored plumes admiringly.

The bartender leaned her way, handing Claire a drink.

"It's from some guy...I dunno what happened to him..."

Claire found this to be mildly amusing, as her custom-made Indian costume seemed so...*unisex.* Claire took the drink and slightly lifted her mask to take a sniff. It was a hi-ball. Claire drank it down. Her throat so parched, it didn't matter what she imbibed. The bartender shouted if she wanted another...Claire waved him off with her gloved hand, and looked up.

She was standing directly in front of one of the Adonis boys, who was grinding and gyrating in gold-lame' briefs and wildly feathered black and gold mask, puffing a slender cigar while older men drooled, tucking dollar bills into his briefs as he ground his body down to a sexy squat at the bar, a sort of slow-motioned reverse *Jack in the Box.*

Claire watched in pure fascination, as the men grew even rowdier, stuffing more money, while one of the revelers in an Elton John mask reached out and groped the sexy dancer's privates—*squeezing his lemons*, as they say.

Claire gasped and laughed in her gloved hand. The young Adonis slapped the man's hand silly, sprinkling ashes from his thin cigar all over his hand. But the masked suitor seemed to welcome the attention.

Winnie made her motions around the dancers, as she was shimmying and duck-tailing her tush to the music now blaring from the D.J. station. Winnie arrived just in time to catch the nasty scene and admonished:

"Now, you quit that right now, boys. You know better!"

Noting Claire right below her, Winnie winked, bending down with a cupped hand:

"You freakin' yet, Dorothy-girl?"

Claire shook her head, the great Indian headdress feathers wafting to and fro as she slipped onto the recently vacated barstool in front of her. Claire slowly swung around to watch the crowd. The costumes themselves were a show like no other, and of the sort that no one would ever see back uptown, that's for sure. The man who groped the dancer was sitting next to her now, and the place was becoming mighty warm. The fellow peeled off his Elton John mask and fanned himself with it. Claire struggled to keep hers on for fear of being found out. She knew she looked way too young and innocent to be in such company. Besides, she's female. But she, too, fanned her veiled neck with her gloved hands. Suddenly, the unmasked man looked over to Claire and mumbled some incomprehensible words her way.

Claire was totally awestruck by the person now in full frontal. It was amazing, actually. The unintelligible words (it was obvious the man was a bit tipsy) were of no importance. No, not at all, for the man who sat before her was none-other than the snooty, punctilious and irascible, Hugh Gruber, her World Lit teacher back at *Immaculate Heart*. The one who gave her a hard time during last week's pop quiz; the teacher who ridiculed her and scoffed at the sincere effort Claire had made in writing an impressive essay on that French Renaissance writer. But Claire maintained her stance, aiming to keep le cool, but it was hard not to laugh under her mask. Instantly and instinctively, Claire's gloved fingers searched her satin pant pocket for her cell phone. Claire fished it out and held the little device in her lap.

As the man continued to talk, this time, to the person on his other side, Claire waited patiently for the moment when he'd swing his face back to hers and just as the Adonis dancer returned to deliberately shimmy in his unmasked face, and unbeknownst to the two of them, Claire quickly aimed and clicked her cell-phone camera.

◆ ◆ ◆

Say what one will, but it's time I claim credit for this one, dear readers. It was none other than ' yours truly' who initially nudged that little bastard schoolmarm to turn his face to our girl, and it was right then that I prompted her to go for the camera-phone. Maybe all my efforts at making contact are beginning to make a dent. I surely hope so, dear readers, for I fear I am becoming desperate in my search for clues to my own great mystery, and of course, I don't really need to tell you what that is, now do I?

It has crossed my thought-emotion being that, perhaps, I might have a clue arise in this den of decadence, but no, nothing registers. Only my concern for our girl here keeps me glued to the scene and I see that she is going to be well and in good hands despite the gluttony, and lustful scenes about her. She remains only amused and entertained. And I see there are some discarnate spirit entities drifting about, enjoying these scenes of flirtation and debauchery, as I expected there would be. After all, it is the feast before the more austere time of repentance and restraint and then where will they go, these decadent spirits? So, perhaps, everyone is taking full advantage of this day of frolicsome fun! Except for me.

If I can just ask you to pull up your chairs so I can tell you what's truly troubling me since my nocturnal adventure in the inner cranium, the psyche and soul that dwells there in our Sister Mary Boniface. Although I may seem to be jocular on this festive day as I fancy my way into Claire's first real show- time gig, though the environment is a bit mature, if not a bit frisky, I continue to look for a way out of this maze of mystery, dear readers. I realize our good nun is clueless and is currently in a brain-racking session, discussing your Sigmund Freud and your Carl Gustav Jung on the nature of dreams as the two cloistered ones shell pecans in the kitchen and chatter away the afternoon. It's just that I am slowly, ever so achingly slowly, beginning to recall some very slight things. But these slivers of memory are only small clues. However, there is one incident that came back to me as I was winding in a maze of dream imagery on the part of my hostess for the evening, the unconscious, Boniface, and it was when I first realized that I was no longer in physical form. It may be of some importance, perhaps, as it was this matter that initiated my downfall. And somehow from that point I lost connection. But here the very scene was in my midst. And it slowly unfolded.

And I found myself in a place where there is much darkness and frigid cold, and so much snow; sheets of soft, crunchy snow, adrift near a thickly wooded forest. I do not know where this place is, but there, above me, in this frigid winter setting in the deepest nocturnal silence, I recall a most radiant being, an entity asking me to join him (her?) and I am somehow suspended above it all, looking back at this scene of a human body lying face-down, and deep rivulets of blood pouring over this icy white blanket of snow and I am curiously staring at this human form lying there and this kind spirit is gently pushing me away and upwards and yet, I keep looking back. And it all dissipates from there. Nothing. Just thin light wisps of a vaporous nothing.

♦ ♦ ♦

Of course, as Mardi Gras day enfolded upon this *City that Care Forgot,* there were those few souls who managed to bypass the spell of reckless reverie for more sensible recreations—Sister Mary Boniface being one of them. Sister Boniface, whose holiday took on a relaxed and lackadaisical feel, took advantage of the vacated quiet of her abode. She and Antoinetta had the day to themselves and Boniface was relieved that her side-kick didn't pester her about her winnings, enjoying, the both of them, the afternoon in their cozy convent kitchen, sipping hot drinks and cracking roasted nuts, including the pecans that fell from their backyard tree. Yes, Boniface and Antoinetta had a time of it, talking about the old days and catching up on some recent gossip in between scant speculations on dream theory, both Freudian and Jungian. Now Antoinetta admitted that she might have lacked the vast knowledge for any discursive exploration on the subject as she read various essays here and there while in college. But Boniface located a volume on Jungian dream symbolism in their communal library and planned on diving into the rich material starting at bedtime that very evening. Boniface felt somewhat hopeful on the prospects that she would glean some insight, as she remained troubled that there were no answers to the phenomena she experienced while in her thirty-odd hour slumber. That there were some aspects best reserved for deep spiritual thinkers, and yes, Jung notwithstanding, surely he had some fascinating input into the subject, but how could she explain the sensations of an actual communication she sensed from some unexplained source?

"Are there spirit beings among us?" she wondered aloud.

"Well, then, with all our training, we know that's a likely probability." Antoinetta opined, gingerly cracking a Brazil nut with a nutcracker, adding,

"...and Carl Jung surely seemed to be open to such things. Some people think he went crazy, himself, as he delved further and further into the morass of human consciousness. You better be careful, girlie."

Boniface shook her graying pageboy head,

"Well, then maybe I should take a light look at his findings. Perhaps, I need to explore this on my own because I don't think there's anything in these books that explain what I actually experienced. I believe the Molyneaux girl's soul somehow slipped into my dreams as she was trying to tell me something. I think I'll have a talk with her when class resumes. Hey—I almost forgot—guess who I ran into on the gambling floors?"

Antoinetta listened with rapt attention as Boniface described her unexpected meeting with the former Sister Mary Katherine.   Afterwards, Antoinetta nodded, shrugging her shoulders,

"Well...I knew about *that*, Boniface. She also had a pretty serious thing going with one of our PE teachers. The girls knew about it, too. Where were you?"

Boniface winced,

"In case you don't remember, I was busy running the show around here. Not an easy job. I had my school to run. PE teacher, huh? The one with the short cropped, sort of slicked ducktail—50's*do*? Yeah, now I remember. She was nice, though. Helluva basketball coach, too. Moll Dupuy. So they were better friends than I had imagined…well, I just don't know how to deal with such things, Antoinetta. We are spiritually *married* and devoted to *Our Lord* and that's that. I don't know about all these other matters that come up with some of our more wayward sisters."

Antoinetta solemnly shook her head as she shelled another pecan noting,

"But at least, she's now content, then. Our Kate."

Antoinetta assisted the elder nun from her perch as the two rose from the rustic kitchen table, bringing their goodies to their beloved living room. With a slight wave of her hand, Boniface turned the conversation to the more staid matters of needed repairs and improvements to the school. As the two nuns wiled away the afternoon, a glorious sunset penetrated the picture window in their parlor, streaming the little crystal ornaments Constantine's been hanging there for the last ten years into splays of dazzling color throughout the room. Boniface looked up and marveled at the dancing flecks of light, recalling something from her slumber, an image of a bright emanation gleaming in a dark winter's sky as a figure lay motionless in a mound of snow. *Now what could this mean*? Boniface wondered to herself, as Antoinetta obliviously busied herself with her treasured needlepoint.

At just about the time the two nuns settled into their comfy, velvet covered chairs in their quaint parlor, Claire was anxiously finishing up her second set at her gig, having no idea that the old nun had concerned thoughts about her. Of course, Claire might have felt some consolation had she known this, but the reality she faced was her need to finish up her time in the club before any incident would upset the applecart of what could end up being an almost perfect Mardi Gras Day. Darva Jean showed up, standing beside Claire as she played. Darva Jean invited another cousin to came along with her, all in full Indian regalia, as they broke away from the crowds in the Faubourg, curious to see their more exotic, though distant kin relation, perform.

Outside, thousands flooded the streets along the parade routes as this brisk, cool, Carnival day started its slow, drunken descent into an interminable dusk of even more rowdiness. Earlier, Anne and Warren flanked young Marc, all bedeviled in his crimson red gear, pulling their wagon of iced drinks while Squires walked alongside the trio, hi- fiving many of his cronies along the way. At some point, Anne, getting mighty frustrated with her 1800's floor length habit as she was dressed as Saint Bernadette, decided to shuck her voluminous skirt, rolling it up and storing it their little wagon, as she pranced around in her nun's veil and half slip most of the way. This seemed to draw even more attention from the crowds and of course, their cronies in the *Bergeron Street Steppers*, their marching club.

Warren also grew more frustrated with his get-up as the day wore on. He often had to stop to scratch himself under his heavy faux hairshirt get up—the one he made out of potato sacks he had stashed in their garage-storage room. Dressing up as Saint Sebastian, the martyr, was turning out to be equally as troubling as Anne's cumbersome nun's gear.

But it was a chilly Mardi Gras Day, and Warren wore a thermal T-shirt under his burlap tunic. This would have been fine had he not decided to add the many arrows appearing to pierce his chest and back. They had a way of unhinging from the stick-up pads he patched to the arrows. The basic idea was to resemble the depiction in that famous painting by Sandro Botticelli, but he would've had to place too many arrows all over himself, down to his knees, and he also didn't exactly have the kind of young, muscular body required to pull it off. Anne knew it would be too much work and tried to get him to settle for a mellower saint, like Saint Dominick or Bernard of Clairvaux. Besides, Warren just looked more like a fat friar left aloft on some dusty, great western plain after being run out of town by a posse of wild Indians.

Marc found his unexpected hosts to be mildly amusing, as they offered him a beer, but only because it was Gras, as they were acting as his chaperones for the day. This made him feel a bit brighter about things, but still, as he walked along, he pondered his decision to remain with them, along with the marching club, most of the parade route. Should he continue to perambulate as they make their way downtown? He wasn't so sure, but Phil wasn't answering his cell phone, so he plodded along with the troupe knowing that they were unlikely to allow him to roam the streets unsupervised.

However, there was the prospect of venturing into the *Vieux Carré,* and that was a big plus. To be ensconced in all the madness and debauchery would be a welcomed diversion from the usually restrictive routine of parade viewing with his mother's uptown crowd. Of course, Marc slightly winced whenever his mom came to mind. Before leaving the house, Anne left a note for Rita, indicating that Marc was joining them and would be home in a few hours. Anne got the impression that Rita was napping and simply assumed she needed some rest.

As they thronged along with the crowd down the vast parade route that eventually led them into the French Quarter, Anne made attempts to probe young Marc's mind a bit further, but she didn't get too far. True to his mother's instructions, Marc insisted that his big sister flew the coop to be with her older boyfriend. When Anne remarked that she found that to be rather odd, as Claire was always at her school, according to *other classmates* she happens to know of, it just didn't seem to fit the profile.

"I don't really know much about that, Miss Anne." Marc grimaced.

Catching the tail end of this little exchange, Warren shot a scouring look his wife's way, but soon waved the matter off, swaggering over to her, carrying another cold long neck beer from their ice-chest wagon and handing it to Anne, two beefy fingers locking the bottle at its dripping neck. Yes, the Leblancs were beginning to look a bit piqued and a tad sloppy, actually, a sure sign that Mardi Gras Day was soon coming to a close. Besides, their costumes were falling apart. Anne trounced around in her half-slip awhile before taking off her nun's veil and swinging it around as she strutted down Bourbon Street.

Several costumed figures took note of the rowdy middle-aged gal in her black fishnets, half slip and clunker rosary now tied around her waist, along with her swinging nun's veil. Anne shimmied and shook with fellow random *revelers,* spinning and gyrating in circles in the middle of the crowded street, and for a moment, she glanced down at the little guy in the red-devil costume, wondering exactly how she knew him, only vaguely recalling the situation hours earlier when the day was young.

Scores of people filled the heart of the *Vieux Carré*, which seemed to grow more rambunctious as Warren, Anne, young Marc and Squires walked deeper into its fascinating throng of celebratory fanfare. The various costumes, so colorful, so creative and varied, Anne felt dull next to some of them while people kept pulling at Warren's arrows. It sure looked like their visit to their friends' house party would be a brief one.

Now Squires seemed to be having a very good time, not nearly as inebriated, but partying all the same, as he often stopped to greet familiar faces that approached him. As he smoothly perambulated through the raucous crowd, with a few maskers stopping to admire his cool duds, he caught a glimpse of a familiar face. A young, dewy, and rather pretty visage; one he vaguely knew, as he believed it was one that belonged to the daughter of a former client. She was standing near the entrance of one of those questionable establishments where males frequently exchanged their looks and dress for a female's—*and to a rather extreme degree.*

The girl chatted with another teen, a white gal, Squires noted, both holding feathery masks under their arms and puffing cigarettes. The two of them looked like they had on Mardi Gras Indian costumes, which was odd, in this part of town. The *Indians* always hung in the Faubourg, not Bourbon Street, and certainly not in front of a gay bar. Besides, the Gras Indians are usually male and black.

Her mother must have a challenge on her hands, Squires mused. Now what's her name? *Ah, Lucy. Lucinda. Nice and nice-looking, that Lucinda,* Squires recalled.

Squires continued to survey the scene as he slowly walked behind his friends, now slightly wobbling, pulling their wagon ice chest behind them, as they paused to two-step with other couples passing by. Be-deviled Marc looked agape as he swung his head from side to side, taking in the more risque' costumes in this part of the *Quarter.* But as Marc stopped to take in a guy dressed only in the barest briefs, his body completely spray-painted silver, he noticed Squires looking across the way. Marc, too, turned his gaze to the crowd gathered at the far side of the street, and there, he spotted her, and just when he did, his heart leapt. It was his forlorn big sister, Claire, smoking and laughing with her black friend from *Immaculate Heart*. Who would have ever imagined? Marc thought. *And in all this madness!* The boy did not hesitate to make his way through the wall of bodies to where his sister was standing, and unbeknownst to him, a curious Squires soon followed.

As they approached, the girls were now sipping drinks through colorful straws, giggling at the varied, crazy costumes of passersby. Apparently, Claire was enjoying a break before her final set of the day, glad that she could share it with her best friend. Now that the day was sagging along in inebriated over-kill, Claire felt relaxed enough to remove her mask, and Scheherazade-like scarf, if only during her break outside. Zee—Darva's tag-along cousin—stayed inside the club, dancing with the crowd.

The two chatted and hooted away, taking sips of their drinks, feeling a bit buzzed and enjoying every minute until Claire paused mid-sentence, curiously studying a reveler in a red-devil costume standing before her. He was covered in bright red facial makeup accented with gold and silver glitter, and remained silent as he continued to stare back at her. Claire lowered herself slightly to get a better look at the curious figure as it was beginning to grow dark.

Claire spoke up:

"Hey! Do I know you?"

Darva instinctively grabbed her friend's arm. The red devil figure nodded its head, and as he was about to respond, Squires approached from behind, squeezing the young boy's shoulders, and smiling directly at Darva Jean.

"Well, hello, Darva Jean! It's Mister Montgomery, your dad's lawyer! How're things?"

As Squires and Darva continued their chat, the red devil and Claire locked stares. On closer inspection, Claire realized that it was her younger brother, Marc. The boy whispered, under the on-going exchange between Squires and Darva Jean,

"How are you doin? We miss you. I hate her. I hate her and hope she ...she…"

Claire reached out and gave her brother a warm hug. She whispered: "What are you doin down here? Who brought you here, Marc? Wow. Crazy down here, isn't it? Phil has my number. Call me later, okay? I gotta go… I'm working here."

And while Darva Jean and Squires continued their discourse, Claire swiftly stepped back into the darkened bar, a warm tear rolling down her soft cheek as she reapplied her mask and scarf.

◆ ◆ ◆

And as one of your clichés of yesteryear goes, "the show must go on". Yet young Marc is intent on following his sister inside, however, our Holy One of India still has his gentle brown hands clamped on the boy's shoulders as he chats way with Darva Jean, fellow person of African descent who are now both American. Oh, well, I am trying to control my own tears, if they can be describes as such. What a warm, heart-felt reunion—though brief—between tender-age siblings! But I see that Warren and Anne Leblanc, the emcees of this little adventure-foray, are now dancing in the street amid the crowds as music is now blaring from a balcony above. Showers of trinkets and strings of colorful beads are being tossed to the partiers below. The Leblancs are oblivious to the scene outside the bar, and have practically forgotten the other participants in their group. Thankfully, our solicitor-Ramakrishna-costumed fellow is keeping his eye on things, otherwise, who knows what would happen with the boy?

Though Squires Montgomery may seem aloof, he is not—no, not at all. He has his eagle-eye on everything, including the scenes taking place in back of his head. This fellow is a sharp one, all right. But as I penetrate my thought-emotion being a wee closer, I see he is a tad lonely. His spouse of twenty-five years passed into our realm a couple of years ago, and since representing Darva Jean's dad in an old charge during his hippie-dippy, "Panther" years in your state of Michigan, he has been a bit charmed by Darva's momma, who, as I speak, is making her way up Rue Bourbon, in search of her daughter as she took hold of someone saying, during the Indian costume festivities, that Darva Jean left to go see her drag math-wizard cousin perform.

But now they are wrapping up their conversation, and Mr. Squires is leading the boy back into the crowd to meet up with Anne and Warren. Squires looks back briefly and notices young Darva walking back into the bar—the name, "Fidel's Finale" flashing in soft-lighted lettering around its entrance. 'Now what would she be doing, hanging out in there?' our counselor wonders.

Well, I tell you, Lucy Darlene is now only a few blocks away, but on this rowdy eve, with wall-to-wall humans filling the streets, who knows how long it might take her to get here? (As soon as I pose the question, it is revealed to me. But I will pretend I am human like you are and lack the abilities I possess for the sake of proper storytelling). And of course, the same goes for our little troupe aiming to make its way to a final destination, a festive gathering at their friends' home on Rue Esplanade—the boulevard that divides the old city from the Faubourg.

Now, I checked in a wee bit earlier on our nuns who are now both gently snoring on their respective velvet upholstered chairs in their quaint parlor. It seems the afternoon discussion had gone on longer than the two anticipated, and perhaps the sugar from their cakes and pastries brought on a languid fatigue. But as they napped, I found myself making telepathic suggestions to Sister Boniface's interior psyche; that I believe it might be a very good idea that she shepherd our Claire.

That she might make a bigger effort in assisting her in her endeavors and ambitions. I am not sure why I suggested this, outside of the fact that I am fond of the child, of course. I just feel the two will meet heads and somehow come up with something that might alleviate my purgatorial mystery. Yes, I realize how self-serving that sounds. But the idea of ameliorating a situation for one, might benefit the other, is one that makes sense to me, no matter the whimsy on my part. Perhaps, I grow desperate as I blindly navigate my way in a sea of unanswered questions.

I now recognize Ms. Lucinda Darlene, elbowing her way through the crowd, intent on seeing her niece and daughter in this den of decadence, this "Fidel's Finale" establishment where our Claire has made her professional debut. (It's a start, as they say). Inside, our Claire is fingering the keyboard at full throttle. The lively trio now playing catchy pop tunes as Claire continues her conversation with her friend at timely intervals.

At one point, Darva Jean leans in and gets an earful about a seemingly heavily intoxicated Hugh Gruber, the pugnacious schoolmarm back at their school, who is now casting his fate to the winds as he attempts to dance with one of the male entertainers on the bar before being nudged off, and actually, gently kicked off by Winnie's pointy-toed pumps. I swiftly cue our girl at the piano for a possible snapshot from her little metal device, the one she talks and types on, but to no avail.

Winnie shouts, as she shoos the fellow off the bar:

"There's none of that here, boyfriend. Git!"

Winnie looks down and catches a familiar countenance, one she hasn't seen in a while.

She pauses and shades her sweating brow with her hand, focusing on a face looking up at her from below.

"Is that you, Miss Lucy? Lucy Darlene, is that really you down there? Honey—don't you dare move. Do I have a tune for you!"

◆　◆　◆

The number Winnie referred to was none other than an old favorite, *"I Will Survive"*—a disco-era tune performed in drag shows the world over. It was such a popular request by the *Fidel's Finale* crowd that Winnie wondered how she missed singing that beloved anthem of every woman in America for the last few decades. But here was Lucinda's cousin, bringing back fond memories. Winnie waved her arms before moving the microphone close to her frosty pink lips, looking straight at Lucinda as she spoke to the crowd.

"Now—you girls remember how it used to be? How I was just so scared to lose that man. That he'd walk out that back door and me, leavin me with nuthin but the cat food and no cat, cuz he done slunked it over his shoulder with him, as he slipped his self-righteous butt out the door? Well... I mighta been a little...scared. Sometimes, I wuz just downright *petrified*...but...as time went on..."

Claire got the cue and swiftly shuffled the sheet music stack, finally flopping the notes in front of her. It only took the tinkling of the opening notes down the keyboard for the crowd to go wild, flipping over tables, standing-up on barstools, shouting out at Winnie,

"Whatchew think I'm waitin here for ya, then, huh?"

"Jaysus. Sweet lovin' Jaysus!"

You could say Lucy was quite taken in by it all. So much so that she just stood there transfixed, her mouth slightly hanging open, taking in every delicious moment as a tingling sensation crawled up her arms and back. She marveled at the rowdy jubilation of the crowd now breaking into a *Saint Vitus Dance* as the sheer joy of that old disco tune resounded through the club. Lucy wondered why it took her so long to check out her cousin's act. Wilfred/Winnie had only been doing this sort of thing for the past ten years or so. *Or has it been longer*? Lucy wondered. Actually, Lucy was so entranced that she nearly forgot the main reason for forging her way through the Bourbon Street madness in the first place. Where on earth could her daughter be in such a dark, cavernous, decadent venue? But Lucy could barely scan the place, making it easy to bypass the little trio playing in the corner, her daughter now standing in the little nook, next to the bass player. Just as Lucy was beginning to relax, someone from behind lightly pinched Lucy on her shoulder. Reflexively, she spun around.

"Who in the heck?"

A vaguely familiar face winked at her. Lucy squinted her eyes, but to no avail. She had no idea who this strange looking person could be—this man in a goatee and wire framed glasses, with a twisted sheet running diagonally across his bare chest.

The voice asked:

"You remember me, doncha?"

Well, it didn't take long for Lucy to bring to mind the memory of Squires Montgomery. Especially the sound of his rich, resonant voice as it fell in a courtroom not all that long ago. How he diligently defended her husband of those old charges and succeeded. In fact, she was relieved to run into someone she knew, but what on earth brought him to such a venue?

"You, first!" Squires retorted.

Lucy filled him in on her cousin, who was still bellowing out tunes until he /she finally closed with the immortal Supremes' tune, "*Someday, We'll be Together*". And as they chatted away, Squires filled Lucy in on his day. That he spent it with another lawyer friend and his wife, joining their Mardi Gras marching troupe, and winding things down there in the *Vieux Carré* for the remaining hours. His friends had decided to head home as they had a minor with them, a neighbor's boy. So he figured he'd check things out. Of course, Squires casually mentioned that he noticed her daughter, Darva Jean, talking to another gal out front.

Lucinda added:

"Oh, you must've caught Darva with her cousin. Little Zee. I can't find her, either."

Squires shook his head, correcting her,

"No, this girl's *white*. Both of them dressed like Indians, if you can believe that one! That white girl, she's the one over there playing the piano. Pretty good, actually, for someone so young. Look at those crazy plumes she's got showering over everything. It's a wonder she can concentrate so well."

◆ ◆ ◆

If it were not for the gentlemanly Squires Montgomery, perhaps Mardi Gras evening would have turned out worse than it had. Lucinda, though, sort of lost it when she approached the little ensemble finishing up their gig at the club. Darva, puffing a *Nat Sherman's* the bass player had given her, let the cigarette slip through her fingers and fall to the floor, stomping on it as if it were a live firecracker as she jumped back and shouted at the sight of her mother, arms held akimbo, smirking there in the dark. But Lucy could see well enough that the girl at the piano was the imposter that shared the SUV ride earlier that morning. Claire leaned back in horror as she tried to finish her last number before jumping up and high-tailing it to hide in the backstage dressing room.

Grounded, grounded, grounded. For the first few somber days of the Lenten season, Darva could only see drab grey awashed over everything. And she certainly didn't want to conjecture the prospects of earning her mother's favor again. Sure, it was the big holiday and all, but the thing Lucy couldn't get over was the fact that her friend stayed in the back cottage for several nights without her knowing. How could Darva be so plain recalcitrant? But if the truth be known, Lucy wasn't really all that angry. She was actually more embarrassed than anything. That she didn't even know that the girl sitting next to her in the SUV was an imposter— a white imposter, thank you—seemed to floor her completely. But when she sat back and thought about it all, *Gras* turned out to be more fun than Lucinda was willing to admit. Even though her unreliable, estranged husband did not show up as he had promised, Lucy was beginning to brighten to the idea of moving on without him. She was tired of waiting, and tired of the promises—the idea of hubby being at least devoted to the twins her last hold on the hope front.

But Mr. Montgomery surely looked like he wasn't doing all that badly. After Lucinda got over the fact that Darva was playing some tomfoolery numbers on her, she realized that Squires turned out to be a most welcomed surprise. And what of all that talk about spiritual matters? Lucy mused. Surely, that was refreshingly different, coming from a male, and actually, after Squires informed her of the stunning profundity of the *Vedanta,* Lucy bought a couple of books on the subject—or topics that seemed close to the subject. For the past few days she was spending her free time reading *Divine Mother According to Ramakrishna,* aiming to bring it up in her next women's group.

Claire met with good fortune as she was paid in full and had the cash to return to the hostel with one dorm bunk bed waiting. It wasn't the usual, albeit funky, private suite she so luckily had before, but being that the hostel was so jammed packed with drunken, traveling college kids, she settled for the miracle dorm bed that became available. She had the money now. And all of her things were still being stored, as if waiting for her victorious return. But of course, getting there did not come without challenges. Darva Jean, with the help of Squires Montgomery, had to block her mother from following Claire back to the dressing room.

Darva shouted:

"Ma! Blame *me*—don't get angry with her. I was just tryin to help! What'chew so mad about, anyway?"

Lucy scolded:

"You realize how nervous I was thinking she was you when she ran outta the car? Do you know how bad I felt thinking you were all freaked out about your father? ." Lucy—stopping midsentence—sent a sheepish look Squires' way before continuing:

"You had me worried to death! When Tante Suzette toll me you were already there, I had myself a drink...okay...two drinks."

A dramatically made up face suddenly eclipsed Lucy's view.

"Suga…my sweet suga plum girl, cousin, you."

Lucy put her hand to her chest.

"Ah, God, Will—ie—you scared me there! Oh, my, you were fantastic! Just fabulous, Will—er—innie?"

The club's starlet was now making *her* way back to her dressing room with a fistful of cash. She had just paid her bassist and drummer and was now headed to pay Claire.

"How d'like that piano-player, huh? I think she'll go far. I just know it. Excuse me, honeys" and tapping Lucy on her shoulder "…but don't leave now. I wanna talk to you, Lucinda"

And chat away they did as the crowd in the club slowly began to disperse. But as soon as Claire was paid, she was undressed and out of there—through the back door, leaving her Indian costume in Winnie's care, and wearing the leggings and sweatshirt she had with her in her trusty duffel bag.

Claire sure had it down, all right. Actually, she was becoming quite good at this. That is, her entrances and exits. And she wisely clicked her cell phone off. She just couldn't deal with her friend tonight. She had worked her fingers to the bone for all of Mardi Gras day, but it all felt so good. She was actually hoping that she'd get a call again to play another gig for Winnie, her new employer. No more table wiping, drive-thru-order-taking, burger and fries establishment jobs for this gal.

Claire loved the way the two crisp Ben Franks and single Ulysses S. Grant bills felt in her fist as she securely rolled them into her coin purse nestled deeply in her bag. Golly-gee, life was good! But when she thought of her little brother standing there, looking up at her in his cute costume, she felt sad. Surely, she missed her old life: clowning with her brothers, sleeping in her warm, elegant bed, and enjoying hot food every night, even though the latter days of dining there kept her in a *Rapunzel*-like tower during mealtime. As much as she enjoyed her first foray into the world of entertainment jobs, and her newfound freedoms, she sure felt weary at times. Especially given the fact that her best bud was now in trouble because of her. Gads.

Claire pulled out the fancy pink cigarette with its gold-foiled filter, the *Nat Sherman* given to her by her musician-associate. She lit it up and walked along, puffing the pungent smoke as she tiptoed her way down a garbage strewn French Quarter street, the crowds thinning as the wee hours of Ash Wednesday began to unfold.

Now Rita didn't exactly understand, at first, what was going on when she finally arose from her bewildering, all-day snooze. It was practically dark by the time she did so and if she hadn't come across the friendly note posted to the refrigerator she might have panicked. Anne and Warren had come by and being that she was sound asleep they asked young Marc to join them. *"Will return by early, early evening, babes. See you then!"* the note in flourishing script declared.

God, she's a clever one, Rita mused, conjuring up all sorts of possible scenarios. Of course, Rita was frightened at the prospect that Anne might ask her son all sorts of questions about his rebellious sister. As soon as her disheveled son, in smeared red-faced make up—smeared because of some sloppy hugs and kisses he received from his hostess (okay, Anne drank a wee bit more than she intended)—appeared at the great front door, Rita stepped out to greet her neighbor.

Rita, now changed and out of her feline costume, smoothed her hair and waved, mouthing a thank-you. A disheveled Anne blew back a kiss.

"No problem! He was a dreamboat, wasn't he, Warren?"

But Anne was looking a bit wobbly and inebriated, her half-slip sagging and pulled down at her hips, her nun's veil askew on her head, as she slightly staggered down the driveway, waving back to her bridge buddy— actually, her *former* bridge buddy as Anne has been excusing herself out of playing cards altogether lately and this, of course, made Rita suspicious. Oh, those two were a pair, all right. One minute, buddies, next, cool-shouldered acquaintances. One could never tell where the weather vane of their so-called friendship would spin. What kept their association going really had everything to do with Rita, as she was always intrigued by Anne's pedigreed upbringing. Rita studied Anne like a book. She had all the privileges Rita dreamed of having: a high-class, convent education, debutante breeding, a summer home on the Gulf, a college degree from *Sweet Briar*. Okay, so her husband Warren was a bit of a puzzle, but he was successful, at least.

What truly forged their friendship, however, was a little incident of several years back when Anne ran outside one summer afternoon to referee a hose fight Rita and Mrs. Deschamps (who has moved from their neighborhood since her husband passed) got into after Rita learned that she had called her a *tramp*. Well, to Rita, this was the lowest of the low, and being that the two were outside respectively tending their flower gardens and lush, verdant trees, Rita got the inspiration to just hose *the bitch* down. Now Lorraine Deschamps was adjusting a sprinkler she had just bought when a stream of water arced over the quaint, tree-lined street and landed directly at her back. Defenseless and soaked, Lorraine shook her fist and unplugged the hose that was attached to the sprinkler, running across her lawn to return the gesture. This went on for quite a stretch as the neighborhood children looked on in utter fascination as the two adults had at it.

At the time this was going on, Anne was polishing some silver in her ornate dining room as she and Warren were preparing a dinner for some guests from out of town. Anne couldn't help but overhear the commotion and soon found herself outside, aghast at what she saw. Rita was about to cross the street and confront Lorraine Deschamps, dragging her still spraying garden hose behind her.

Anne approached Rita just as she was about to drown her neighbor.

"What on earth is goin on around here? Stop! Now stop you two!"

The both of them looked embarrassed and disbanded, but only after Rita said through clenched teeth that she did not deserve to be talked about in *that* manner. That she learned about what Lorraine Deschamps said while in line at the *Piggly Wiggly* as two members of the Bienville Club committee were standing ahead of her, discussing the list of new applicants. When the Molyneaux name came up, Rita cocked her ear as she hid her face behind a *Globe* tabloid. "*Lorraine says she has no idea where this Rita Molyneaux came from. Besides she's Italian. And according to her, not of our sort.*"

It was right after that that she learned of the crass remark.

"I was utterly appalled by that wisecrack." Rita bellowed.

Anne scowled back at her neighbor, Lorraine, and took Rita's arm in hers as she walked her back across the soaked street, telling her she should join her for coffee some afternoon over at the Bienville Club as a "we'll show'em" sort of gesture. And that was the beginning of their friendship, or *acquaintance-ship*, depending on the situation, of course.

And right now, as far as Rita and Anne were concerned, it was back to being mere acquaintances. It's just how things go when you are in and around the upper societal echelons. One never really knew where one stood when one is an *aspirant* like Rita Silvestri Molyneaux. For those from Rita's station in life, one was always on a social probation from the societal elite. It was the price she paid despite her husband's old French lineage.

After waiving off her neighbor and sometimes friend, Rita quietly shut the front door and stared down at her son. Phil had not returned yet, as it was only 7pm. Rita figured she had a few minutes to spend interrogating young Marc about his adventuresome day with the neighbors. Marc smirked at his mother.

"Ma, she only asked how Claire was doing. That's it! Of course, I gave her the bs you've been forcing us to say since you kicked her out…"

Marc was tempted to give away the juicy bit about his miraculous run-in with big sis down in the 'Quarter, but he held his silence.

"Well…okay, then. That's that. You want some dinner, son?"

Rita was especially making an attempt to be easy-going with Marc as she felt a tad guilty about falling asleep the way she had. Waking up with the bottle of bourbon next to her head didn't help matters, either. *Did I really take the whole bottle upstairs with me?* Rita wondered. She also noted that hubby, Hilaire, called and left a message on the answering machine, wishing them all a happy *Gras*. Gads.

She knew she needed to say 'hello' to him. It had been two weeks since they last chatted, and always putting off the fact that Claire was not there when he called yet again. How long could she keep this up?

♦ ♦ ♦

I would say, not very long, dearie. 'Your days may be numbered', as the individuals that populate your flat-screens—especially in these daytime dramas—say. As you can imagine, good, loyal, readers, life is very different in the Arabian desert land Hilaire is now inhabiting—so that he can 'bring home the bacon', another phrase I catch from your flat screens. One might note that "bacon" wouldn't exactly be a term used with such fondness by the humans that dwell where Hilaire is living given that the animal of which bacon originates is considered unsavory and unholy.

Hilaire, so preoccupied with his obligations in spearheading such a massive project, an office building in a dolphin shape that, one would suppose, honors the sea life in the Persian Gulf of which these massive buildings now flank. No, Hilaire, being the devoted boss and loyal husband to his family on the other side of the world is just too focused on his work. And, of course, dear readers, hubby Hilaire remains clueless as sons Marc and Phil stay true to their mother's commands, never to spill the proverbial beans, as they say—well, not yet, at least.

The two boys actually fear being met with the same fate as their sister, although our little one often likes to imagine an adventure of being on his own. I have to tell you, though, I just noticed two questionable spirits surrounding their mother, Rita, and have actually been with her since she woke up from her long-Mardi Gras day nap.

I decided to patrol the premises as Rita roused herself from the pitch-black darkness of an early dusk. She was truly puzzled, not knowing the day, the time, the situation. That's when the dark spirits approached her, making suggestions of which she did not respond.

I was relieved when she changed out of her silly costume, washed her face, her teeth and then headed downstairs to turn on the flat-screened device in the family room. She then left it blaring as she walked into the kitchen to clean up the breakfast dishes. I stayed behind to view one of the 60-second skits the flat screen was showing on medications. Sorry, I just find them so delicious in their deceptions; they're a marvel, actually, "a money making machine", as the business men say in your country. And it's usually the same line-up. The "skits" I noticed on other occasions were repeating, except there was one in particular I found amusing, one that features a pill that seems to stimulate the phallic function of the male human.

The parlor flat screens seem to show this one quite often, actually. I found this rather intriguing until the usual litany of warnings came through. It's the bad news that always follows these presentations after they're swooned over and idealistically presented by rather attractive, middle aged or older, silver haired individuals. What fascinates me is the enormous profitability these manufacturers make (I looked into the little company name at the bottom of the flat screen and soon investigated) in spite of all the horrors that might ensue if there is: low blood pressure, alcohol consumption and worse yet, the priapic function lasting more than six hours.) My. Just as my thought emotion being was learning of numerous emergency visits in the wee hours of the morning on the part of many partakers of this phallic elixir, Rita re-appeared, picking up the rectangle device and flipping through the various programs. Then she flicked the screen back to its black, motionless state.

I passed by the two spirits hanging around her and wished for divine protection on younger brother, Marc, as he walked in to greet his mother. I then 'high-tailed it' to investigate some items over at the Archbishop's mansion. Earlier, I noticed some things of note as I checked up on the nuns who were having a time of it, catching beads and colorful aluminum doubloons as the parade floats passed them while standing on the much-coveted, mansion's veranda. As our Archbishop here naps in his robe and slippers near the low-ember fire in his handsome study, I flip through texts and volumes at a most rapid speed— searching for information that might help me. Now you may be asking: "Why on earth am I here, of all places?" Well, I'll tell you why: it's a better library than what our good sisters have and besides, as I am flipping my thought-emotion being through the pages of this tome on dreams by this brilliant fellow, this Carl Gustav Jung, I am getting the full run down on what possibilities lurk. I just rifled through "The Undiscovered Self", of which I am sure you would not be surprised that I found much too ironic for me to bear, but I am intrigued with this third volume, "Synchronicity: An Acausal Connecting Principle". Very curious, very interesting, yes, but could I ever suggest such an activity? Perhaps, I need to investigate more.

My thought-emotion being rivets back to the good sisters' abode, as the parade-viewing nuns return for their evening dinner hour. As they frolic about, in a rather convivial mood this Mardi Gras evening, greeting their Rip Van Winkle nun who just announced the news that they had received an extra seventy-five thousand dollars; that the "donor" she went to see out west simply handed her the money. Antoinetta is attempting to keep her cover, resisting a smile or a wink in order to avoid any sign or clue as to their bogus front. She busies herself serving the nuns a supper of steamy lentil soup, hot bread and a crisp salad. The relief was met with much humor and happiness. Now they could at least repair more things and avoid the possible takeover from the Jesuits over at St. Jerome's, at least, for a while.

"We have much more to do, girls," Boniface reminded them. "Let's just keep our prayers humble for Ash

Wednesday, shall we? Let's just bend our heads in gratitude this Lenten eve and pray we get more guidance."

"Or more big donors!" Constantine, bless her heart, announces, as she passes the basket of tasty bread to her fellow nuns.

♦ ♦ ♦

But Ash Wednesday came with its usual somber implications, as many revelers from just the day before were now sore and tired and hung over, yet willing to show up for the stamp of ashes on the forehead, reminding all of the flesh's mordant inevitability. Hugh Gruber even remembered to stop by his local church as he drove to *Immaculate Heart*, ready for a fresh, six-week session of tests and instruction. But if one were to inquire, Hugh Gruber wasn't having a very good time of it these days. Perhaps, going to Mass and receiving the ashen seal as a stamp of approval, as it were, would be a sign to a better tomorrow or something close. Gruber checked his in-box at the school on his way to his first class noting that there was a single memo in the distinctive script of the school's principle, Sister Mary Boniface.

While so many revered the old nun for her tenure as head of the school, it was important to note that the good sister was also someone's boss—in fact, Hugh Gruber's boss.

Boniface had her back to her visitor as she finished up an email on her trusty computer. Waving her hands, she barked:

"Sit down, Hugh. I'll be with you momentarily."

Hugh Gruber sat in the dainty tufted satin chair and twiddled his thumbs impatiently—anxious to be done and out of there. He was certain that this was simply a routine inquiry into the usual matters pertaining to the students in his classes. Surely Boniface was calling him in for a general assessment of things. The last time they had a discussion, Gruber complained about his students' lack of interest in great books. Boniface breathed a sigh of relief and swiveled around in her great chair to face Mr. Gruber, who was fastidiously picking at his nails with a fine, manicuring instrument he kept in his breast pocket.

Boniface emitted a slight smile,

"Well...thank you for coming in, Hugh. I know how busy you must be in getting things done after our customary *Gras* break and all we need to get done before Easter."

Hugh Gruber, head bent, continued to pick away at a hangnail on his left thumb.

"Mr. Gruber..." Boniface, now with a broader, forced smile, announced, "In my office, I ask that you give me your undivided attention."

Hugh looked up, placing the file back in his breast pocket.

"Fine, Sister, excuse me."

Boniface studied the man sitting before her. He had been part of the faculty for going on ten years now. Not the most favored teacher, but a good one. A bit tough, but Boniface liked his old-fashioned, hard-nosed style. Of course, she thought he was a bit *heavy* on the girls. At times, *medieval*, as the girls are wont to say, given that the tomes he often assigns are a bit on the hefty side.

Boniface cleared her throat.

"Well, I just find that this spring's selection—among the varied shorter works and story collections—*Moby Dick*, is a tad cumbersome for the girls, Hugh."

Hugh Gruber replied:

"Well, Sister, that's precisely why our alums end up thanking us years later—as they find they surpassed their "colleagues at *Sophie Newcomb* and *Loyola U*. Many have said they got through their college classes in absolutely florid..."

Hugh stopped himself, blushing slightly at his choice of words, "...flying colors. As we speak, Hallie Montclair is a Masters candidate in *American Lit* from that stellar, name-dropping U in suburban Boston, you know, the one that starts with an *H* ? It was only last year, that I received a note from her, where she actually *thanked me* for all the hard work I put her through. Preparation, remember sister?"

My, he's a tough nut, Boniface thought as she grinned like a cheetah back at her employee.

"Well...lighten it up...just a little. How's about something like *Jonathan Livingston Seagull* for a change? It's a modern classic—yet a heck of a lot lighter and concise. Just as profound, though."

Hugh chimed in,

"Oh, no it isn't, Boniface. It's like having *Velveeta* after a good *Camembert* and you know it."

Boniface grinned, adding,

"Well, we all like a little snack once in a while, don't we?"

Assuming he was done with his little *tete a tete* with the good sister, the punctilious instructor abruptly got up to leave. Boniface gently waved him to sit back down. Hugh Gruber swiftly resumed his perch like a trained rhesus monkey.

Boniface continued:

"Before you go there, Hugh, I want to ask you something—How's the Molyneaux girl doing?"

Hugh emitted a heavy sigh.

"She's still a mediocre student, Sister. Her last essay on Rabelais got her a C plus. She repeats things and then pads her essays with fluff before making a simple point, why do you ask?"

Boniface grew quiet, a pensive look formulating on her face before adding,

"Well...she's ambitious, but maybe not exactly *academically* ambitious. She's more of a *creative* type, Hugh. She's into music."

"So?"

My, he's a sour one, Boniface thought, adding,

"Well...I'd like to give her a hand. Maybe if she's not a stellar student, then let's look at what she *is* good at."

Hugh Gruber shook his head, saying with a sigh,

"I'm not impressed. She may not even get into a good *music* college. Her test scores were bland. Not so terrible, just unimpressive. She isn't up for it, Boniface. She's also lousy at math from what I understand."

"Well...give the girls a break and assign a lighter book, won't you?" Boniface asked, chortling to herself: *I know he wants a raise, for goodness sake*.

Hugh emitted the slightest smile and shrugged his lean shoulders.

"Well...maybe one."

"Good!"

As much as Boniface wanted to lend a hand to musical aspirant, Claire, she didn't realize that the girl had just had her first professional gig and that she had recently landed a new private client who would pay her handsomely for a weekly private session as this individual (a patron at the bar that *Mardi Gras* afternoon) had ambitions to be a cabaret-style singer. Of course, Boniface had no idea of what was going on in her student's life. As far as she knew, Claire was still inhabiting her comfortable home, dining on fine china every night and slipping into clean, warm clothes before bedtime in her great canopy bed instead of the grim, slim-pickings situation the girl faced on a fairly regular basis for several weeks now.

Hugh Gruber smiled, nodded at the clock as he got up to leave. Boniface smiled at his back, adding,

"We realize, Hugh, that you will be celebrating ten years with us here at the *Academy*, and I know you'll be interested to know that we'll be reviewing a pay increase."

Hugh paused at the good nun's office door, turning around to face his employer, adding in a rather unctuous tone,

"Well, then, I would so appreciate that. And you know…now that I think of it…there are so many masterpieces that are pithy, concise works. I'll be looking at that during my lunch break, Sister!"

But Hugh Gruber felt that things wouldn't really lift much for the Molyneaux girl even if he did assign a *Jonathan Livingston Seagull*. Besides, what's all this about her being a musician? Perhaps such lofty ambitions rubbed Hugh the wrong way.

Maybe it reminded him of his own youth and the hope he once held in becoming a writer. Perhaps this is what irked him so about the girl. To his way of thinking, Claire had all the advantages of a moneyed background that he never had. No, he had to work jobs after school and had to fight his way into college by earning a hard-earned merit scholarship. Maybe Hugh could find a way to keep the Molyneaux girl's privileged nose to the grindstone in spite of lightening the course load so he could garner favor with his boss and get his salary increase.

◆　◆　◆

Claire surely felt grateful that Mrs. Gaynor had answered her telephone that afternoon, especially after she had slept in a coarse-blanketed bunk bed back at the hostel for so many nights. Although the "room with others" arrangement –about eight girls-*max* to a room –all in depressing, waffle-thin bunk beds—cost only ten dollars a day as opposed to the usual, twenty-five dollars Claire paid for a single (with a weekly rate of one hundred and forty dollars), Claire didn't feel much comfort knowing she was shoring up some serious dough. *What was it?* Claire wondered each afternoon when she asked frisky Gabe about a single-room availability and the prospects of anything opening up. Claire suspected that the management wanted to discourage any long-term stays and felt Claire had basically worn out her welcome there. Mr. J.J., on the rare occasion that he was around, would usually duck into the management office whenever he noticed Claire traipsing the lobby.

Well, so what? Claire realized that Mrs. Gaynor was really her best option even though she feared running into her brothers, or mother, God forbid. But things were going quite smoothly. Thus far, Mrs. Gaynor never got wind that Claire would leave by the kitchen side-door (the only entrance she used, actually) and through the back alleys whenever she had to do an occasional gig or practice session with her new high paying client, Gigi Letourneau.

Claire initially met Gigi when masked as a Greek nymph he slipped her a note during her stint on *Mardi Gras* day. In fact, this was the anonymous person who approached the bartender, asking him to offer Claire a free drink. Claire didn't much mind that she had to meet Gigi and his significant other, Ray, at a small nondescript club in its back room to practice singing some old show tunes. Turns out, this young man (all of about 25) was apparently well-off and didn't mind paying Claire about forty dollars for a mere hour and a half practice session she'd do with him once a week— usually on Tuesday evenings. It meant extra money given that Mrs. Gaynor only asked Claire to clean, dust and mop her great house twice a week in lieu of any payment she might have charged. Claire rather enjoyed her weekly time with her singing aspirant, Gigi and his partner, Ray. The only problem was whenever Gigi would hit a certain high note Ray would gingerly ring a brass cowbell he wore around his neck. Claire had to resist breaking into laughter every time Gigi's friend did this—which was fairly often—and sometimes she couldn't resist.

Recently, in last week's session, Ray sat perched on a stool, seeming to busy himself with his new electronic gadget whilst Gigi bellowed one of his favorite show tunes made famous by the torch singer, Helen Morgan, the 1920's hit, *The Man I Love*. If having Gigi belt out this old standard wasn't amusing enough with its opening line, *"Someday, he'll come along, the man I love and he'll be big and strong, the man I love. He'll build a little home, that's meant for two..."* the cowbell touch added just the right tincture of unintended humor to send Claire into a paroxysm of laughter. Claire held her hand to her mouth attempting to smother her giggles in a loud faux cough.

But this evening Claire was busy running a dust-mop over the wooden floors in Mrs. Gaynor's hallway before setting out to practice at the nun's convent parlor instead of the *River Road Bar* she so preferred. It was her final two months of school and it was becoming impossible to keep the late hours at the bar. It was also her last chance to beef up her grades as every spare moment was spent cramming for tests. Claire was beginning to show remarkable progress in her classes except for the dastardly *World Lit* and *Advanced Calculus*. How she ever made it to *Calculus* was a miracle in and of itself, but *Advanced Calculus*? Claire wasn't very hopeful in pulling up her grades in these classes, perhaps, a B minus in each, at best. So far, she was right at a mere C. Two schools of music had already rejected her with one in an obscure town in North Carolina giving her the ok. But it wasn't exactly a stellar college. Claire needed better grades. So what of her musical ability? Darva pulled her aside after school recently one afternoon, suggesting that she needed to make *the threat* and make it soon, but Claire was apprehensive. Even though she saved the photo she took of an intoxicated Hugh Gruber on *Mardi Gras* day in his highly compromising pose, his grinning face to the camera as he's about to grope a male dancer's gold lame bikini brief right in the gonads, Claire was hesitant to take the bold step of nailing the creep.

"It's blackmail, Darva."

Darva furiously resounded:

"So? So what? It's worth a try. The draconian dude is dyin to flunk your butt anyway. I say, forget propriety and give it a go, girlfriend."

But Claire had to give it more thought. Were things *that* bad that she had to stoop this low?

"Yeah, girl." Darva said, bobbing her head like a yo-yo as they walked, "you darn right they are."

But as Claire finished up her cleaning chores—hot water now running full blast as she rinsed the assorted rags and sponges in Mrs. Gaynor's utility sink—someone was thinking very intently about her situation. Of course, Boniface had no idea that the girl was living as a rent-free *Cinderella* of sorts in a wealthy old widow's home a few houses down from her own former dwelling. Nor did she know of the hardship the girl endured while putting up a brave front everyday at her school. No, she didn't know any of these things, but still, Sister Mary Boniface had her concern.

In fact, the good nun wrung her hands as she sat in an attempt to meditate in her favorite upholstered chair near the great window in her office, a Thomas Merton book resting in her lap. It was late afternoon and the sun was making its slow descent into dusk. Sister had just had another call from 'Nate over at *St. Jerome's*, asking for a meeting next week in his office. If that wasn't nerve-wracking enough, she was searching for a way to have a genuine conversation with Claire, who was now showing up more regularly to practice her piano playing there at the convent. But any attempt to engage the girl in a talk beyond the usual formalities was becoming impossible. Either Claire would stand there in the atrium of the convent with her stack of sheet music in hand simply answering the nun's questions with polite, but blunt statements or she would eye the wall clock interrupting Boniface mid-sentence, at times, as to her demanding study schedule.

Boniface had not forgotten the strange sensation she had after her hours-long slumber when she returned from her Las Vegas foray a couple of weeks ago and was wanting to probe a bit further as to what might be going on with the girl. She couldn't put her finger on it, but the old woman knew *her girls*. She had dealt with teenagers since the 1960's and she knew when there were troubling matters going on just by the way the very air wafted in their presence. No, the Molyneaux girl didn't seem to be pregnant or overly involved with a boy. It seems the girl was dealing with something odd, though, and it seemed she was under some terrible pressure, but getting her to open up was becoming quite a challenge.

Boniface sat in her chair watching the sky turn into the somber purples of evening, and as she did so, ideas began to formulate in her ancient mind. She was not going to give up her interest in Claire's welfare, but any attempt to engage the girl would have to wait, at least, for tonight. The thoughtful nun looked over at the invitation again to remind herself that she had made a promise to attend this gathering of spiritual women. There were some women of note, from the community, who would be there and Boniface felt it would be most rude not to show up.

◆　◆　◆

As dusk enfolds, I am twinkling my thought-emotion being just slightly above the good sister's head as she reads the words of her favorite Cistercian monk. I follow along like a little bouncing ball of television animation yesteryear. Actually, I rather enjoy these words of the holy contemplative, but to tell you honestly, I have other matters that seem to be in the way. I thought that I did a rather effective job of it late last night when I decided to give the dream-session matters another 'go', but it seems it is still not having much of an effect. Actually, in an off-hand way—a term I caught in a luminous television interview blaring from the good sister's flat screen the other night—I feel she is getting a signal, but is misplacing its source, or so I believe. For some reason, our good sister believes it is our Claire who needs her fastidious care and attention, and not me, your patient, albeit unintended, host of this tale of misadventure and mad-capped capers.

My orb-like self calls out:

"Yooooo-hoooooo! Over here! –or is it—Up here?"

Of course, I bamboozle myself in believing that, somehow, there has been some miraculous breakthrough in my reaching human senses. Hence, my maladroit attempts at entering the inner dream life of which I am still not so certain to its effects. Now the good sister is lifting the invite and reading it over again. Perhaps she is having second thoughts about attending this women's spiritual group—the one Darva Jean's mother, Lucy, belongs to and tonight's guest of honor, and for the first time, is a man, one we know. One we have seen here on these very pages: Squires Montgomery.

I attempt a nudge, suggesting she pop in for a few minutes as I believe she and Mr. Montgomery, a potential donor and idea-conjurer in connecting the convent to the Hindu and Buddhist communities, if not local, then at large—in fact, I perceive a potential money-maker in the near future that Squires could very well orchestrate. I attempt to suggest with my thought-emotion essence that this may be a worthy adventure. "Please, Boniface, get up from your chair"—I nudge my thought-emotion being closer, alas, her open book slips from her lap to the floor.

Boniface leans down to grab her book and realizes that she had better show up. She glances over at the grandfather clock, figuring that an hour or two wouldn't hurt. Maybe it'll do her some good.

♦ ♦ ♦

It took a while, but Phil and Marc decided that they had done the right thing. After Marc took Phil aside one day after school suggesting they stay out of the house awhile and have a pizza somewhere, Marc showed his older brother the pictures he'd taken of his mother with his cell-phone Mardi Gras morning.

Phil examined the two photos on the little screen.

"Wow. She must've been pretty tanked. Look at the bourbon bottle. Yeah. That's not good. But we need to think this over more."

Marc shook his head.

" Why? We need to email these to Dad. And then give him the lo-down on Claire. He wouldn't like this one bit and you know it."

Older brother wondered aloud,

"Yeah, but do we really need the scene? He'd come back and all hell would break loose and then what? He'd lasso her back here. Maybe she's happy this way. I think she likes being on her own. Actually, I wouldn't mind it one bit, to tell you the truth."

"We don't know where she's living, Phil. And he'd die if she's living with some dude."

Phil shook his head.

" I know where she lives, Marc. And you'll laugh. It's not with some dude. It's never been with some dude. I won't tell you because I promised her. But she's fine and dandy. Fit as a fiddle as they say. We better tell Dad she's been living at a friend's house from school, so he doesn't freak."

The afternoon went on this way, and after ordering a second pizza—which Phil paid for with his tutoring money—they decided to email a letter to their dad simply because they had grown weary of making up excuses as to Claire's whereabouts in their once a week conversations. Rita had delegated that duty to them these past two weeks and the boys just didn't feel comfortable lying to their father anymore. From what they could piece together, Claire was intent on finishing up at her school and graduating. And that would be in a matter of weeks. Dad was going to be there anyway.

So they nixed the idea of a phone call and decided a letter would be best. It seemed to be the right thing to do.

Claire Ange

Phil waited two days to check his emails for a possible response. He figured with the time difference and some trepidation, that it would be sufficient time. But there was no email from his dad. Instead Phil's phone vibrated like crazy in study hall one afternoon and he had to take the call outside in the school courtyard.

Father and eldest son talked for a very long time. Hilaire mentioned that he just got off a call with Sister Mary Boniface. He was assured that the girl was fine and attending class, but he hesitated to ask much further. He hadn't been in touch with his wife and daughter and wished to know if she was still attending school as his sons speculated. Hilaire was not going to call Rita. He explained to Phil that he simply could not go into this with her, that he was far too bogged down in his work and would not be able to get away until May—when he's due to return for a long break anyway. He asked for Claire's number, but the two brothers laughed, saying her phone only takes local calls. Phil volunteered to contact his sister for him. Their dad assured them that he would deal with Rita later. In the meantime, not a word about this to her.

Marc emitted a slow grin.

"Wow. This isn't goin' to be good, dude."

That very afternoon, Sister Mary Boniface was mulling things over after she got off the phone. She was, indeed, curious that Mr. Molyneaux had called, and all the way from the other side of the world. But she did not push the matter. He was a friendly man, kind and seemingly thoughtful—gentle, even, so unlike his brusque-mannered wife. But opposites attract, as they say. It was a bit odd, though. Asking her if his daughter was *still* attending school. Odd, also that several weeks ago Mrs. Molyneaux had called one morning, asking if her daughter was there at school that day.

"Aha!" Boniface slapped her thigh. Of course, now she understood, at last, as to the girls' taciturn ways, her mysterious manner; her reluctance to talk. *She's not living at home!*

Boniface rose from her great desk chair, buttoning her simple white cardigan as she prepared to walk to her appointment with 'Nate over at *St. Jerome's*. They were to have their follow-up meeting. To see where things stood. Her last meeting with Father Ignatius was in late February, right before she made her big win during her little trip to Vegas, so she had a little more 'ammo' in the till. But instead of being nervous, the good sister was mighty excited about a new plan to save her school. The one she discussed with that fine, articulate lawyer who was the guest of honor at the *Minerva's Dream* women's group she had attended the week before. In fact, Sister leaned over her great desk and picked up the business card he handed her. Yes, it was an interesting conversation, very enlightening, actually, as he seemed to have a very creative idea to get the alumni off their *collective* and donate! A meeting between East and West right there in the school courtyard! Perhaps it's not a complete solution, but one that could at least stave off another year from falling into the clutches of those opportunistic, entrepreneurial-minded, Jesuits. As the good sister flicked off her desk lamp, smiling to herself, a thought came to her: *Then where, pray tell, is the girl living?*

♦ ♦ ♦

Claire poured the steamy hot water into the dainty china cup, allowing Mrs. Gaynor's tea to steep. A soft-boiled egg wiggled on a plate as a slice of toast popped up from the old toaster. Mrs. Gaynor wasn't feeling well this morning, and actually, neither was Claire. But with her, it wasn't anything physical, per se. Actually, her head throbbed probably from lack of sleep, and her much desired coffee was still brewing. What distressed Claire this morning was the third rejection letter she received the day before from one of the many music schools of which she had applied. Of course, feeling lofty, not all of the universities and colleges Claire targeted were *middle of the road*. Some were quite selective, and Claire was just too shy to ask for help. She had no letters of recommendation from anyone. She was too unfamiliar with doing such a thing. Yet now she had to think of a new strategy, and fast. What made matters worse was the very untimely request that she contact her dad via her brother, Phil. She decided that she could only email him. That she wanted him to know she was doing well and applying to colleges and planning on graduating and her friend's family that she fictionally claimed was hosting her is treating her well. No talks. If she called him, she was afraid she'd break down in a torrent of tears. And Pops might roar and make things worse by confronting Rita. So email Hilaire she did. Claire smartly minimized Rita's antics and just said she was touched that Phil and Marc cared so much. Claire loved being out of that house and though it was a challenge, she would rather that any day over living under Rita's roof. *Please, Dad. I'm really ok!* Claire wrote.

But right now, she had to think of how she could possibly save herself from being a complete reject at all of the colleges of which she so naively applied. Asking for help was a very scary prospect for Claire. The shame she held from the constant onrush of criticism and denigration from brash mom, Rita, seemed to win out over any gusto she might muster in even writing a list of potential letter-writers on her behalf.

The daring act of asking for any assistance seemed too much for her to bear. Poor Claire. She could scarcely admit to herself that she had this problem. But it was becoming clear that her way of applying to college wasn't working. It was a waste, actually. And each application cost her at least thirty dollars of her hard- earned money. By contrast, Darva Jean got two acceptance letters and scholarship offers from the few schools of which she applied. But Darva stayed up late consoling her friend as they chatted on their phones the previous evening with Darva insisting that she start all over again.

And Darva—being a stellar champ of a buddy—encouraged her friend:

"Think of the schools you really want to go to and write a list of everyone who might be of help. Forget the grades, girl. You need to broaden your scope!"

And on this fine early spring morning, Claire settled down at Mrs. Gaynor's kitchen table with a cup of steaming coffee and attempted to write her list. One had to make up for the so-so grades and the so-so SAT scores. Actually, to conjure a rabbit out of the proverbial hat seemed to be in order. And for that to happen, one had to get creative in coming up with a strong list of candidates to pen those letters of recommendation. And this meant everyone she knew. Perhaps, Winnie and maybe Gigi Letourneau—her only private client-could lend a hand? Let's not forget Claire's old piano teacher, Mitch Logan. But to say that Claire is stellar as a musician might not be enough—and in acknowledging any obstacles to that, one had to consider Hugh Gruber.

"I told you, it would be a good move, girl." Darva said in their conversation the previous evening. But Claire remained silent as a stone.

Darva then offered:

"If you don't do something, *I* will. Just leave it to me. I get to school earlier, anyway…we'll just slip a little reminder note about things in his in-box, okay?"

Later, that very morning, while Claire was catching the streetcar to make it to her first class, Hugh Gruber was about to pass on opening his in-box in the faculty area, figuring the little note he spotted lying there by itself was just a flyer about some upcoming school function or the like.

But open it he did. In plain typed words it read:

*"We have the evidence of a little incident on Mardi Gras Day at Fidel's Finale. Be fair with **Claire M.**, that brilliant musical composer, and we'll forget the photo we have of you lewdly fondling the boy-toy in the gold lame' briefs. You still want your job, don't you?"*

Hugh quickly crumpled the note and shoved it deeply in his trouser pocket as he slinked away from the teachers lounge area and into the main atrium of the school building. His intention was to step out and get a bit of air, but he didn't get that far and feeling woozy, he took hold of the banister on the great staircase. A lightening bolt of fear struck the very core of him.

Who could possibly know of this? And who typed this note? The idea of Boniface—this seemingly kind little nun—doing such a thing seemed too far-fetched.

I know she's fond of the girl…but this? No, I can't be thinking of the same person. And besides: how could she know where I was on Mardi Gras Day? Furthermore, aren't my after-school hours my own business?

Still, the thought of a possible photo of his carousing with half-dressed male dancers made him most uncomfortable. Throngs of schoolgirls now charging up and down the staircase as the first class bell rang out, went unnoticed as Gruber continued to stand there, his hand frozen in place on the staircase railing, his head woozy and wooly at the shock of it all. Hugh pursed his lips and narrowed his gaze down to his chocolate brown, Steve Madden boots, *Okay, so I was carousing on Gras day—so? I still don't get how anyone could know of my whereabouts… After all, I was masked.*

◆ ◆ ◆

Not for the entire time, bud. Ha! I must admit I rather enjoy watching the nitpicky, nefarious schoolmarm squirm. Thanks to me, we got the evidence. All I can say is: better be prepared—change is coming 'round the bend. Victory for our girl, at last! And as we pause here while Mr. Gruber whirls himself into a sea of worry, I need to report some good news, dear readers. Yes, I believe I see a crack in the code as to my own mystery, for my old "visitor" slipped in to see me late last evening, as I was bouncing my orb-like self on the ceiling of Claire's comfy room at Mrs. Gaynor's.

You may recall, it was the spirit that happened upon me some time ago, the one who called out to me, saying he once knew me, and tried to send some clues my way as to a life I once lived, perhaps, my most recent life of which I am so incapable of recalling. A life where it seems I wore Cossack chapeaus as the region of where I might have lived seemed mighty cold in winter. Yes, it was the friendly entity who wished to be of assistance, but was intercepted by cosmic beings far more advanced than either of us.

There I was, ruminating on whether I should try, yet again, to gain the good nun's attention in any possible forthcoming dreamscape, my orb-essence bouncing lightly—not unlike the smallest of helium balloons—on the ceiling and he called out to me, slipping me a hint. A much needed clue to my own mystery, dear readers. I was so thrilled for this unexpected assistance.

And so he showed me a scene, with many men sitting at tables dressed in uniform-like greatcoats, and Russian fur caps gloriously crowning their skulls, and it came it me: sitting at the sturdy, hobnailed boots of these men, were these objects lying about. But as I looked closer, I could see that these items were worn leather cases, in different shapes and sizes, lying about on the floor, our two large tables nestled together. And in front of me, on the table, was a leather portfolio of some kind, and stuffed inside, barely peeking out, was a stick or a wand of some kind. Oh, my, I knew these men. We were a club within a club, an association of sorts. We would meet for a coffee or spirits in the late afternoon, and in this particular scene, it was snowing outside, and the cases around us were wet, sitting in slight pools of water— obviously from the thaw of cozy heat inside.

It seemed that we spent hours in this place, discussing an array of subjects—and then, my mysterious visitor conveyed something else to me, and for a moment, I shivered, and spun in the air—it startled me so, but its nature wasn't particularly anything that would evoke such a response for it had something to do with prayers and joy—laughter, even. It was something a friend had shown us, as he grew up somewhere in the Far East. It was something of great importance to me, later, at a time I was to experience and of which I was too timid to re-visit, as I was lead to a further vision of a doorway in a dank, decrepit building of some kind. A barn. A shed. A—I am not so sure, but I shuddered and in doing so, I was brought back to my cozy spot above the main atrium of our girl's convent school.

◆ ◆ ◆

It had been a few weeks since Squires began to actually spend some time with Lucinda Mobray. At first, Squires wondered if he was doing the right thing—a former client's wife, and all, but given that they would only meet for coffee and a casual chat about things didn't really feel like dating, *per se.* Squires was all too happy to take his time with women, in general. He found it most daunting to be even attempting to date after being married for all of twenty-five years and then having to deal with the whole process of losing his wife to an untimely death. But was he getting too enthused? That is, in his general aim with Lucinda? Was he being too much the *Dudley Do-Right* by interjecting his ideas into Lucinda's women's forum? *"It never fails. When it comes to women, I always feel I must do something to resolve whatever dilemma a female might be dealing with. What is it about men that we must rescue?"* Squires asked his friend, Warren Leblanc, after the two of them played their horns on the Leblanc screened-in porch one evening, assorted smoldering cigars and long neck beer bottles lying about. And yes, as far as his recent guest of honor appearance at Lucinda's women's group, Squires wondered if he said too much already. He didn't intend to paint such a rosy picture when he walked over to talk to the demure, septuagenarian nun sitting in the corner of the room, a cup and saucer in her lap as she listened intently to an impassioned speech by one of the regulars at the *Minerva's Dream* women's group. Maybe he felt sorry for the aging nun and her flailing school, and felt that he could empathize with her. After all, Squires graduated from *Aquinas Academy,* a well-established, all-male institution, which continues to be well endowed and standing. But to be honest, Squires had a special interest in one of the women in the group, in fact, the very person who had invited him to speak, and it didn't hurt that Lucinda Mobray had a daughter who also happened to be finishing up at the beleaguered institution, either.

"May I join you for a moment, Sister?" Squires, in his smooth, smoky, oak-cured voice, inquired, sliding an ottoman chair across the carpet with his high-polished, wing-tipped shoe, in order to speak more directly to the good sister. Boniface was rather impressed with the bespectacled Squires, as he waxed eloquent on his esteemed, Christian Brothers education, and when she went into her situation, the pending takeover from Aquinas' rival, *St. Jerome's,* Squires lit up, his nostrils slightly flaring, "Well…now that doesn't have to happen, Sister. You just need a good fundraiser—pique the curiosity of the alumni association…and I think I might have an idea for you." Squires immediately made some intriguing suggestions. "I'm sure they—your former students—would probably love a Maypole like the one they have here. An East meets West and a little Goddess culture thrown in. That should get them interested!"

Boniface took a bite of her teacake and dunked it in her cup. In fact, she let it float there as she speculated on what the good man just said.

Now, two weeks later, Squires sat in his desk chair, slightly pulling at his goatee. *Maybe I got a little carried away*, Squires mused to himself, *I shouldn't have said that I could actually provide her with swamis and Zen Buddhists as if I have them sitting around my living room!* Squires very well knew he didn't really know any swamis or high profile—or any profile, actually—Buddhists. Still, he awaited a call from Gus, his old friend in Malibu. *Maybe he could make some suggestions,* Squires thought as he gathered his documents in preparation for an upcoming trial. And just as he was about to leave, the office phone rang.

Nestled in a leafy college venue, eminent mathematics professor, Dr. Wilfred La Rouse, sat in his office taking advantage of some free time between classes. He busied himself with writing out suggestions in resolving an algorithm problem for a young gal he happened to find favor with as her desperate plea into his voicemail prompted him to action. Upon waking-up this fine weekday spring morning, Wilfred intently listened to the three-minute spiel on his voicemail on *speakerphone* as he quietly shaved, trimming slightly the thin mustache adorning his full upper lip. On and on the message went, with sobs and tears spilling into the receiver, a nose-blowing session in between rushed words about college applications, and math class quandaries.

"Okay!"

Wilfred, responded a couple of hours later, as he softly spoke into his cell phone, walking across campus, attempting to make it on time to his first class.

" Now you don't think I wouldn't help my favorite of favorite pianists now do you, suga'? Didn't *Miss Winnie, herself*—tell you that *she* would help you with any math quandary you might git yo'self into? So shush. Forget all that weepin' and freakin'—Just tell me what your Calculus question is and we'll get you some ideas."

Dr. La Rouse continued to listen, making mental notes in his vast, geodesic mind,

"Ahha...so we have us a situation with Advanced Calculi in creating a possible algorithmic solution. I see...Okay—give me the question...okay...I got that resolved and stored right in my noggin. Now, I'm not going to actually write out the answer, dear. I'll just give you the main triggers, ok? I will point you to it. Horse to water, baby. So relax. I'll email the sequence suggestions to you later. I know not everyone loves math like I do...but I realize you feverishly write music when you blank out in class, so I will grant you this one exception. Everybody knows a musician aces her math, girl."

Claire emanated a smile through joyous tears, snapping her cell phone shut as she and Darva skipped down the breezeway near the courtyard, aiming to take in some morning sunshine during their break.

Darva shook her head, saying,

"I knew my cousin would come through. Now all you need to do is get a solid testament to your musical prowess and write a better essay for yourself. That's it!"

Claire beamed:

"She…I mean, Wilfred La Rousse, said he'd be willing to provide a referral as *Winnie*. But when I think about it, would anyone be impressed with *Winnie the Wonder, Performer Extraordinaire?*"

"Well…" Darva pondered, "At least it's a plug. Who else have you asked?"

Claire squinted her eyes in the morning sun.

"I'm not sure who else…I'm working on it."

Claire remained taciturn and basically unconvinced that anyone would step up to the plate to give her a much needed boost. Besides, she was nervous about meeting with Sister Boniface after lunch, as per Sister's request. While Claire and Darva enjoyed the late morning sun, legs outstretched, plaid uniform skirts hiked to the thighs so they could fan themselves with their notebooks, as it was an unusually warm day, Claire ruminated on the recent change in the way her *World Lit* teacher had been treating her lately.

"I still can't believe Gruber asked to look at my papers again. He was particularly interested in re-reading the last two. And he actually changed the grades to B's. Instead of the C's I originally got. Now, Darva, please tell me you have nothing to do with this, girlfriend."

The girls sat in silence as they munched away on their mid-morning snacks. While blithely peeling a banana, Darva smiled as she stared straight ahead. Her eyes slowly drifted sideways to meet her friend's unabashed gaze— and the two of them broke into giddy laughter.

Claire blurted:

"All right! So he's being mighty nice lately, but it's hard not to smile when he practically falls over himself every time I stroll into class! Not that I'm complaining! You musta scared the *bejesus* out of him, that's all I'm going to say!"

The two carried on, stretching themselves out on the grassy lawn, giggling about their recent conquest. Claire suddenly propped herself up, resting her chin in her hands,

"Yeah. I just wish I knew someone, like a famous musician who could write a glowing assessment of my musical abilities. But I only have Mitch Logan, my former teacher, *Winnie* and maybe my new client, Gigi."

Darva sat up, peeling the paper wrapping on her bran muffin.

"So then ax the nun. She likes you."

"You mean, Boniface?"

Claire mulled over this idea as she walked up the flight of stairs to the good sister's office later that very afternoon. Surely, she knew the nun liked her. After all, she gave her full permission to practice in the little parlor room any time she wished after school and in the early evenings undisturbed. But the idea of actually inviting the old lady into the parlor some evening where Claire would perform her own compositions made her blush right down to her toes. Claire didn't feel she really had enough talent or mastery to actually ask anyone's opinion. Usually, she just buried the stacks of sheet music from her own hand in the bottom dresser drawer in Mrs. Gaynor's quaint guest room, her home at the moment. It was a wonder Claire would include some of her compositions in her applications, with two of the schools returning hers, as Claire seemed to have absent-mindedly avoided that very important inclusion. Claire's music was actually quite good, but she kept it hidden deep within the corridors of her very soul—out of habit. She was too frightened of any ridicule or insult, as Rita, in her persistent, spirit-raking criticism so trained the girl to expect. Claire flushed with shame, remembering her mother's crass remarks of only a few months ago, some weeks before she had her treasured piano moved into storage.

"You'll be broke if you think you're goin' to get anywhere with that tepid, lackluster talent. Give it up, Liberace, and pray that, someday, you land a hubby to save your sorry self!"

Claire shuddered at the memory. Was she crazy to pursue this idea of a music career? Perhaps, the good nun would guide her. Steer her in ways Claire couldn't have imagined for herself, for Sister Boniface was not exactly a passive bystander to the girl's presence in the little downstairs parlor most evenings. In fact, Boniface rather looked forward to hearing the girl walk down the convent hallway and into the quaint room to practice, unlocking the door with the golden key she had given the girl so many weeks before.

Actually, Claire wouldn't have to ask the good sister for any assistance this afternoon. For it was the very reason she had wanted to talk to the girl in the first place. For the past several evenings, Boniface was moved by Claire's passionate practice sessions—recognizing some of the melodies she played, while not exactly being able to pinpoint others. *Maybe these are from her own hand*, Boniface mused with pursed lips as she listened intently from the upstairs landing as the lovely music flowed into the grand atrium of the old convent.

After hearing the child play on one occasion, in what had to be three straight hours of practice, the nun couldn't help but be moved by the girl's ability. For it wasn't the array of show tunes, and some of the child's own works—which seemed quite promising—but a selection of classical composers' works, spilling off the keyboard, one right after the other in rapid succession, each piece brilliantly played, some a bit challenging for her level, but performed all the more passionately and deftly, still. But there was one composition that stood out.

And it was earlier in the week, while busy with some paper work, Boniface rose from her desk and cocked her ear outside the doorway of her upstairs parlor—listening, quite intently, to the brilliant touch and style of the girl's playing. The passion that would come through and the way she played this particular piece- though awkward, as its complexity would be more for the seasoned professional, which Claire simply was not at that point- was so tenderly played. Despite her missteps, the rich layers shone through. The good woman just had to creak down the stairs to lightly tap on the door to ask the child the name of the piece she was playing. Claire answered the door, flushed with embarrassment, her black hair a stringy, sweaty mess as beads of perspiration gathered at her brow.

"Too loud, Sister?"

"No, child. I'm just curious as to the piece you were just playing."

Claire shrugged:

"Oh, it's a complex one…I hardly know it, Sister, only certain segments…it's probably over my head—it's a Franz Liszt composition. A sonata with an unusual name—*"After a Reading of Dante"*, I believe it was after he read *The Inferno*, from the famous *Divine Comedy*?

"Such passion… but what a subject, eh?"

The good sister chuckled, quickly adding:

" I would like to have a chat with you in my office. Is Thursday all right with you? Say, after lunch?"

Claire thought back on that moment, wondering what the old nun might wish to discuss. But Boniface well knew the girl was struggling with her college applications and warmly greeted her when she walked in.

◆ ◆ ◆

Anne took a quick glance at her husband as he polished off his beer. It had been several weeks since Mardi Gras and Anne was a tad curious as to what may be going on over at chez Molyneaux.

Anne corrected her husband,

"I didn't exactly say I heard they are headed for a divorce. My womanly instinct, though, says that's more than likely the case, that's all."

Warren settled into his favorite porch chair and looked out at his yard, taking a swill of his beer as the sun made its evening descent. Warren was in a rather pensive mood given that he had just returned from a funeral. It was an old high school friend's mother who passed. Warren filled his wife in on some of the details:

"She wasn't extremely old, you know. About seventy-five...and her death was unexpected—so much so that Buz Muldoon and his siblings didn't know how to go about this funeral stuff. But it didn't take them long to figure it out. They had the old lady take care of her own last tab, that's for sure. They put the casket, hearse, limousines, even the flowers and little Virgin Mary holy cards—actually, the whole she-bang on *her* American Express card."

Anne waved him off,

"Oh, Warren, please…that's ridiculous…on *her Am-Ex* card? It *does* require a signature, you know." Warren returned his wife's gesture with an elfish grin.

"Yeah, I thought so, too, but the mortuary indiscreetly went along with it and looked the other way. That Mollie Muldoon wasn't so bad off. But…still…I thought there'd be, at least, some propriety—given the situation. I mean, we all know about *not leaving home without it*…but who would ever say… "oh, and while you're at it, *don't leave your life without it, either…*"…heh—heh…I can't believe Buz just came out and admitted this to me, but when you're a lawyer as long as I've been at it, people tell me things. They just loosen their lips and spill it all out. Sometimes I think I'm more of a confessor than a lawyer, especially with an Irishman like Muldoon. What are you lookin' at me like that for, Annie? It's the truth."

Anne shooed her husband with her newspaper, opening it as she sat back down on the couch.

"I can't believe that's even legal, but if it is, I would hope that bizarre purchase brought in some good points, at least…"

Warren quipped:

"Points? For what, her next life?"

Anne shook her head, laughing behind the society page, her face emerging from the folds,

"Warren, why are we talking about those *Irish Channel* friends of yours?"

"Cuz you asked me about my afternoon and I told you. Want to fill me in on yours, missy?"

Anne really didn't know where to begin, with the earful that she got at the Bienville Club about shrieks heard in the wee hours of the night, and Rita rolling the SUV down the driveway to retrieve her sons who both decided to rebel and leave the premises, shouting back at her that they wouldn't be returning at all. (Anne wondered if that was the same evening when she was awoken by a car horn blaring, as she quickly drifted back to her nocturnal slumber). Or that there were some photos floating about of an intoxicated Rita with her arms around a bottle of prime Kentucky bourbon on Mardi Gras morning—thus the reason for her being knocked out for all of Mardi Gras day. It was an earful, all right. In fact, Anne was just giving Warren's trusty binoculars a test-run, scrutinizing the great side window of chez Molyneaux before he pulled up in the driveway.

However, there was nothing unusual going on. Actually, things seemed very quiet and rather peaceful. But it was no wonder that she was curious given all the talk. And the fact that Hilaire was planning on returning from his assignment in a matter of weeks. Anne finally announced:

"Well, the girls confirmed it at the club today that the child was kicked to the curb. Locked out, as soon as Hilaire left. I understand Claire's shacking up at old lady Gaynor's down the way…it's why you saw her dragging all those trash bags down the street."

Warren smoothly remarked,

" Well…that was weeks ago and I haven't seen little Claire since…but that doesn't really surprise me about Rita. She's a real piece of work. Yes, she is…I never told you this, but my dad knew about her family. I'm not sure how. I think it was someone who worked at *Chez de Roche* who actually knew Rita, or her family. The *Silvestris* were first generation immigrants from somewhere in Southern Italy. But when they came here, they lived in Destrahan or some place like that. Rita and her sister, Rosa—the Silvestri Sisters—who were known, "at one time, to have some kind of show biz act. I understand they were left to fend for themselves—not so unlike *Remo and Romulus*, the twins raised by wolverines—when they were still in their teens. And their folks were not too far off the gypsy tree—they were circus performers or something—jugglers, tightrope-walkers, like something out of the *Greatest Show on Earth*. You can't make this stuff up, Annie. Anyhow, one day, her folks, along with some aunts and uncles, were all deported. Seriously. I don't think Rita and her sister ever heard from them again. So, they worked as models at the old *Godchaux* department store when they were in high school. Rita met Hilaire at a fashion show. She was a real dish in her day. I mean, she had to have been—how else can you explain how Hilaire fell so head over heels?"

Anne playfully added,

"Well… aren't you a little *Funk and Wagnalls* on everybody's business these days! I know the bit about Rosa, her sister, at least, to some degree. The only thing I ever heard was that she left town in a huff, after an argument and never spoke to Rita after that. Oh, we really need to talk about something else, Warren. I'm plumb ashamed of myself—talking about Rita's private business and all. You know we shouldn't be doing this".

Warren walked over to his wife, swilling a second beer from the little fridge on the porch.

"Aw, come on, you bad ass. You love every gossipy minute! What else would you do? Crochet like a nun? Come here, you cute little thing and let's go upstairs."

Anne frowned at her flirtatious hubby, gently brushing him away,

" What am I going to do with you—you silly?"

Warren nuzzled his nose in his wife's lovely neck, purring,

"You're my cookie, my cupcake and my butter cup, you know that? And you're a shining jewel next to that Rita."

Warren slightly pulled away, adding,

" She isn't all Italian, either, *that* Rita. I understand she's part Albanian or something, but she keeps that under wraps. And as far as her daughter, well, she's probably happy to be away from her. Who could forget Rita's little bonfire rampage she set on the girl's stuff a couple of years' ago? Whole neighborhood looked like it was sending smoke signals! Scared the hell out of us, remember? Well, if you must know, Hilaire called me this morning, seeking my advice about possibly serving some *papers* Rita's way come May, when he returns."

Warren resumed his position, his nose softly brushing against his wife's soft nape,

" Here's to that woman's intuition of yours, baby."

♦ ♦ ♦

Rita wasn't exactly sure when she started doing this. This business of taking mirrors down around the house and placing them behind sofas, under beds and chairs, but the boys surely began to take notice.

The two of them, conspiratorially huddling together in the hallway, shrugging their respective teenage shoulders, and glancing over at the their mother with puzzled looks, seemed to be a rather common scene these days. Perhaps, it was none of their business, but heck if it didn't feel a tad creepy.

"Guilt, anyone?"

Phil quipped, as they passed the assorted serving bowls of steaming food around their little dinner table. Rita shot a scouring look her eldest son's way.

Phil countered:

"What? You think we don't notice anything, Ma?"

Actually, this was one of the last occasions where the boys would actually sit down and have supper with their mom, as the situation was just getting a little too weird for the boys. Phil could not contain himself from speaking his mind and Rita was becoming more intolerable of any critical comment.

Rita blankly stared at her sons,

"You think you two know everything? You saw how Claire was. She never obeyed me. She insisted on playing that piano for hours at a time. She really isn't all that good, anyway. I don't know who she thinks she is. She's just a hard-headed, difficult and stubborn girl—destined for trouble."

It was much later that evening, when the boys returned from one of their school games, that the two decided that enough was enough and threatened to leave the house permanently. Thus the ordeal in the driveway so many hours later while most of the neighborhood slept. However, there was one individual who awoke, slipping from her silky bed sheets to tippy-toe to her opened, moonlit window to peer at the goings on so many houses down. Claire pushed the French window further and stepped out onto the upstairs veranda of Mrs. Gaynor's grand old house, hoping no one would see her. She noticed the two familiar figures in the driveway as they walked to their dad's car. For a moment, Claire was tempted to call Phil on his cell, but hesitated. She didn't want Rita to get any idea that her daughter was actually watching the commotion from her new home. Claire was doing so well at deftly walking through the back alleys whenever she came and went from Mrs. Gaynor's house until she finally got to the major boulevards where she would usually catch a streetcar or bus.

Days later, Phil reassured his sister that he revealed nothing as to her new living situation and promised that the two of them didn't mention it to their dad. Both boys were back at the house after staying with friends for a few days during their spring break. They awaited their father's imminent return.

But this afternoon, while the Leblancs were chatting away on their screened in porch, Rita comfortably sat on the plush sofa in her ornate living room. The walls did look somewhat barren without the presence of the much-beloved, gold-leafed mirrors Hilaire had placed there so many years ago. Rita carefully removed them, placing the heirlooms that had been in the Molyneaux family since the mid-1800's, in the cool of their storage closet near the back hallway.

My, but the boys have been difficult as of late, Rita mused, taking a sip of her plain soda, an orange slice floating nicely at the glass's rim. With the removal of most of the grand specula about her lovely home, Rita decided to turn over a new leaf by taking better care of herself—no more whiskey shots or languid afternoons of sipping fine chardonnays. It was a time to be clear-headed. And given that mirrors, at least to Rita's way of thinking, were emblems of vanity and self-indulgence, she thought it best to remove some. That is all. Why her eldest son was delving so deeply in the matter, she did not know. While she definitely favored her boys over their difficult sister, it seemed that Phil, in particular, was becoming much too severe in his thinking.

What's he reading these days? Rita mused, recalling an afternoon where she asked about this *Thus Spake Zarathrustra*, by this brooding, German pessimist, this Friedrich Nietzsche. True, Rita never completed high school—a secret she kept from everyone, even her husband. But who is this *Zarathustra*, a demon or something?

"*Sounds devilish.*" she said to her son, Phil, who shook his head and laughed as he climbed the grand staircase to his room, arriving late from the library.

Well, it sure seemed odd, as of late. Rita always considered her sons to be more congenial, sanguine sorts, quite like their father, but things were beginning to change. Where Rita often found that Claire was too deep on the matters of life, and would often scold the child on being overly pensive, her sons now seemed to be shifting into that murky place of just too much seriousness. To her way of thinking, life was simple. Not deep, dark, or lugubrious, God forbid. Rita thought she made life easier for her daughter; that all Claire needed to do was circulate in the right circles, preferably, among the wealthy elite.

It was why she insisted Claire be a debutante and show up for tea and petit fours at *Miss Duvall's*, the junior league club, so she could be introduced to the finer things in life.

"A life I never had, mind you," Rita would often bark whenever Claire shrugged her shoulders with the slightest indifference to such matters. But Rita wasn't one bit worried about the threats her sons were making. It was fine with her if they chose not to formerly dine with their mother, the both of them preferring to eat in their respective rooms, in honor of their exiled older sister.

But what were these strange books her sons were reading? Rita forgot that she discontinued their Internet service. This seemed to encourage the boys to hang out at the school library, or their friends' homes after school only to later return to the house to do their homework, instead of *twaddling and doodling* online, as Rita called it. Now they were reading books—big, hefty and dusty old books. This brought out Rita's contempt all the more.

"You're becoming like your sister more and more every day!" Rita shouted after them just the previous evening, as the two bounded up the stairs. Marc bellowed back to her,

"Great! When's kick-out day?"

Rita fluffed the satin sofa pillows in an attempt to get more comfortable as she preoccupied herself with a glossy fashion magazine. Since her sons' recent rebellions, Rita decided it would be best to give Hilaire a call.After many tries, Rita finally decided to leave a very long message in his voicemail.

This was about four days ago. Rita took a sip from her drink, *I don't understand why I haven't heard back from him,* she wondered aloud, jolting slightly at her own reflection looking up at her from the polished silver serving plate resting next to her sparkly glass.

◆　◆　◆

I am as still as the ceiling's brassy lighting fixture as I observe the crusty, callous matron sitting comfortably on her satin sofa below. Perhaps, it's startling to recognize one's own visage when it presents a very different reflection than what one assumes. (I can empathize in a way, readers, as I got no further clue when I tried the mirror experiment on myself one desperate afternoon). Instead of the youthful, dewy-complected countenance Rita is accustomed to seeing—thanks to various expensive facial products and the like—she saw before her a rather hardened and frightened aspect—if only for a micro-second. There was a time when I foolishly wondered if I could see my thought-emotion being reflected in one of the many mirrors I have come across since finding myself here in this strange, boggy city. Sorry to say, I did not notice myself at all in any possible reflection, including your refrigerators, blank computer screens, parlor flat screens, as well as any beveled glass adornment that fancy the walls of these fine homes. My goal was to see if I could recognize myself in a different way. I also had this idea that, perhaps, my slipping into a mirror's glossy surface might transport me to an alternate reality waiting on the other side. Ah, in my wildest dreams! Still, I amuse myself while observing Rita as she attempts to assuage any uncomfortable feelings she may have about her misdeeds toward her daughter, and now, perhaps, against her sons. It seems her wicked behavior is finally getting the best of her, as they say. Evidently, time may be running out, and not simply for her, but for 'yours truly', as well.

Yes, it seems the answers I've been seeking are not forthcoming. Apparently, my little experiment with interspersing my orb-self into the dreamscape of our good Sister Boniface, has ended somewhat unsuccessfully. I thought that by now, I would have been able to piece together a narrative of a life I once lived. Perhaps, I bamboozled my thought-emotion being into believing that my discarnate "visitor" would again show up and sprinkle more clues my way. Even though he did make a solemn promise that he would return, I have yet to see the likes of him, bouncing about in all his luminescent glory. There have been moments when I questioned my own senses. Perhaps, I misunderstood, but I've been waiting for my discarnate "visitor"—the one who has so graciously shown up these past few weeks in unexpected intervals—to arrive. Although he shows me scenes from a life I still can't quite remember, I somehow maintain a degree of faith. I amass these clues in the hopes that the final pieces of the puzzle will miraculously show themselves. Lately, I've entertained this notion that I might be rescued out of my predicament at any moment. The trouble is, I've been thinking this for quite awhile now, and as much as I'd like *to believe that because time is irrelevant in my realm, I am reliant on it more than ever as I traipse about in your human world, looking for clues to a life I once lived.*

As our curious humans here bumble about their business, I continue to wait for new discoveries. But there doesn't seem to be any news of any kind for me. My discarnate "visitor", who showed me curious images the last time I met with him, told me that he would appear again, but he has not shown up.

I wonder if he might have forgotten about me, as it has been so many weeks now since he last attempted to prompt my memory. However, I have revisited the café scene in my thought-emotion being's memory—I have gone over things innumerable times, examining the details right down to the tablecloths adorning the café tables. I have looked into the faces of these individuals and recognize no one. I land at one individual there, and I feel it is me, but I look for a flash of recognition in the visage itself and nothing registers—yet it all feels warm and familiar. How can I explain such a thing? I then examine the greatcoats that adorn these men and the supple black sable fur of their elaborate hats as they rests atop the tables, thawing as an interminable afternoon snowfall pounces the cobbled streets outside. I have examined the town square where the cafe is situated and admire its central tower and its grand, brassy clock, but it's all amusement and speculation. I curiously zoom in on the objects that sit at the hobnailed boots of my fellows, and try to make them out. They seem to be cases of some kind—not exactly those for clothing or the like, but for something else altogether. I re-examine the leather satchel case set atop one of the cloth-covered tables.

I peek inside to examine a baton or wand of some kind slipping out of it. And I pause. Oh, readers, I know what this might mean. But as soon as I feel the slightest tingle of recognition, my thought-emotion being instantly zips away from this scene and I am back where I visited before, where I see a beautiful, celestial being in a night sky speaking to me, beckoning me and giving a loving, but stern warning not to look back at this bleeding figure lying face-down in the snow.

◆　◆　◆

Late spring blossomed in a rich flourish of radiant hues about the old city. Rows and rows of pink and white azaleas abounded the meridians that graced the grand boulevards making the world, itself, seem fresh and renewed with a resurgence of life and all its wondrous promise. By mid-May, magnolias and gardenia joined the floral celebration, just in time for Claire and Darva's long-anticipated graduation day. Yes, the two chums were a giddy and happy lot. *Senior Prom* went amazingly well as the two acquired handsome dates. Darva's new beau from *Aquinas Academy*, a second cousin of Squires Montgomery, admired her from afar, and geared up the nerve to ask her out once Squires introduced the two at the recent *Convent of the Immaculate Heart* fundraiser. Perhaps, it was destiny or just good timing, but the nascent couple hasn't taken a weekend off from each other since. Rolf Dumont, Claire's 21 year old love interest from a few months back, (handsome, former hostel dweller from Montreal and rumored housemate-paramour), accompanied Claire as they continued to email until his imminent return—making his way back from exploring the ruins of Mexico. Of course, many a classmate were rather dazzled, with a few betting heavily that neither Claire nor Darva would secure dates, much less such impressive, if not handsome ones.

But the gossipy girls got over it and actually admired the twosome's taste in their respective, prom dress choice. Like a latter-day *Cinderella*, Claire maintained a low profile; putting aside her earned money from her private lessons with Gigi LeTourneau and bought a lovely cream silk designer gown, (on sale, of course), transforming her into her true swan-like beauty. Darva and Lucinda created Darva's gown, an exquisite satin sheath in a rich peacock blue.

Both looked radiant as the two friends danced and partied the night away, riding in a rented limousine with their dates, drinking champagne and dining at *Chez de Roche*, a favorite of the high society crowd. It sure was a hoot, with Mrs. Gaynor swilling her tall glass of gin and soda as she waved the couples inside for a photo-op before taking off. Rita parted her living-room curtains just as the limousine crawled by, and stepping out on the porch noticed the youngsters laughing and carrying on before slipping into Mrs. Gaynor's great front door. Rita had no idea that her daughter was among them, only wondering why the old lady would be part of such youthful dalliance.

But none of it would matter for long, anyway. Hilaire Molyneaux did show up, as promised, and beamed proudly at his daughter's accomplishments. Only he and the boys attended Claire's graduation ceremony, as Rita wasn't invited. Nor did she show an interest when the boys left to meet their father in their suits, carrying gift-wrapped boxes and bouquets of flowers.

When Hilaire initially contacted his daughter, Claire insisted that it was she who voluntarily left the house, yet Hilaire knew that his sons wouldn't make things up. Still, Hilaire withheld further commentary on the matter and smiled at his lovely daughter while the two met for a quiet dinner at the fancy restaurant of her choice. Claire did not wish to discuss where she was living, but as father and daughter chatted away, with Hilaire filling the girl's wineglass twice and he swilling a bit more than usual, himself, Claire broke down and told him that she was living just down the street.

"Dad, promise that this is between you and me. And it remains my own business. I come and go through Mrs. Gaynor's kitchen door, and walk through the alleys to the main streets so Mom never sees me. And I want to keep it this way. Let's face it: Mom and I don't mix. We're really not at all compatible. I'm happy. I really am. And I like being with Mrs. Gaynor. I help her out, clean and dust mop her floors, hose down her garbage cans. Sometimes I rub cream on her legs before she gets into bed. I don't mind."

Hilaire listened to his daughter with mild admiration. *How could I have such a fine girl as a daughter? So kind and unspoiled, she is,* he thought to himself as the girl chatted away. Claire was grateful for the breaks that have come her way. Although she didn't exactly want her dad to know about everything she had experienced in her four-month stint out on her own, she did speak about her helping a certain vocal aspirant, a young man, her first real client. Also, that she performed in a jazz trio here and there—but avoided going into too many details, for the obvious fact that Hilaire would be a tad appalled that his darling, seemingly innocent daughter was playing in a floozy gay bar deep in the bowels of Bourbon Street. Claire assured her dad that she performed mainly for private parties and usually, in the afternoons. As his daughter spoke, Hiliare thought of what he should do. He knew about Rita's troubled past. He knew more than his wife ever suspected. But from what the boys told him, he felt he had to make certain that she get professional help. Of course, the two had a long history of seeking therapy, but this time, he had to insist, or else. He didn't really wish to divorce his wife.

Claire looked up at her father as she finished speaking. She took a bite of her dessert and briefly looked away. *Love sure must be strange*, she thought. It must, because somehow, her father loved her weird mother. She was a pretty creature, and at times, a very vulnerable one, but surely, Claire thought, *Dad doesn't see just how ghastly Rita is. He just doesn't see it, doesn't want to see it, and brushes it aside.* Claire realized that he was rarely around when Rita would torment her with her rants. Usually, he was still working or only walking in from the office after one of their many hair-raising scenes, and by then, Hilaire was pretty much exhausted and barely alert enough to comprehend the true situation, but he wasn't stupid. He knew his wife had deep emotional wounds; *abandonment issues*, as one of the therapists put it. But she also had a mean streak and he caught glimpses of that chilling trait and never knew what to think of it. The Rita he knew was a fun-loving, delicate creature.

He's kind of a fool. Claire thought, as she watched her dad pull out a credit card and flopping it into the little plate over the paper bill that sat there. *A sweet fool*, Claire corrected her thoughts, as she smiled at him: *maybe too sweet.*

Claire spoke,

" Dad, I know we both said we'd leave her out of it, but are you seeing Mom soon?"

Hilaire brushed his shirt of any crumbs that gathered there.

" I already have. And I'm not going to be seeing her again until she gets help. But your brothers and I may take a trip. You're welcome to join us. We're going to Colorado."

Claire told her father she would give it some thought. It would be a couple of weeks out of her schedule. She just started her internship at the

Duquesne Musical Archive, a position Sister Boniface secured for her, as the old nun had a few connections to its board. And it was a good paying job, working for a musicologist, a collector of rare archives and obscure and lost compositions

While her bud, Darva, got a full scholarship at Loyola U. in Chicago, Claire had not been accepted at the music schools she so wanted to attend, but managed to get on a *waiting list* at two of the conservatories, thanks to the help of Sister Mary Boniface and the stellar letter of recommendation she wrote on her behalf.

"Then your summer job might be the thing to do". Her dad said, gently squeezing his daughter's lovely arm resting on the table.

"You get into one of those schools, I'll take care of your tuition. So don't worry!"

Claire felt the warm tear making its way down her soft cheek, and this time, she didn't fight it. After several months grinding her nails into her delicate palms so she could get through her classes, so she could, at least, graduate, and keeping a tight lid on this humiliating and shaming situation, she finally, in a spontaneous burst, returned her dad's arm-squeeze, saying,

"Oh, gosh Daddy, thank you. Thank you for being my dad. I wish you wouldn't have to be so far away, but I know you care about us. About me, about my life."

Hilaire was disturbed that his daughter would speak this way, but didn't want to show the weighted concern that coursed through his veins. He playfully threw the cloth napkin on the table and smiled,

"Ah, forget that stuff. You never have to thank me for anything, Rochelle Claire."

Claire's eyes were now red with tears,

"Oh, yes I do. I thank you and my lucky stars."

After dropping his daughter off at the corner of Evangeline Way and Beaumont Drive, at his daughter's insistence, Hilaire drove back to the quaint, bed and breakfast inn where he was staying. His wife was furious that he refused to stay in the house with her and the boys, given the situation, but he stood his ground. *Get help, or else!*

"I feel like I'm dealing with an addict."

Hilaire told his friend and legal advisor, Warren Leblanc.

"And I'm going to just wait and see. I can't just outright divorce her. Everyone abandoned my wife when she was young. Everyone. But she's the mother of my children, and I well-know she doesn't mean to be this way. I don't think she even realizes it."

Warren could only listen intently and gently shooed Anne away when she inquired who might be calling at eleven-thirty in the evening. But it would take a while for Hilaire to figure these things out, and he had the rest of the summer to be with his sons, and he didn't want to have the subject hover over every spare moment he had with them.

As for Sister Mary Boniface, things couldn't have been more resplendent. Yes, Sister had a new advisor, this miracle man, Squires Montgomery, of whom she and Antoinetta were thinking of dedicating a commemorative spot in their garden as his ingenious idea of holding a fundraiser for the sisters and members of the Vedanta Society along with some Zen Buddhists from their center in Bogalusa, drew an unprecedented crowd of alumna.

The checks and online payments poured in like much needed rain in a Nevada desert, and given their fiduciary success, Father Ignatius and his ambitious Jesuit brethren backed off from any merger idea.

"At least, for a year or two…we shall see, Squires."

Boniface barked as she relaxed in her office, a box of *Krispy Kremes* lying atop her great desk, as she,

Antoinetta and Constantine were in a rather celebratory mood these last days of the academic year. Squires couldn't have been in a better frame of mind, after helping the good sisters put their financial house in order. He was glad to offer legal advice-*pro bono*- when asked, but offered to refer most of her questions to his friend, Warren Leblanc.

"I work with the bad guys, Sister. So perhaps, it's my way of refreshing my soul. God knows how unpleasant my work gets. I have more homicides and other sordid matters I wouldn't want to soil your good spirit with, so believe me, I am delighted to be of help where I can."

Boniface chuckled, taking a bite of a glazed *Krispie Kreme*, one of those *little cuties*, as Sister fondly called them. Sister smacked her lips,

"Well, you know, we cloistered types are known to deal with some *baddies,* ourselves. Only they aren't always here in our world. But sometimes, I think they show up just to test us. And I believe there's a little demon right beside me, making me eat all these donuts."

"But you're celebrating, right?"

Squires countered.

The good sister gave a shrug of her shoulders and lifted another glazed goodie from the box. After the two ended their conversation, Squires thought over the events of the past few weeks. Things surely have turned out well. He enjoyed spending time with Lucinda Mobray, and thought it was a good idea that they both take their time getting to know each other.

Experience seems to have a way of steering things on a safer, more careful course, yet it is a diametrical contrast to youth's folly, as young Darva and Squire's second cousin's son, Travis, seem to be *head over heels*, as they say. But Darva still found time to hang with her best bud,

Claire, and the two of them would often laugh over the crazy escapades they shared. It wouldn't be long before the two of them would go their separate ways, especially for Darva, as she was soon to be northbound and in Chicago in a matter of months.

♦ ♦ ♦

Dear patient readers, I believe there is a saying about the season of summer. That it is a time where—like its abundant fruit—its promise is also ripe for the taking. Well, if there isn't such a saying, then there should be. After much fretfulness, I finally resigned myself to an existence of blindly following along the lives of these curious humans, especially, our Claire.

I truly felt that it wouldn't be such a terrible way to exist, after all. And just as I was settling in my cozy spot up at the ceiling of our girl's room at Mrs. Gaynor's one evening, I felt a light sparkle near my orb-like self. It was my old discarnate "visitor" showing up like the first inklings of a new day. I was stunned at his sudden appearance and felt my orb essence glow in warm, happy colors. He conveyed to me that my attempts to enter the dreamscape of Sister Boniface were not in vain. That she did register my presence and my plea—although subconsciously—that the results would be forthcoming; that my mystery would soon be made clear. That he, too, would be there with me, to guide me, not unlike Virgil in his assistance to Dante as he stood before the Gates of Hell in the immortal 'Inferno'.

Naturally, upon hearing this, I paused a bit, taking in this concept, and his orb-self jiggled with glee.

"I have been appointed to assist you. The Big Beings sent me here. Don't worry, we're not gong... there!"

Still in a convivial mood he added,

"Why do you think your girl there dug up that Liszt composition? You remember, the complex, passionate sonata she tackled at the nuns' parlor piano so many weeks ago? 'Apres une Lecture de Dante: Fantasia quasi Sonata', as it is known. I was trying to tell you—that was your sign that more was going to come your way. You needed only to be patient, friend."

So said my yet to be identified, "visitor", my sole guide in this mysterious morass of subterranean spirit existence. He kept saying he had something to show me, and I was puzzled as he brought me to this strange, dark place. I wasn't sure where I was, but I stayed with my fellow spirit- friend, trusting that there would be more clues. We waited in this dark, shapeless space and then my "visitor" showed me more scenes from the life where he says he once knew me. I continued to not recognize these things, but he said it wouldn't be long before everything would come together for me. That he would be there beside me to assist when more information would be revealed and that, by then, I would be ready.

◆　◆　◆

It was turning out to be a magical summer for Claire. Being out of high school was sheer bliss. No more did she (or Darva Jean, for that matter), have to tolerate the triteness of high school and the silly girls both friends knew they'd not much mind ever encountering again. After only a few weeks, *The Convent of the Immaculate Heart* seemed like a distant dream. The only tenderness she felt in regards to her old stomping grounds was the consistent and caring support from Sister Mary Boniface.

Claire would sometimes drop in at the old convent and actually stay for supper with the nuns, laughing on her phone later with Darva Jean as she described the nuns' playful jokes and banter at the dinner table. Yes, Claire truly felt grateful for all the blessings in her young life. Dad, Hilaire, and her brothers took off for their Colorado vacation, while Claire stayed behind. Dad kept mum about Claire living at Mrs. Gaynor's, and encouraged her to be hopeful about attending college in the fall. But Claire wasn't all that worried as she was deeply entrenched in her new job, which she found utterly fascinating.

The Duquesne Musical Archive is housed in a former stately, 19th century mansion in the leafy university section of the city. It is affiliated with an eminent musical conservatory in faraway Boston, one that Claire had applied to, but failed to gain entry. With the recommendation from Sister Boniface, Claire secured a spot on the conservatory's waiting list for fall acceptance. In the meantime, thanks to the pertinacious Sister Boniface, Claire landed a very good job for the summer assisting a musicologist, Dr. Andras Najman, in the area of rare manuscripts at the archive. Claire had no idea that such a place even existed, but the ever-mindful Sister Boniface learned about the archive from her associate and former *mergers and acquisitions* foe, Father Ignatius of *St. Jerome's*, who happened to know some of its associates.

Claire didn't know what to think of her new job when she first entered the quaint building obliquely hidden behind lush foliage and greenery in the lovely uptown neighborhood. Her boss was a serious-looking man of about sixty, with a full head of longish, salt and pepper hair, and an ample, graying beard. Wire-framed spectacles slid down a long, bony nose as he perused manuscripts, always making notations on a pad nearby. Magnifying glasses in various shapes and sizes were often spread out over his desktop as he pored over materials most mornings, a steaming cup of strong coffee always set on a side table away from his great desk.

Claire silently observed the professor in quiet fascination and awaited his instructions. She was to catalogue and enter documents from bound packaging in a great storeroom, and often, she was instructed to take the manuscripts out with care and always with white-gloved hands. It was odd, but kind of exhilarating. Among the material were recovered works from mostly European composers, both famous and obscure. Many were worn, delicate, yellowed pages from places as faraway as St. Petersburg and Krakow. One, in particular, was a rare piece by Chopin—which was immediately put in protective coverings and sent off to a sister archive in London. When Claire observed the writing and scrawls, with the florid signature of the said composer, she emitted a joyous sigh as goose bumps formulated on her slender arms.

Dr. Najman smiled and nodded jubilantly as the two of them carefully took out the sheet music—their respective, gloved fingers delicately handling the yellowed pages as if they were fine crepe or rare silks.

During her lunch break (where she'd usually eat her sandwich alone in the small sunny kitchen area in the back), Claire would often daydream of possible scenarios that launched these works on their strange odyssey—one that brought them to this charming, welcoming place on a different continent and in a new century. *Something they would have never dreamed of when they were living,* Claire thought, taking a bite of her chicken salad sandwich, which she made at Mrs. Gaynor's before setting out for the day on foot, as the archive was only a twenty-minute walk away.

But on this particular June morning, Dr. Najman was at his desk, staring at a large parcel sitting unopened before him when Claire entered the building. Claire lightly tapped on the doorframe of his handsome office, not wishing to interrupt, but to let the professor know that she was awaiting his instructions for the day. The professor hovered over the parcel and enthusiastically beckoned Claire to join him. Shaking his head, he said,

"I'm marveling at this daunting package because I've finally mustered the nerve to deal with it. I had this in the cool storage area for the past six months and today, I decided it was time to take a look. My search for this has gone on for quite a while. It was only about a year ago that I began to get warmer, but the search took me to Prague then, Lithuania and on to Budapest and back to Prague. It's time I open this up. But I'm still hesitant. There's the dreaded thought that it may not be what I've been searching for, after all."

Claire slid onto the chair next to her employer's and excitedly rubbed, then clasped her hands, a pair of white cotton gloves resting in her lap.

"Wow. I can only imagine what it could be!"

Dr. Najman nodded and smiled,

"More than likely, you probably don't know of him. He was an up and coming composer, one that most may not find all that extraordinary. But he was good, from what I know."

Claire looked down at the large package and politely spoke,

"If you don't mind my asking, then, why's it so important?"

The avuncular professor with a Czech name Claire had to practice pronouncing before showing up on her first day of work, shrugged his shoulders,

" No, I don't mind. This little known composer, this man—whose work, hopefully, is in this package—was responsible for saving my father's life."

◆　◆　◆

My discarnate spirit "visitor" has ushered me into this cozy office after we waited in the cool dark storage area most of the night. I am not so certain why I have been brought here, but I feel a tingling formation of knowing within my orb. It's as if, all along, I had been blindfolded, and now the golden sunlight streaming through the floor-to-ceiling window in the good musicologist's office warms my thought-emotion being in a way I've yet to experience. A joyous radiance comes over me. My thought-emotion being is stunned with a clarity that has parted me from this former existence of unending occlusion and unfathomable mystery. I am a guest of honor at my own surprise party, for I didn't think it would all come about in this way, dear readers, and perhaps, I am amazed that this darling girl had somehow held a clue without not only her knowledge (remember, she has not a whisper's knowing of my presence) but mine as well. Still, it is all so wondrous. And it's only now that I finally realize what brought my befuddled spirit-self here to this time and place. And yes, to the New World, and in a new century (as Claire mused over her homemade chicken sandwich one recent lunch-hour), but not too far off from when I last lived.

My orb essence floats here, above the scene where our girl and music prof-employer take out scissors and carefully open the parcel that has quietly sat in its sad little place in the cool storage room since about the time I found myself here last December. That, dear readers, is my life there in that brown paper package, shipped all the way from Prague in what is now known as the Czech Republic. It was there that I last happily lived and my spirit "visitor" is beside me here, explaining that I would not have known this until now, when our girl was to meet up with this aging musicologist, this man of sixty, who was not yet born when I helped his father escape.

Clear streams of memory come to me without hesitation, frothing with rich details of a life fully lived. It all unfolds in lucid clarity. Yes, I knew this man's father, all right. His name was Viktor Najman. He was a splendid, virtuoso violinist, and I was the conductor of one of the finest orchestras in all of Europe. (my spirit-"visitor", my personal Virgil, reminds me that with my newfound memory, comes my distinct flaws of ego, one of which is a tendency to boast. So my orb essence rightfully blushes, readers, but alas!)

With his customary gloved hands the astute professor is taking out the carefully packaged bundles of sheet music. I see that they are all there, and I had so wondered about them when they finally took me, and imprisoned me, never knowing what became of my work. And many an evening, I also wondered what became of the people I helped, musicians from my orchestra which was ever-evolving, or devolving in a way, since all of the musicians I replaced mine with were young adults and even university students, and that is when the authorities grew suspicious.

As most of my original orchestra consisted of middle aged and young adult musicians, I had to lead the most vulnerable to where my 'associates' were at the various borders. There they issued visas to anywhere that was vastly outside the stronghold of German occupation. In the meantime, I ended up with a young, lithe, handsome, almost teenage orchestra, thanks to my friends back in Andrassy Street at the music conservatory where I had studied. I had to somehow keep my seats filled as it was becoming obvious that someone was allowing musicians of a certain pedigree and their families to flee.

When the fascist-police finally arrested me for covertly assisting the 'enemy', I gladly let them handcuff me and take me away—never had I doubted my decisions. I had no reservation when it came to helping those I cared deeply for. I had gotten by, I believe, for such a good while because my family was well regarded. My mother was Hungarian, my father German. I was educated in Budapest, but I lived and worked for much of my life in Prague. By the time the authorities caught up with me, I was ready because I knew that most of my musicians, the ones who needed protection, safely got out—and the musicologist here, the one with the Czech surname, bears my Hungarian given name. It is moving to learn this. After he was taken to the borders and got to your Ellis Island, and eventually finding work as a violinist in New York City, and later marrying, Viktor Najman named his first-born after me.

My name was Andras Sandor Baumann And now that I have finally been able to properly introduce myself to you, dear readers, as a former human, as one who was once like you, I ask that you come along with me, as I traverse the path of a life I once lived, and I am told by my spirit "visitor" that, perhaps, by the time I am done, I will meet up again with the celestial being who tried to stop me from looking back at where it all had ended.

I begin my story with a scene you may recall—the one my discarnate companion, "visitor" showed me—where a group of men, mostly from my orchestra, is sitting at café tables on a frosty winter's afternoon, snow falling incessantly outside. Our fluffy, sable chapeaus that we all wore with our great overcoats are drying near the cafe's ceramic, pot-bellied stove.

We would often arrive here at this favorite spot after rehearsals and the like, and usually our instruments would be in their cases on the floor, while my leather satchel case filled with sheet music and my baton lay on the cloth covered table in front of me. We would order rounds of coffee and sometimes, brandy, and we would talk and sing songs and share thoughts on the topics of the day. Sometimes we would be there for hours discussing philosophy, literature and life's unsorted mysteries. And I recall, Roland Cerny, who played the French horn with such deftness and mastery it could make you weep. Roland was also quite the storyteller, as he would weave intriguing tales of life in the Far East. It turned out that he had spent much of his youth in Japan, as his father was a missionary. It was there that he had learned a laughing meditation, and he taught this to us one afternoon—with the entire café staring at us as if we had all gone mad. Little did I realize that in my darkest time in that horrible prison, that awful, dank, and dark camp, where I was locked up for months in solitary confinement, that the memory of this would save my very life—at least for a time. During those harsh, lean months where I lived in virtual, unending darkness for hours at a time, all I could do was compose music in my mind. It was how I kept my sanity. I would also run through entire symphonies from memory, and attempt to recall them backwards until I would finally drop off to sleep.

One evening, while still in isolated captivity, I had a wild idea. I thought of Roland Cerny and recalled his laughing meditation that he brought with him from his adolescent years in rural Japan.

Desperate for comfort, I started to do this laughing routine that went on to an incessant degree until a guard came by, unlocked my cell door and threw me out in the rain. I was only trying to keep myself sane, I had no idea that the guard, in his ignorance, was thinking the very opposite and he, along with some fellow officers, marched me to the infirmary. It was the most ingenious idea I had ever come up with, and I thanked the spirit of my French horn musician endlessly, as I got to rest and eat better food and actually shower again.

But that was only a brief respite. After I recovered, I was sent to hard labor. I was considered young and fit, although I was about thirty-eight years old at that time, in 1941. Perhaps, the Nazis were desperate, as many prisoners had already expired due to dysentery and disease—which was rampant in those camps. So each morning at 5 am, my fellow prisoners and I would rise to eat stale bread, drink a cup of tepid tea and march to a vast field where we would dig ditches 'til sundown. This went on interminably. Perhaps, my strength was my fortune as I was spared being taken out back and shot like some others who were getting too slow or weak in their limbs. But there came a time when I saw an opportunity.

It was December, and the first heavy snows had already arrived. The guards and the staff, you could say, were preparing to have a Christmas celebration, if you can imagine. While we prisoners were barely given meager portions of thin soup and bread rations, perversely, there were treats being baked in the guards' quarters and on Christmas Eve morning an evergreen tree was brought in and later decorated with much fanfare. I knew of this because I was assigned to a small detail hauling debris near their quarters. As I was passing a window to the guards' barracks, I noticed two of them laughing and talking as one guard tried on an outfit, a St. Nicholas, Father Christmas costume.

At a side window, I deliberately dropped some items on the ground to give me more time to take note of that particular locker and the guard trying on his costume. As I proceeded along, I made this plan for escape. "What better opportunity", I thought, " than to run in the night when the guards were celebrating Christmas Eve in their quarters?" I thought I could easily go to this fool's footlocker and change into his uniform. He didn't seem to be any larger or smaller than I. Now, readers, I knew we were somewhere in Poland. I memorized the route when they brought us here, and when some of us in my work detail were driven in trucks to where we worked, I memorized the thicket of forest and any roads that might have lead out of them. I did this day in and day out, especially in good weather, so I would know if I ever had the chance to escape. And so, here was my moment.

Later that evening, just as I knew, when the guards loosened up their routine, heading for their dining hall to decorate their tree, and to eventually drink rum punch and eat their baked treats, I deftly slipped into their quarters and headed for 'St. Nick's' locker. I trembled like leaves shimmying in a ferocious storm as I swiftly changed from my rags to not only the guard's uniform, but to his coat as well. I could hear "O Tannenbaum" being sung by these bleary-eyed fools and prayed that their drunkenness would topple them over in a heap to the floor of their little makeshift tavern. In fact, I prayed for a lot of things that night, including that I would not only make it back to safe harbor, but that my concert master, Ivan, made it out of Prague with my music, as promised. But I was more concerned about my concertmaster's well being, and if he had managed to collect my effects (including my compositions) and bring them to safe harbor, then fine. But where was he?

In fact, what became of our friends and fellow musicians that I knew for so long? Half had escaped to better pastures, but the ones that remained—some of them, from what I knew—were taken in as I was. But at that moment, all I could focus on was escape.

I frantically scoured the guards' empty barracks for a gun, any gun that I could protect myself with, but there was none to be found. Be damned, I thought, and—as you Americans say in your flat-screened, TV dramas—I ' high-tailed' it out of there.

The snow had long stopped falling by the time I made my way into the guard's greatcoat and out onto the roads that lead to the great forest outside the camp. Were it not that particular evening when the guards were singing in their hot rum drinks, I never would have had a chance. But sometime during my escape, word had gotten out that the guard's coat was missing. Perhaps, he had gone back into his barracks to retrieve it and noticed that some of his other clothing was gone, never mind the heap of rags I had forgotten to pick up from the floor. It didn't take long for a group of them to catch up with me. I ran as fast as I could carry myself in that ridiculous, over-sized coat. I had forgotten how I had lost so much weight while incarcerated, but I ran anyway, and I heard their shots and I reached a wall and foolishly tried to scale it. That's when the first shot stung my leg, then another my ankle and finally one that hit straight through my back and into my heart. It's strange, but I had no idea that I died. At that moment, I was recalling a piece, a symphony I had composed some time before, back in my little practice room in Prague, and I was running it through in my mind, thinking, I really should change a part in the first section, and so on, and I was floating above a body, a strange, alien form laying about in a beautiful mound of snow where rivulets of crimson spread into splayed formations, like the poinsettias of the Americas, their flower for Christmas.

◆ ◆ ◆

Both apt pupil and professor carefully took apart the packaging, slowly pulling out the bundles of papers, not knowing whether they were the compositions Dr. Najman had so ardently pursued. But the professor smiled when he carefully took out one set of yellowed pages and nodded enthusiastically. It was all there, everything that he had researched and had known about from his own father and others. Or so it seemed. Claire listened intently as the professor told her that the bundled compositions were found hidden in a wall in the basement of the symphony hall where the young Andras Baumann was its conductor for over ten years. The sheet music remained there for almost fifty years, and once discovered, the material was moved about to various parties in Budapest and then on to a distant relative in Lithuania before they were sent back to Prague where a collector held them in a file cabinet in his office for so many years.

The musicologist fidgeted with his spectacles as he glanced down at the pages before him,

"He wrote symphonies—and I believe this is one of them. He also wrote an opera or two, from what I know. Maybe they're in this other bundle".

Claire marveled at the yellowed pages, reading the complex bars and notes as she carefully took the sheets out. But she was curious as to this man, who he was and what became of him.

The professor glanced over at Claire, as if he could pick up on her thoughts.

" My father was devastated when he learned so many years later that Baumann had been captured and killed. But he died a true hero. He was part of a resistance group "that involved a variety of people—but many were his fellow musicians. They all knew each other. It was preposterous for the conductor to think that he wouldn't protect his musicians, as they were also his friends. Still, he was quite courageous and noble. But there's only so much I know about him. Since he was killed in the concentration camp where they held him for two years, I only know of him through the stories my father told me. How much he liked his conductor and friend. So I got curious, especially after my father died and recently, I was able to learn more about the resistance efforts at that time. But my father told me Baumann was also a composer, and as a musician, I had to find out if anything was out there for me to discover. Someone cared. Someone hid this music away."

Claire speculated,

"Maybe he, himself, hid it. Maybe he knew they would find him."

The elder man shook his head.

"It's fascinating, isn't it? What might have gone on there—well, someone felt it was best to keep it hidden and away from intruders. How else can you explain?"

The professor leaned in closer, his gloved finger touching the faded sheet music.

"But here, look at the signature. Such flourish—a bit flamboyant!"

Dr. Najman suggested that they take some of the pages into the next room where there was a state-of-the art Steinway piano.

♦ ♦ ♦

And I am listening, dear readers, to the opening bars of a little sonata I wrote, admittedly, not one of my better ones. I believe it was the wish to retrieve my music back in Prague that fostered my desire to break free, a mission that I had clearly failed. But apparently, that wish is what eventually brought me here, and kept me bound to this world and its ephemeral aspect until the mystery was finally revealed.

While the two of them explore the delicate pages that I wrote out some seventy years ago, I am intent on telling you more of my story. The musicologist and eager acolyte, Claire, may find out more in due time. Of course, they have no idea that I've hovered among them since that parcel arrived here in this swampy, New World city so many months ago. No, that honor is yours, dear readers, and given that you have allowed me to take up residency on these very pages, I'm going to attempt something here. And I must do it, fast, because I see I am being called to move along into another realm. Now that my own conundrum has been resolved—thanks to our budding young composer and her missing piano—yes, for that was the first thing I noticed when I arrived. And I now realize that that piano was of the same make as my own, the one I composed so much music on back in my private quarters at the lovely symphony hall in Prague. It was part of the lure, you could say, when I took notice of the haulers that December morning and this lovely girl buckling to the ground in tears as her mother seemed to relish in her child's sorrow. Yes, I wrote my music, as I hovered over the ivory keys of a similarly made piano, manufactured also in the former Czechoslovakia. And I see why I became even more enchanted with our Claire and her world. I will miss her.

And I will miss this subtropical city and its intriguing inhabitants. And I may wonder about the fate of our Claire, her friend of African descent who is now American (which I now understand the phrase is a more pithy one), her family, her wretched mother (well, maybe not so much her) and Sister Mary Boniface. And you, dear readers, for I feel I am floating again, like I have done before, a long time ago, way before my reappearance on your plane. Before I left my safe, nebulous hammock of sublime non-existence. What my orb essence is feeling is similar to when I last was met with this phenomena of leaving my human body. And I am, somehow, re-visiting that occurrence. And I can tell you, when it first happened, I felt myself entering a most extraordinary experience. I looked around confused, of course, being that my movements were exquisitely light and my thoughts had a quixotic, three-dimensional quality to them. How do I express this? Thoughts took on fanciful shapes of which I had never seen in physical form, and thus, could not identify. It's foolish of me to attempt description of what space and form is over there—inside of that reality. How does one attempt to describe what is ineffable? I can only say that it is so entirely remarkable. And I remember, I felt myself swimming in this vast, unfathomable space of lightness, mesmerized by it all. My emotions took on colors and form. I was dazzled by a panorama of illumined tones both subtle and stark, yet I remained confused but not in an unpleasant way. Time moved forward and zoomed past. In grand sweeps, I felt myself entering actual periods from my life at the blink of an eye. I grew amusingly disoriented. Felt myself expanding in a most extraordinary way—only to contract again as if I were inside a microcosmic version of a breathing being that was the universe itself.

When the realization came over me that I was no longer in my physical body, I became quite relaxed and actually, mellow and comfortable—as if I had just slipped out of a wetsuit after a long and difficult swim.

I was a bit astonished at this, at first, but then a knowing crouched around the periphery of my mental being. It really was as if I had done this before. Life. A body. An inner inkling nudging me—that I was vaguely familiar with this bizarre routine and its strange offerings. The notion made me shudder with a tingling delight. I soon accepted my lack of physicality and exhilarated in this feeling of airy floatation. I breezed along for a while, whirling in weightless somersaults—so it felt—as if I were inside a gently spinning orb of light.

It was soon after that I felt something—a gentle force—sweeping me upward and away as if I were floating on the back of a soft, comforting creature. (Perhaps winged?) I felt myself rising upward for a while, quite pleasantly, and then everything stopped. I was immersed in an atrium-like space of radiant, golden light. The energy that surrounded me had a feeling of pleasant anticipation. And I wasn't alone. It was a voice. Actually, it was a collective voice that spoke—very earnest, very clear. This unified 'voice' said to me, in a most matter-of-fact tone:

"If you have something to contribute, please…please …*do* come in."

As this was spoken to me, I felt an incipient opening, a shift in energy that if a celestial welcome mat could be formed into a feeling, it would have been this energy emitting from this collective voice. Understand, it was not said with the slightest intimidation.

The 'voice' was warm and friendly, like a group of jolly scholars or professors, inviting you into their privileged, smoked-filled club for a game of pinochle and a drink by the fire. Only this convivial feeling surely was not the life I had come to know. And most recently had endured, that's for certain. It was too stark a contrast to what my life had been. Or rather, what it became.

*And, of course, it was the surprising and unexpected:
"...If you have something to contribute..." that made me
take pause.*

*Now this is where it all gets even more perplexing
for me. I remember I suddenly became—and to put it in
human terms—quite bashful. As if the lights on a stage
suddenly came up and I was caught unawares, yet
expected to give a performance. On the spot, as they
say. (My thought-emotion being blushed—I could see
colors of orange and reds around me). And I felt rather
unworthy of this warm, amazingly intelligent and clear,
collective voice and whatever went on behind those
gossamer golden columns of light. Surely, this was
some kind of mistake. I somehow ended up in the wrong
place. Such was the feeling I had. After I spun in light
circles around in the small, orb-like space of my being,
I did an about-face, and left. And by that, I mean
whatever now contained my feelings and thoughts,
because I no longer had a body. I tumbled, and fell
down what seemed like a vast and seemingly
unfathomable shaft of light and rather swiftly, because
something–some soft sweet slippery arc of light—caught
me just as I was about to re-enter that life. Yes, that life
that I had so suddenly departed—oh, goodness, in such a
shocking way. And I actually saw my former body—lying
there, in a strangely beautiful drift of snow and the stark
contrast of crimson pools coagulating about.*

*But I was stopped by this loving being—as it
slipped right under me. Its arc of light spread across my
former body—preventing my spirit's re-entrance. And
in that instance, I expressed that, surely, I had much
more to do in that life—alas, I was gently instructed
that this was not to be so. There was no hope for re-
entry. Or, at least, this is what was indicated by the
kind, incandescent entity as it lay over my physical
body that was dying there in the snow.*

Claire Ange

I tell you, it is a strange sight to behold, your own former physical body, as mine lay there empty and abandoned like a shell. But I was particularly troubled. I tried to explain to this kind entity that I had too much more to do. I was not yet forty years old. I was worried about what would become of my work. I wondered about the people, the friends that were left behind. I thought of Ivan Markovic, my concertmaster, and if he were safe and if he got out with my effects, mainly, my music. Perhaps, it was this selfish notion that weighed on me and prevented me from joining that kind entity who attempted to bring me forward. And there I lingered, missing any last cue to leaving the human world and its cumbersome concerns. Then everything familiar folded into itself like a black hole, creating an island of interminable amnesia.

But now, I see the familiar opening, with its gossamer aspect. And as I move forward and through diaphanous columns of light, I hear them, that collective 'voice' in the distance. I notice my "visitor"-guide, my personal Virgil's shape, as it's reconfiguring and I see now that he is, indeed, Ivan, my dear old concertmaster and friend, and he is coming toward me with some others. As I enter, I am being greeted by an overwhelming and joyous chorus of laughter—reminding me of that strangely wise, yet exotic practice Roland Cerny learned from his years in the Far East—the exercise we all so heartily partook to shake off the winter gloom outside.

Note to the reader

This is a small-press effort, a *little train that could* among publishing giants. If you enjoyed this read, the author would be most grateful if you could let others know about this unusual story. Putting the word out on social media sites, book forum pages (such as **BarnesandNoble.com**, **Goodreads.com**, and **Amazon.com**) or just to your local bookstore would be most appreciated. Thank you. And thank you for reading *Claire Ange*!

About the author

M.A. Kirkwood was born and raised in New Orleans, Louisiana, graduating from Loyola University, New Orleans, before continuing with additional studies at U.C. Berkeley and Stanford University. She went on to write professionally for stand up comedians, MTV and similar channels in the early days of cable television, and the advertising industry, both in San Francisco and New York City. The author currently resides in Northern California. This is her second novel.

For author appearances, please contact:
spiritspress@mail.com